Beautiful Game

by

Kate Christie

Bella
BOOKS

2011

Bella Books, Inc.
P.O. Box 10543
Tallahassee, FL 32302

Printed in the United States of America on acid-free paper
First published 2011

Editor: Katherine V. Forrest
Cover Designer: Judy Fellows

ISBN 13:978-1-59493-245-8

Other Bella Books By Kate Christie

Leaving L.A

Solstice

Acknowledgments

Thanks to my parents for providing room and board while I wrote this novel back in the day. Also, thanks once again to Katherine V. Forrest for her invaluable editorial assistance and her willingness to read revised scenes on the fly. And, finally, thanks to Bella Books for giving this story—and the others—a home.

To Alex, the first round draft pick for our home team

About The Author

Kate Christie was born and raised in Kalamazoo, Michigan. After studying history at Smith College, where she played the beautiful game Division III-style, she earned a Master's in Creative Writing from Western Washington University. Currently she lives near Seattle with her wife, their two loyal mutts, and the newest addition to the family—a beautiful, amazing, incredible baby girl, worthy of as many superlatives as her entirely unbiased mothers can conjure. *Beautiful Game* is Kate's third novel.

CHAPTER ONE

At first I didn't think I liked Jess, back when I still believed that surface appearances could be reliable measures of character. Even though the '90s were just beginning, I think I saw the world then through a sort of 1950s lens as one long series of uninspired binaries: good vs. evil, right vs. wrong, black vs. white. At nineteen, I hadn't experienced anything yet to make me question my version of reality. My family was healthy, my parents happily married, and I was in college in sunny Southern California playing my way into adulthood.

Probably I believed in hard-and-fast boundaries because, like Jess, I was a college athlete. Only instead of a tennis court like her, my playing field of choice was a regulation hundred and twenty yards long, sixty yards wide, anchored at either end by goal posts that measured eight feet by twelve: a soccer field. But even soccer is subjective, as any fan will tell you. Referees oversee every match, and with human ego in the picture, you might as well kiss objectivity goodbye. As much as I genuinely love the game of soccer, it's still just that—a game. It took me most of my college career to realize that sport can sometimes distract you from what's real. Almost four years to notice the gray in the world all around me.

I miss that time, when soccer was all I could think about and I woke each day knowing exactly why I was where I was, happy to be doing what I was doing. Because once I noticed the gray lurking at the edges of the people and places and things I loved, the colors around me never seemed quite as vibrant again.

I met Jess in the spring of 1991, my sophomore year of college, on seemingly just another night at the San Diego University cafeteria. I never thought our food service was all that bad. I appreciated the luxury of institutional food, liked having my meal ready and waiting, guiltily enjoyed having other people clean up after me. Ever since I could remember, my older brother and I had been the reason our parents never owned a dishwasher. Most evenings when I was growing up in Oregon, my family sat down together around the oval oak dining table to a dinner of vegetables, bread and meat, amiably wrangling over Reagan's mismanagement of the federal government, the Republican-guided depletion of natural resources, the state of communism in the Soviet Union. Every once in a while my father, a high school special education teacher, would try to make something unusual for dinner, like fried bananas or sushi. Those nights typically ended with the four of us piling into the family station wagon and heading for Balboa's, our favorite Portland pizza joint.

At SDU, I was almost always late to dinner because of practice. In the fall I played intercollegiate soccer. Over the winter, I played intramural soccer. And in the spring, I worked out with the middle distance runners on the track team. The track coach had offered me a spot on the team, but I didn't want to be away at meets every weekend. Besides, I needed my Saturday mornings clear for the occasional spring soccer scrimmage. My attendance wasn't optional—I was at SDU, a Division II state school with just over eight thousand students, on a partial soccer scholarship.

As usual, I was running late that Tuesday in March when I parked my mountain bike in the rack outside the student center and got in line behind Jess Maxwell, SDU's very own tennis phenom. Everyone on campus who followed sports knew Jess was currently ranked number two nationally in singles and had been voted NCAA Division II Rookie of the Year the previous spring, our freshman year.

As I stood in line, I tugged on the bill of my worn navy baseball cap and checked Jess out. Whenever I saw her around campus or made it to a tennis match, I always noticed her legs. Beautiful, long and lean, not as thick as you might expect for a tennis player, and evenly tanned, except for the sock line that sometimes peeked out from the top of her short socks. She always wore Nike tennis socks and Nike cross trainers. There was a rumor floating around campus that Nike had offered to sponsor her.

Jess must have felt my eyes on her legs, somehow, because I glanced up to find her looking over her shoulder at me. I lowered my hand from my cap. Busted. Our eyes caught, hers a lighter brown than I expected, almost copper-colored, and one of her eyebrows lifted as if to say, *What do you think?* I smiled at the quirky eyebrow. She smiled back, and we both looked at the food up ahead beyond the plastic guard.

For my part, I gazed upon the cooked broccoli trying to convince myself that yes, Jess Maxwell had indeed smiled at me. This was momentous mainly because Jess was known around campus for her chronic unfriendliness to anyone not on the tennis team.

"You play soccer, don't you?" she asked.

I looked up from my contemplation of the vegetable selection. "Oh, yeah," I said. "You play tennis, right?"

She nodded. Her dark hair was pulled back in a ponytail that swung with the movement of her head. A few curls had come free and framed her oval face.

The line moved forward a couple of steps.

"I like your shoes," I said, offering a lame explanation of why I had been looking at her legs. I wondered if she would shoot it down. She had to know she had great legs.

But she said only, "Thanks." Apparently she was willing to participate in the cover-up.

As we moved forward again, I tried to think of something else to say. The most obvious line, one I'd exchanged with literally hundreds of fellow students since coming to San Diego, was, *Where are you from?* But I'd seen her hometown, Bakersfield, listed in the tennis program. Central Valley had the reputation of being hot, dry, and ultra-conservative—not exactly the place for self-professed homos like me.

At her turn, Jess picked mashed potatoes, turkey, and a side salad. A glass of water. No dessert. We chose the exact same meal, except I opted for different salad dressing. Ahead of me, she handed her meal card to the cashier to run through the register. As she walked away, she smiled at me again over her shoulder. "See you around, Cam."

Cam was short for Camille, a name only my professors ever used, and usually only once.

"See you," I said, waving a little as I handed over my own meal card. Jess Maxwell knew my name? She had a nice smile, I decided. I was used to the frown of concentration I'd seen on her face whenever I watched her play tennis, the stony gaze she wore like a mask around campus.

Orange plastic tray in hand, I surveyed the cavernous seating area. A couple of guys I knew from the swim team were just finishing up their meals, so I slid into a chair next to them.

"Hello, boys."

"Yo," Jake Kim said. His black hair was just growing back. He'd shaved his entire body for nationals a couple of months before.

"Howdy, Cam," Brad Peterson said. Slightly in love with Andre Agassi, Brad liked to think of himself as a rebel. He defied swimming convention by wearing his hair in a ponytail and had still managed to set a D. II record in the butterfly in this, his junior year. "Was that you we saw actually conversing with the tennis goddess?" he added.

"Can you believe it?" I drowned my salad in dressing. "She caught me checking out her legs and didn't even freak."

Jake winced at my liberal use of dressing. "You know you're exceeding your daily fat intake with that stuff," he couldn't resist saying.

Brad and I rolled our eyes at each other. I dug into my mashed potatoes. "You forget, Jake, I'm a soccer player. The bigger I am the better."

I had added ten pounds to my five-foot six-inch frame since coming to SDU, but it was all muscle. Or mostly muscle, anyway. The weight had helped. In the fall, I'd been named all-conference first team and all-region second team—not bad for a sophomore defender. My coach had told me if I kept up my level of play and avoided injury, I might even make All-American. The awards were political, I knew. Someone would have to owe my coach a favor for me to make All-American. Still, it would feel good. Hell, who was I kidding. It would feel amazing.

"We know, you're a brute," Jake said. "So what did Maxwell have to say?"

I shrugged and took a swallow of water. "Not much. Oh, she knew I played soccer."

Brad leaned forward. "That's a good sign. It means she's noticed you."

"There aren't that many non-football playing athletes on campus. I bet she knows you both swim, too."

"She's never said anything to either of us," Brad said.

"Yeah, well, she probably knows you guys are a couple of fairies."

"I don't know what you're talking about," Jake lisped exaggeratedly. "Just because a man is in touch with his feminine side doesn't mean he's a fag."

Brad threw his crumpled napkin across the table at Jake. "Of course it does, sweetie."

The conversation moved on. The campus Lesbian/Gay/ Bisexual Alliance was hosting a dance Saturday night, and one of Jake's friends was planning a pre-party in his graduate apartment if I and some of my buds cared to attend.

"Bring along that cute girl we saw you with at Zodiac last weekend," Brad added.

Zodiac was a gay bar in the city that held eighteen-and-up nights once a week for the college crowd.

My smile turned sheepish. "I would, but she has to go up to L.A. this weekend. She kind of has to break up with her boyfriend."

"Another straight girl?" Jake shook his head. "If you're not careful, you're going to have a posse of dissed boyfriends after you by the time we graduate."

I was a little leery of that possibility myself. But I couldn't help it that somehow I always ended up with women on the verge of coming out. I had going what my best friend from soccer, Holly Bishop, called the twelve-year-old boy look: short dark hair, delicate features, freckles, and small breasts that were just substantial enough to assure you I was in fact a nearly twenty-year-old woman. Straight women were always telling me how cute I was. I just smiled and went along with it. I was young, in college and playing the sport I loved. Even I knew enough to appreciate these years while they lasted.

A couple of days later, I was walking toward the gym for track practice when a red Cabriolet pulled up alongside me on College Lane. A dark-haired woman in sunglasses and a black sweatshirt leaned out the driver side window. Jess Maxwell.

"Want a ride?" she asked.

"Sure." I walked around the car and hopped in, resting my bag on my lap. "Thanks."

"No problem. You are going to the gym, aren't you?" she added, smoothly shifting gears.

"I am."

Unlike the cars of most college kids I knew, you could see the floor in Jess's. It even appeared to have been vacuumed recently. Only the back was slightly cluttered, plastic containers of tennis balls sharing the seat with a sports duffel, two jacketed tennis racquets and a backpack.

"Where's the bike I always see you on?" she asked.

"One of my suitemates snagged it this morning. I'm Cam, by the way."

She smiled a little, eyes hidden behind her sunglasses. "I know. I'm Jess."

"I know," I echoed.

We drove across campus, past brick buildings and under palm trees, the sun warm on our shoulders and bare arms. Back at home in Oregon it was probably rainy and fifty degrees. Once again I thanked my lucky stars I'd landed at SDU.

On the floor at my feet was a textbook, *Art: Context and Criticism*.

"Are you an art major?" I asked, surprised for some reason by the idea.

"Art History. What about you?"

"Education."

My father was a teacher, as had been his mother before him and her mother before her. My older brother, an extreme sports junkie, couldn't stand to be indoors for any significant length of time, so it looked like I would be the one to take up the family educator mantle. In my intended future career as a high school history teacher, I was hoping to land a position at a school that needed a girls' soccer coach. But that future seemed a long way off yet.

Jess downshifted to turn into the athletic building parking lot. The gym was only three years old, an impressive modern structure with a glass-walled atrium that spanned three floors.

"You have practice?" I asked unnecessarily as Jess parked the car. Of course she had practice. Tennis was a two-season sport, but spring was the "real" season—the most competitive tournaments took place during the last two months of the school year.

"Yep. You work out with the track team, don't you?"

"Just to keep in shape for soccer."

Only five months now until preseason, that twelve days of hellish double sessions that strained every leg muscle until it hurt even to sit on the toilet. I couldn't wait.

She reached into the backseat to grab her bag and a racket,

her arm brushing mine. This close, I could smell her shampoo, a delicate floral scent that somehow didn't seem to match the image she projected.

"Can you lock?" she asked as we both slid out.

"Sure." I did, slamming the door a little harder than I meant to, and thought I saw her wince behind her shades. We stood facing each other for a moment on opposite sides of the car. "Thanks for the ride."

"No problem."

Still we lingered near her car. The sun was out, hardly unusual for Southern California, and a slight breeze rustled the trees at the edge of the lot.

"How's tennis going?" I asked. I knew the team was doing well, mostly thanks to Jess. Everyone was saying she would get All-American this year for sure.

"Not bad. We've got Big Eights up in San Francisco this weekend. Shouldn't be too tough." She paused. "I heard you guys did pretty well this season."

"We made it to quarterfinals at nationals. And we hosted Big Eights earlier in the fall and ended up beating Southern State in the finals."

"I know. I was at that game."

"You were?"

I bit my lip, remembering how I'd nearly gotten red-carded in the finals. A tall forward I was marking had actually punched me when the referee wasn't looking five minutes in, and the rest of the game had been a thinly veiled battle between us. Her, to mentally knock me off my game and score. Me, to stop her from scoring and take her down legally without getting called. I succeeded, mostly. She never did score. But I got a yellow card midway through the second half for slide-tackling her from behind at the half line. I could tell the ref thought about red. A yellow card is a warning, while a red card gets you ejected and makes your team play down a man for the rest of the game. I'd gotten lucky that day.

Jess tilted her head slightly. "You kept picking on some girl on the other team. I thought she was going to have to be carried off on a stretcher."

"She hit me first!" All at once, it seemed inordinately important that Jess Maxwell not think I'd instigated the fight. My rule in soccer was simple: Never start anything, but finish everything. "Seriously. She kidney-punched me when the ref's back was turned. *I* almost had to be carried off on a stretcher."

"Uh-huh." She raised her eyebrows again, and I realized she was just teasing me, pushing my buttons to get me riled up. If it had been someone other than Jess Maxwell, I would have sworn she was flirting.

"At least I never busted a racquet on the court after double faulting a game away," I said slyly.

At one of the matches I'd attended the previous year, Jess had done just that despite the fact she was leading 6-2, 4-1.

She appeared to color slightly. "You saw that?"

"Your McEnroe impression? Uh-huh."

"Guess we're even, then."

She took off her sunglasses and slipped them into her bag. Then she smiled, and I noticed the coppery glint of her eyes again.

I checked my watch. "I should probably head up. Thanks again for the ride."

"De nada. See you around, Cam."

She turned away, and I did too a moment later, heading in the opposite direction. As I walked toward the track, I pondered the fact that her "de nada" had a Spanish lilt to it, which might have to do with her slightly darker coloring. Maybe she wasn't as WASPy as the majority of the tennis players I had met in Southern California.

Curiouser and curiouser. Not only did Jess Maxwell know who I was, she seemed to want to get to know me better. I could dig it, I thought, only just stopping myself from skipping all the way to the stadium.

CHAPTER TWO

Whenever I think of spring semester sophomore year, I remember listening to Melissa Etheridge's self-titled album on Friday nights with Holly, my best friend from soccer, shouting along with the songs while we drank Rolling Rock beer and got ready to go out to a party or check out the scene at Zodiac.

Holly and I had been inseparable since the first day of preseason freshman year. I wasn't even sure why we'd latched on to each other at first. We were about the same height and build and we both had freckles, but there the similarities ended. I was dark-haired, fair-skinned and comfortable in faded jeans and hiking boots, while Holly was blonde, blue-eyed and nearly always dressed fashionably in the latest J Crew ensemble. She hailed from an L.A. suburb, her family as different from mine as possible. Her father was a corporate lawyer, mother a stay-at-home mom despite the fact there weren't any kids left at home, older brother president of a fraternity at UCLA. They were all blond and, far worse to my mind, card-carrying Republicans.

But Holly and I had been tight ever since that first day when we ran the timed two mile together and pushed each other to make it in under twelve and a half minutes and then walked off our cramps, barely speaking the entire time. She was the first person at SDU I told I was gay, and she was cool with it. She even said she thought she might be attracted to women herself. Now, a year and a half later, Holly had canceled her assorted catalog subscriptions, joined the SDU Democrats and was dating a woman for the first time, a junior who lived in her dorm and looked even straighter than she did.

I had dated a few different women since arriving at SDU—Beth, an intellectual writer-to-be who lived one floor away my first semester on campus; Sarah, a beautiful redhead who lived off-campus and kept trying to get me stoned the previous spring; and Tina, a rower for whom sport came first. Most recently I'd hooked up with Elissa, the girl with the L.A. boyfriend, but she'd gotten way too serious way too fast for me. I was soon single again, and happy to be so.

Single or coupled, Holly and I reserved Friday nights for each other. Usually I would get dressed up in jeans and a collared shirt and swing by her dorm a couple of buildings away. There, we would blast Melissa and drink beer and get ready to head out. "Like the Way I Do" was our favorite song that year. As we ritually bellowed the verses, rewound, and bellowed the words again, I couldn't help but feel that something was missing. I was having a good time casually dating, but I had yet to fall in love with anyone in California. As my sophomore spring progressed, though, the feeling of something missing was overtaken by the sense of something about to happen. Maybe it was just the mood of springtime, of new life everywhere, but I felt as if I were on the verge of a kind of discovery.

In the weeks that followed that first car ride, I saw Jess Maxwell around campus only a couple of times in passing. By April, everyone at SDU seemed to have spring fever except me. Summer for me meant returning to Oregon, going back to my job as a maintenance worker for Portland's Parks Department, spending ten hours a day in my spiffy green uniform mowing lawns and trimming hedges. I didn't mind the job really, and by living at home I could save enough money to support myself the coming school year. But sometimes I wished I didn't have to work quite so hard, especially when my friends didn't have to worry about their tuition payments.

My parents didn't have a lot of extra money for school. My mom had stayed home when my brother and I were little and gone back to work the year I entered third grade. Her current position in development at the local university, along with my dad's public school teaching career, didn't exactly bring in big bucks. My older brother Nate, who was up in Alaska putting his obsession with the great outdoors to good use working for a Fairbanks outfitter, had gone to college for free at the school where our mom worked. Unlike him, I'd wanted to get out of Portland after high school. My soccer scholarship covered partial tuition but not room and board. That meant I could either hang in San Diego for the summers and take out extra loans, or go home to work. Kind of a no-brainer, I always thought.

Fortunately, I didn't have to head back to Portland just yet. The second week of April, I attended a home tennis match with Holly and Laura Grant, another soccer player. The three of us were always doing anything remotely athletic together. Laura, unlike Holly and myself, was totally straight and slightly clueless, even borderline homophobic at times. But the three of us had bonded over soccer as freshmen, a connection that seemed to transcend difference. Holly and I loved Laura, even if we wanted to strangle her sometimes. Whenever we all hung out together, there was an unspoken agreement that Laura wouldn't talk about boys—much—and Holly and I wouldn't talk about girls. Our conversations centered around our team, other sports teams, our coach, other coaches and soccer. Especially the inaugural Women's World Cup we'd heard was slated to take place in China that summer.

The day of the tennis match, the three of us climbed into the stands during warm-up, picking seats near the court where Jess, the number one seed, would be playing. It was a Saturday morning, warm and sunny, only a slight breeze coming in through the hills. I could smell coconut suntan lotion in the air, a familiar scent at outdoor sporting events at SDU. I ran a hand through my still-damp hair. I'd gotten up around eleven. It was only a little before noon now.

"There's Jess," Laura said, adjusting her light brown hair beneath her baseball cap.

While Holly and I both sported soccer shorts and Sambas, Laura was wearing a tight white tank top and faded cut-off jeans shorts, bordering on the Daisy Duke variety. I'd noticed a couple of guys checking her out as we picked our seats, and thought again that if I didn't know Laura, I'd probably have the hots for her myself. She was the consummate athlete, all muscle and energy. On the soccer field, whatever individual skills she lacked she made up for with determination. Laura liked to win.

"Didn't you say you talked to Jess a couple of weeks ago?" Holly asked me, raising a suggestive eyebrow that Laura missed.

I ignored the look. "Yeah. She's pretty cool. Seems kind of shy, though."

"Shy?" Laura echoed. Reserve was a foreign concept to her, as was tact, most of her friends agreed. "What does she have to be shy about? That girl can play tennis like no one I've ever seen. I don't know why she didn't go D-one."

I had wondered that myself. In college sports, playing at a good Division II school wasn't nearly as notable as playing for even a mediocre Division I program. I was at SDU because they were the only school that had offered me a decent chunk of money. I couldn't imagine the same was true for Jess.

"Some people are just naturally shy, Laura," Holly said.

I could hear the slight annoyance in her voice and elbowed her, glad I was sitting in the middle. Holly had a lower tolerance for Laura than I did.

"I guess so," Laura conceded, but it was obvious she didn't understand why anyone might be anything but bordering on obnoxious.

"Great day for tennis," I put in, changing the subject.

Holly rolled her eyes at me, and I knew what she was thinking:

Cam the Peacemaker. She seemed to think the nickname was an insult.

Directly below us, Jess was practicing her serves, but she seemed distracted. She kept glancing toward the opposite corner of the court. Curious, I followed her gaze and spotted an older woman sporting a wide white hat, small sunglasses and a tan suit. Her gold jewelry glinted in the sunlight. She was standing just inside the passageway that connected the stadium's handful of courts, almost as if she were trying not to be seen.

"Do you think Jess'll make All-American?" Holly asked, watching her serve.

"I hope so," I said. "She totally deserves it."

Later, I thought we might have jinxed her. Jess was on a twenty-two match winning streak, but she lost the first set 2-6. The girl she was playing, a tanned brunette with short hair and big quad muscles, wasn't even that skilled. Jess double-faulted two games away in the opening set. This time she didn't throw her racquet.

At the end of the first set, when the players took a break before switching sides, Holly leaned into my shoulder and murmured, "Dude, what's her problem? She's playing like crap."

"No kidding."

Sitting on a bench at the edge of the court during the switchover, Jess looked exhausted. It had to be mental, I knew, because she was in top physical condition. She just wasn't her usual zippy self. She wiped her face on a small towel, then looked again toward the opposite corner. I followed her gaze. The woman in the suit had disappeared. Jess sat motionless for another minute, towel draped over her face. Then she flung it aside and headed onto the court.

The second set was like an entirely different match. From the first point, Jess was all over the place, rippling muscles and extra effort and long-limbed reach. She finished the match 2-6, 6-1, 6-2. Afterward, she shook hands with her vanquished opponent and the umpire, exchanged a few words with Adrienne Porter, the head coach, and almost ran off court to the field house. I watched her leave, her head down, long legs eating up the distance.

"She's not shy," Laura said, watching Jess leave. "She's totally got attitude. What a snob."

"Shut up," I said, and it was Holly's turn to elbow me in the ribs. "You don't know what you're talking about."

Laura was staring at me. "Okay, I'm sorry. Take a chill."

As we watched the top-seeded doubles match, I pondered my outburst. Usually Laura's comments rolled right off me. But when she called Jess a snob, it pissed me off even though I'd once thought nearly the same thing myself. Now that I'd met her, I knew my initial assessment was off. There was something about the way she held herself apart from other people that made me want to defend her. Which was ridiculous, I told myself as I sat in the tennis stadium that afternoon. Jess was probably the last person on campus who needed defending.

As expected, SDU won the match easily. In women's sports, tennis was our strongest program. Then came soccer, volleyball, and swimming. The rest were mostly club teams still, even after two decades of Title IX. When the match ended, we headed back to the gym lot where Laura had parked her brand-new Isuzu Trooper.

"I'm going to pee," I said as we reached the car. "I'll be right back."

"Can't you even wait five minutes?" Holly complained. "We're starving here, man."

"I've been holding it the whole time," I said over my shoulder, jogging toward the building. My small bladder was a source of contention among my teammates and friends. I had peed in more shrubbery in my life than I cared to remember.

I flashed my ID at the booth and took the stairs two at a time up to the main floor. I burst through the women's locker room door and headed directly into the nearest stall, glimpsing out of the corner of my eye someone at the sinks. Intent on peeing, I closed the stall door and relieved myself. *Whew.*

When I emerged a moment later, I realized it was Jess Maxwell at the sinks, her back to me as she splashed her face with water. I recognized her socks first, her blue and aqua cross trainers, those fabulous legs. Her hair was wet, dark strands leaving streaks on the shoulders of her white T-shirt. She looked up as I neared.

"Nice job today," I said, and started to wash my hands, trying to ignore the fact that Jess Maxwell had just heard me pee.

"Thanks. I didn't know you'd be there." She seemed embarrassed too and brushed the gym towel with its blue and gold SDU logo across her face quickly.

"I came with a couple of soccer players, Holly Bishop and Laura Grant. They're our year, too." I dried my hands on a paper towel. "We all thought you were great in the last two sets."

"The first one sucked, huh."

I leaned against a sink and watched her brush her hair. "I wouldn't say *sucked*. You just seemed off balance. Was everything okay?" I thought of the woman in the suit.

Her eyes darkened for a moment. Then she shrugged. "Just a slow start, that's all."

"The rest of the team did really well, too. You guys are awesome this year."

She looked a little guilty as she tucked her brush and a pair of dirty socks into her athletic bag. "Did you see if Julie Seaver won her match?"

"I think so."

"Good."

I wanted to ask her why she'd been so nervous today, what had made her fall off her game so dramatically, but it wasn't really any of my business. Besides, Holly and Laura were waiting.

Still, I didn't move and neither did Jess. We stood in the locker room facing each other, the scent of soap and shampoo mixed with women's sweat hanging in the air. For a moment, she looked as if she might say something more. Then the outer door opened and the rest of the tennis team began to pour in, muffled words and laughter echoing off the metal lockers.

"Good luck with the rest of the season," I said, backing away.

"Thanks, Cam."

As I left the locker room, I couldn't shake the sense that, crazy as it seemed, maybe she'd wanted me to ask all the questions knocking about my head.

Outside, Laura blasted the car horn when she saw me.

"Took you long enough," she said as I slid into the backseat of the Trooper.

"Sorry, dudes. Let's roll."

As Laura slammed the Trooper into reverse and caromed out of the lot, Holly flicked the volume up on the stereo. Van Morrison, Laura's favorite. We headed off campus for a late lunch, and I trailed my arm out the open window, watching people and trees and buildings flash past. I forgot about Jess Maxwell as the sun warmed my skin and Holly grinned at me over her shoulder and we sped along the hilly streets of La Jolla, the seaside resort community in northern San Diego where SDU was located.

In the back of Laura's Trooper, I was acutely aware of the passage of time, present receding into the recent past as I sang along to the music and felt my words falling away to nothing. I wanted to hold on to the moment, to the feeling of sun and car and friends and possibilities, the immediate future stretching comfortably, known, ahead, even as the moment slipped past and got lost in a thousand others.

CHAPTER THREE

A few weeks later, the tennis team made it to nationals where Jess performed like the stud she was and captured All-American honors. But I didn't see her again before I headed home to Oregon for the summer.

Back in Portland, May soon blended into June and school seemed a million miles away. Monday through Friday, I drove my parents' old Toyota Tercel from our bungalow just off Hawthorne near Mt. Tabor to work in downtown Portland. I was the only woman on the Parks crew. There was one black man, John Bakough, a Nigerian who had come to the States for university and never left. He and I figured we were the city's concession to affirmative action, since the rest of our co-workers were whitey-whites, as John called us.

Every other week it was my job to groom the lawn bowling

field at Westmoreland Park, but most days I rode mowers, trimmed bushes with weed whackers, and painted signs and fences at any of a number of city parks. Occasionally we acted as security at special events like arts and crafts fairs or outdoor concerts. Then we would trade in our coveralls to wear walkie-talkies in the belt loops of our dark green shorts and call each other things like "Big John" and "Little Joe" and "Daddy Cam" over the airwaves.

This was my second summer at the Parks. The guys were fun to work with, most of the time, but I never seemed to quite fit in. Whether that was because I was a woman, a lesbian—though the guys pretended not to know and I pretended not to be flagrant—or a college student, I was never sure. Maybe all of the above. I only got the job because my mother knew a woman in the city Garden Club who was married to a high-up in the Parks Department. Except for me and a couple of other seasonal student workers, the other Parks employees were permanent and owned homes on the outskirts of the city, the only place they could afford. Several were married with kids.

Not my buddy Joe, though. Joe Bulanski, ninth of eleven children in a Polish Catholic farm family from Wisconsin, was my best friend at the Parks. A natural comedian, he never seemed to run out of funny stories about his ten brothers and sisters. He was also the only guy at work who acknowledged that my being a lesbian was cool with him. I didn't tell him, he just figured it out. He had a sister who was gay, he told me the one time we talked about it at the end of my first summer on the crew. He had lived with her for a month in San Francisco when he first moved to the West Coast.

That conversation was one of the few occasions I could remember Joe being serious. The other instance took place the summer after my sophomore year, on a July afternoon when the air was hot and still. He and I were trimming the grass close to the west fence of Forest Park, one of the largest urban forests in the country, under the wire and around the posts where the mower couldn't reach. At afternoon break time, we left our weed whackers to cool and sat in the shade on the tailgate of our green Parks truck, drinking from our water bottles and gazing out over the Willamette River.

"Do you ever go to church?" Joe asked out of the blue.

"Sometimes. My mom likes the Unitarian church downtown," I said, looking over at him.

He had shaggy, dark brown hair bordering on a mullet and wore a faded Emerson, Lake and Palmer T-shirt beneath his uniform. I had never seen him in shorts. Even during special events in the middle of the summer, he opted for the dark green Parks pants. At the end of my first summer on the crew, I'd asked him if he had some kind of scar or birthmark that disfigured his legs. He'd laughed, lean frame shaking with the force. Then he told me it was a farm habit he had never quite shaken; his legs were merely ghostly white beneath the uniform. Men on farms didn't wear shorts, he explained, because you had to be careful around the chemicals and the equipment and the crops. Flannel and denim were a farmer's favorites for good reason.

Now he squinted up at the sky and took a gulp of water.

"My parents are what you would call devout. They used to drag all of us to the Catholic church in town every week in our Sunday best. Me in my Peter Pan collars and this wide, goofy tie with pink and blue stripes. And brown corduroy pants in the winter, of course."

I had no trouble picturing Joe in the outfit he described. He had told me before that members of his family dressed as if they were refugees from the '70s.

"Wide-ribbed corduroy?" I teased.

"You know it." He nodded, smiling.

His teeth were even, thanks to that great twentieth century wonder, braces. He used to play a lot of baseball, so we had traded ball-in-the-braces stories the first summer we worked together. Now, leaning back on his hands, he looked out over the park, dark blue eyes tracing the evergreen tree line against the clear, sun-shot sky.

"But you know, kid"—he was ten years older, and liked to call me kid—"I decided a long time ago that I didn't believe in their God. I couldn't. Not when their God said that if you judged your neighbors then He would turn around and judge you. It's so hypocritical. The church fathers interpret scripture the way they want to, not necessarily the way they should.

"Once when I was seventeen or eighteen, I was in my canoe on the creek way back in the woods, and this doe brought her fawns down to the water to drink. I got closer and the little ones, they just kept drinking, not more than ten feet away. The doe and I stared at each other as I drifted past, and looking in her eyes, I had this amazing feeling of peace. As I paddled away, I remember thinking that God is something within every one of us, every living being. Animals, people, trees. And this," he spread his arms wide open, encompassing the forested park, the sky, the sun, "this is my place of worship. You know?"

I nodded. "Totally."

We sat together in the hot, still afternoon, surrounded by Oregon greens and blues. And I did know.

He looked away, finally, to glance at his watch. "Looks like story time with Father Joseph is officially over. Come on. Best get on with the fence trim from hell."

And that was that. Back to the hot weed whackers and the feel of shredded grass and twigs whipping against our legs, the roar of the small motors and the smell of gasoline disturbing the peaceful afternoon.

Two-person projects like that one were rare. Most jobs were either solitary or called for four or five of us. In the afternoons, I would take off alone on my favorite John Deere mower, Walkman in one pocket of my coveralls, sleeves rolled up so that my farmer tan wouldn't be too bad, SDU hat worn backward to protect my neck while I mowed. There was something satisfying about trimming the lush summer growth, about making even swaths across a green expanse.

Those days, kicked back on my mower in the summer sun, Melissa Etheridge or Janis Joplin or the Indigo Girls blaring in my ears over the sound of the motor, I almost liked being away from my SDU life. Sometimes I felt like I didn't quite belong there, either. Most of my friends from school spent their summers leisurely touring Europe or working as an intern in one of their parents' law offices or financial services firms. Holly was currently working for a broker friend of her father's three days a week. The other four days she usually spent at the beach, she told me when she called on my birthday at the end of

June. SDU kids tended to be rich. And white. And Californian.

Have you heard the one about the Oregonian, Californian and Texan who go camping together? The first night out, they're sitting around a campfire when the Texan pulls out a bottle of tequila. After a couple of swallows, he tosses the bottle into the air, pulls out a six-shooter and neatly shoots the bottle. When the Californian points out that there was still some tequila left in the bottle, the Texan replies, "That's okay, we have plenty of tequila where I come from."

Not to be outdone, the Californian whips out a bottle of White Zinfandel, drains it, tosses the bottle into the air and shoots it with a 9mm semiautomatic pistol. When the Oregonian gives him an odd look, the Californian says, "That's okay, we have plenty of wine where I come from."

So the Oregonian opens a pale ale from a Portland microbrewery. He downs the entire bottle, throws it into the air, shoots the Californian with a 12-gauge shotgun and deftly catches the beer bottle. When the Texan stares at him, horrified, the Oregonian says, "That's okay, we have plenty of Californians where I come from, but we always recycle."

Pacific Northwesterners tend not to appreciate the perpetual flow of Californians to the north. Our southern neighbors move to Oregon and Washington in droves, driving up housing prices and changing the local economies and communities. But I loved Holly and Laura in spite of our regional differences. After all, they couldn't help that they'd been born in the land of greed and honey.

The great thing about summer was that working so many hours made the weeks pass quickly. On the weekends, I occupied myself with my favorite things about being an Oregonian: hiking in the Cascades with a group of friends from high school, reunited for the summer months; camping out on the beach with bonfires and local brew; catching local minor league baseball and A-league soccer games; pub-hopping with our fake IDs. Summer at home was usually a well-needed dose of normalcy after the school year in Southern California with its tightly-packed houses, abundant strip malls and unremitting sunshine.

I worked for the Parks that summer through the third week of August. Then I took a week off, sleeping until ten and lying out in my backyard, still working out nearly every night. I'd started my preseason conditioning program in mid-July—running distance, lifting at a nearby gym, practicing sprints on my old high school track. Now I counted the days until preseason, crossing them off one by one on the Far Side wall calendar in my childhood bedroom. Waiting for real life, my soccer life, to begin again.

At last it was time to go back to California. At the end of the month, I packed the Toyota, said goodbye to my family and friends and headed down the coast. My parents had decided I should have a car on campus this year, and I wasn't arguing. The Tercel might not compare to the Saabs and BMWs and Troopers at SDU, but it was small and red and in good condition. I loved that car.

In Orange County, I stopped to pick up Holly. She'd crashed two cars in high school, so her parents, Bill and Elizabeth, had decided not to give her a car in college. Yet. They said if her grades stayed high, she might get one senior year. Holly's family lived a block from the ocean in Newport Beach in a huge Mexican villa with a red tile roof. Her parents remind me of the people in that movie, *L.A. Story*, who sit around the dinner table talking about vacation homes and stocks and plastic surgery, then kiss the air near each other's cheeks before taking their leave in a swirl of lounge pants and low-cut blouses. But they were nice to me because I was a friend of Holly's, and even managed not to look too askance at the sight of my eight-year-old Toyota in their driveway. I doubted they had any clue I was gay.

Holly had told me once that they referred to me as her outdoorsy friend from Oregon. "How is that friend of yours?" her mother would ask. "She's got the rosiest cheeks, that girl. What is it she does in the summer again? Park ranger, wasn't it? And what is it her father does? Works with retarded children?"

Whenever Holly did her impression of her mother, I cracked up. Then again, her family stories often left me snickering. Our families had met once after a game freshman year. We both stood back and smothered our laughter as our mothers smiled politely and our fathers shook hands and her frat boy, business-major brother tried to find something to talk about with Nate, my ski bum, outdoor recreation-major brother. I think everyone was relieved when we went to dinner with the soccer team and ended up at different tables.

The last Sunday of August, Holly and I loaded her things into my car and drove away from her childhood home, waving to her mother as we headed out. Her father, an attorney, was golfing with colleagues. As we drove down the palm tree-lined street, passing parked Mercedes, BMWs and Lexuses, Holly rolled her window down, stuck her head out and shouted, "See ya! Wouldn't wanna be ya!"

Freed from our families once more, we headed toward SDU for our junior season, and I felt again that sense of possibility. Our college soccer careers were half over, but we still had so much ahead of us, so many practices and games and tough wins and hard losses. I couldn't wait to begin again.

CHAPTER FOUR

Sunday was moving-in day. Holly and I were in the same dorms as the previous year, only a couple of buildings away from each other. We pulled up in front of hers and started to unload her things. Holly had more clothes than anyone I had ever met. Whenever she got upset, she went shopping with her father's credit card. That was the one thing she had in common with her mother, I used to tease her.

Athletes were the only students back on campus this early: men's and women's soccer, field hockey, football, volleyball, men's and women's cross country, and men's and women's tennis. Lugging Holly's trunk toward the elevator—we would be running plenty of stairs in the stadium during preseason—we passed a tennis player on the front steps. She smiled and nodded at us and we managed mangled "Hi's," and I thought suddenly of Jess Maxwell. She should be back today too. I'd thought of her occasionally over the summer, especially when I watched coverage of the French Open or Wimbledon. Now I wondered when I'd run into her, and, more importantly, if she would be as friendly as she had been the previous spring.

Holly helped me with my room after we'd finished hers, insisting on personally unpacking my posters and threatening to put them up where she liked. I let her. The year before, my posters had remained rolled up in a corner until after soccer season. I'd had a heck of a time getting them to unroll and stay up. A couple of boxes of clothes had remained in the same corner, unpacked throughout the year, much to Holly's consternation.

Unlike me, Holly had good decoration sense. When we'd finished, my room actually looked nice, I had to admit. She had hung my Indian print sheet across one wall, filling the room with its warm colors. The other walls were nicely covered with my favorite Matisse print, "The Casbah Gate, 1912, Museo Pushkin," a couple of Picasso prints, a map of the world, a Nike running poster that featured a woman following a moss-strewn path that I recognized as a trail in Oregon, and a poster of Michael Jordan in silhouette with his arms extended. Jordan was my favorite athlete of all time, even if he did insist on regularly trouncing the Trailblazers. A bookshelf was tucked into a corner, boxes of books just waiting to fill its empty spaces, while a beat-up desk sat to one side of a pair of tall, narrow windows.

The last thing we did was haul my futon and frame up from the basement where I'd stashed them in the spring, once again praising the elevator as it carried us painlessly up to the sixth floor. We pushed the frame up against the wall with the Indian print and dragged the double-sized, extra-thick mattress into place, collapsing together on top of it.

"I have a feeling we're going to be spending a lot of time here the next couple of weeks," Holly said, staring at the ceiling.

"I have a feeling you're right," I agreed, and sneezed from the dust floating around the room.

"Thanks a lot." Holly wiped the arm closest to me. "That's disgusting."

"Sorry," I apologized, trying not to laugh. "It snuck up on me."

"I think that deserves... a tickling!" She jumped on top of me, attacking my underarms mercilessly.

"No! Stop!" I gasped, trying to throw her off. Finally I managed to hook my leg around hers and tugged. We rolled around on the bed, laughing, until we heard a polite, "A-hem," at the doorway. We both sat up, looking around quickly.

Jess Maxwell stood there, holding a box with my name and the words "Soccer Stuff" scrawled across one side. She was smiling slightly. "Sorry to interrupt."

"No problem." I scrambled up off the futon and headed toward the door, mock-glaring at Holly over my shoulder. "My friend here was just leaving, right, Holl? Don't you have that special someone waiting for a phone call?" I didn't want Jess Maxwell thinking that Holly and I were more than friends rolling around on my futon together.

"Oh, yeah. Shit." Holly jumped up. She was supposed to call Becca, her girlfriend, as soon as she got in. Becca had stayed in San Diego for the summer. They'd seen each other frequently, but the constant commuting between San Diego and L.A. was starting to strain their relationship. "I'll be right back."

"By the way, Holly, this is Jess Maxwell," I added. "Jess, Holly Bishop."

"Hi," Jess said with that shy look that always surprised me. She pushed a strand of dark hair behind one ear. "I've seen you around."

"Same here," Holly said. "Nice to officially meet you." She glanced back at me. "Don't go anywhere without me, okay? I'll be back in a minute." She punched me affectionately, smiled at Jess again, and jogged off down the hallway.

"Gotta love jocks," I said, rubbing my arm. Holly only punched people she liked. Lucky us.

Jess was still standing in the hallway, still holding the box with my name on it. My cleats, shin guards, turf shoes, athletic bag, water bottles, ball and pump were all in there, the first box I'd packed the day before and the last one I'd unloaded today.

"Let me take that," I said, finally cluing in, and reached for the box. "Where'd you find it, anyway?"

"Out on the front step." She followed me into the room,

glancing around curiously, and stopped in front of the Matisse poster. "I've never seen this one. It's beautiful."

I set the box on the floor and wiped my hands on my dusty cut-offs, moving to stand beside her. "That's my favorite painting."

"I see why." She stared at the poster, seeming intent on the muted blues and reds and greens swirled together.

It was good to see her. She looked healthy and strong in a green tank top and white shorts, long limbs well-muscled. I wondered what she had done over the summer to get such an even tan. Probably hung out at the beach.

"Thanks for bringing up the box," I said belatedly.

"Figured you'd probably be needing it." She moved away, checking out the other posters and the few books I had unpacked. "I was helping Jenny Lewis move some of her stuff in, and someone said they saw you on six."

"Good thing you found it," I said. "Would not be fun to break in new cleats this week." Not to mention drop the hundred bucks that Copas, my shoe of choice, commanded.

"No kidding." She turned from her vantage point at the window overlooking the courtyard on the inside of the building. "You've got a great room. I can't believe you're unpacked already."

"Wasn't my idea," I confessed, dropping onto the edge of the futon. "Holly's kind of compulsive. It seems she wasn't happy that I had a couple of boxes last year that I never unpacked, so *voila*." I waved my hand.

"Good thing you have Holly around, then."

"Most of the time," I said, noticing the way the sunlight picked out golden highlights in her dark hair, pulled back in a silver barrette. I admired the simple elegance of the style. When I'd had long hair in high school, I'd never been able to figure out any way to wear it other than a ponytail. Now I frequented a barbershop in San Diego that specialized in clippered cuts. "Are you ready for tennis?"

"I think so. It'll be good to see everyone again. La Jolla is really quiet in the summer."

"You stayed in town this year?"

"I always stay." She looked sideways, closing her eyes for

a moment in the sunlight streaming in the window. Then she looked at me again. "When's your first practice?"

The subject of summer break slipped away as we talked about preseason and regular season schedules. They played on Wednesdays and Saturdays. We played Tuesdays, Thursdays and Saturdays. They were hosting fall Big Eights this year, always a major event in the SDU sports world, the second weekend in October.

"You should come check it out," Jess said. Her words were quick, her voice lighter now as we discussed our upcoming seasons. She loved tennis as much as I loved soccer, I could tell.

"I'll bring some soccer players to cheer you guys on," I promised. "Even if we have a Saturday game that weekend, we should be around on Sunday."

"Don't you love Sundays? Whenever I'm in season, Sundays are the best. You can sleep in, eat whatever you want whenever you want, and no practice." She sighed, smiling slightly, already daydreaming about Sundays.

"I know what you mean." We were both quiet for a minute. Then I said, "Can I ask you something?"

Jess crossed her arms over the front of her T-shirt, still leaning against the windowsill. Her dreamy smile vanished. "Sure."

Relax, I almost said. I longed to tell her she didn't have to defend herself against me, that I just wanted to be her friend. Instead, I grinned at her disarmingly, the charming smile I saved for straight girls who were convinced I was about to hit on them.

"I was just wondering, what nationality are your parents? You don't look like a Maxwell."

"My father's mother was Spanish," she said. "And my mother's family was Scandinavian. What about you? Wallace is what, Scottish? Irish?"

"Both. My dad's father came over from Scotland when he was ten. But they lived in Ireland before that."

I leaned back on my hands, trying to appear casual. She'd referred to her parents in the past tense. Were they no longer living? Was that why she stayed in La Jolla during the summers?

Probably they were just acrimoniously divorced, I decided, like the parents of half the kids at SDU.

"What about your mother?" she asked.

"Northern European mutt. Some French, a little English, maybe some German and Italian. Basically every major country in World War II except the Soviets."

This elicited a small smile. She still seemed tense, though. When we were talking about sports, she was fine. But now that the conversation had drifted into the personal realm, she was responding carefully, rationing out details about her past. Definitely a story there. I wished I knew what it was.

As if she could read my nosy thoughts, Jess looked at her watch and pushed away from the window. "I should probably get going. We have a team meeting before dinner."

"Us too."

"Do you need a ride? Or are you riding your bike down?" she asked, smiling a little. Teasing me.

"I have a car this year," I bragged, waving at the Just Do It keychain on the dresser.

"Let me guess. A Saab? No, too conservative. Let's see." She looked me up and down, eyes narrowed consideringly. It was probably my imagination, but her eyes seemed to linger on my legs, freshly shaven and newly tanned from my week off. "You'd drive a Beamer, wouldn't you? Or your father's old Mercedes."

I nudged the soccer box toward the desk with the tip of my sandal. "I don't know what you've heard, but I'm one of those people who probably wouldn't be here if it wasn't for soccer."

She stared at me blankly. Did she not get it?

"I drive a Tercel," I elaborated. "And my parents drive Mitsubishis. Sorry to disappoint you." I picked at the tape on a box of books on the middle bookshelf, catching a glimpse of Virginia Woolf's *A Room of One's Own* packed in next to a *Fundamentals of Literacy* text.

"Oh." Her voice wasn't mocking now. "So you're a regular person, too."

I looked up, caught by the warmth in her eyes. "Exactly."

We smiled at each other. She had probably felt like an outsider before, too, on this campus. That was the thing about sports. If you were a good athlete, your sport could level the playing field of social interaction to the point that no one else realized you didn't truly belong.

Off in the distance I heard Holly rambling down the hall and humming a tune from our mutually favorite Indigo Girls CD, *Nomads Indians Saints*, which we had listened to a couple of times through on the way down this morning.

"Holly, however, is not," I added. "Not regular, I mean, and definitely not normal."

"Did I hear my name, perchance?" Holly glided into the room grinning, and I realized all over again what a cute girl she was with her curly blonde hair pulled away from her face in a style similar to Jess's, her light blue eyes and the tiny freckles that dotted her nose and cheeks year-round. She was hard to resist when she was in a good mood.

"Perchance," I said. "And maybe it was just those voices again. I thought you said you took your meds."

"Shut up, Cam." She slugged me happily in the shoulder.

"I should go," Jess said again, heading toward the door. She stopped near the short, squat dresser just inside the door and examined the framed picture lying on top. I hadn't decided where to put it yet, the Wallace clan photo taken right before Nate headed up to Alaska the previous summer. "Is this your family?"

"Yeah." Nate was already working on his Grizzly Adams beard, as my dad called it, but it was actually a pretty good picture of me. I was tanned and smiling and dressed in my favorite khaki shorts and a dark gray T-shirt. Gray was my favorite color. Matched my eyes, Cara, my high school girlfriend, used to say.

Holly looked over Jess's shoulder. "Doesn't Cam look like a preppy boy in that picture?"

"Shut up, Holly," I said, and punched her. Hard.

But Jess didn't seem weirded out by the comment. She just said, "I don't think she looks like a boy at all. See you guys later. Good luck with preseason."

"You too. See you," I added, following her to the door and watching until she disappeared into the stairwell at the end of the hall. Then I turned back to Holly. "What were you trying to do, out me or something?"

Holly sat down on the edge of my bed, wiggling her bare toes in front of her. "You mean the preppy boy comment?"

"Duh. As far as I know, Jess is straight. No need to scare her off." I sat down next to her, then lay back and gazed up at the white ceiling. Not that I wanted to hide who I was, either. I just wanted to deal with the issue my own way in my own time.

"Come on, Cam." Holly stared at me. "You wore a Silence Equals Death T-shirt to the spring sports banquet freshman year, remember? Do you honestly think Jess Maxwell doesn't know?"

I had forgotten about that banquet. That was the night Jess had received the Rookie of the Year award. I remembered she had walked up to the podium all cool and sophisticated in a black sundress and a black jacket, her hair swept up in a twist. I'd looked at her up there, beautiful and talented and smiling slightly as the athletic director presented her with the engraved plaque, and for just that moment, I'd wished I could be Jess Maxwell.

"Good point," I admitted. Even without my choice of apparel, everyone in the SDU sports world gossiped about everyone else. I'd known Jake Kim and Brad Peterson, my buddies from the swim team, were gay long before I met them. "I don't know what it is about her, Holl. There's something, I don't know, deeper going on with her. Don't you think?"

Still leaning on her side, Holly reached over and patted my head. "What I think is that you're into her. Not that I blame you. She's totally hot."

"That's not it. I mean, she is hot. But it's not like I want to sleep with her. I just want to get to know her better."

Holly sat up, looking around. "Wait, where's your calendar? We have to mark down this day of infamy, this twenty-eighth day of August 1991 when Camille Wallace claimed that she did not want to get an attractive woman into bed."

Laughing, I grabbed a pillow and whacked her on the head. "Shut up, jackass." It was impossible to stay serious around her when she was in one of her moods.

She grabbed the other pillow and struck back. Eventually

we collapsed on our backs holding the pillows to our stomachs.

"We should chill," she said, looking at her watch. "In another, what, forty-five minutes we'll be running the two mile. For time."

I groaned. "Don't remind me! So how's your girlfriend, anyway? What'd you guys do, have phone sex or something?"

"No, we just talked." She flopped over on her side. "But guess what? She's coming over tonight. She has to be at work tomorrow morning at eight thirty and we have breakfast at eight, so it works out perfectly. Pretty cool, huh?"

"Sure, if you like booty calls." No wonder she was so excited. She was going to get laid tonight. Which reminded me. "You know what? I've been meaning to tell you this. I think I'm going to be celibate this year."

She burst out laughing. "Yeah, right. As if! You flirt with every woman you meet."

I moved up on the futon and leaned against the wall. "I'm serious—at least during the season. I'm going to concentrate on soccer and classes and nothing else. Next year is my student teaching internship, and I won't have as much time to think about soccer."

"You are serious," she said, gazing at me. "You think you can make All-American?"

"Maybe. Either way, I want to give it everything I have right now. And I haven't met anyone really, you know, special or anything yet. I hate that word, special."

"Me, too. Makes me think of short buses. No offense to your dad's students, of course. But I think you can make it. All-American, I mean. If anyone on defense gets it, it'll be you."

"Thanks, man." I was glad she was a striker—that meant we never had to compete for playing time.

She slapped my leg. "You're welcome. Now let's get going. I want to get to the gym early and check out the freshmen recruits."

We jumped off the bed and got going.

CHAPTER FIVE

More than one opponent compared our playing fields to a golf course. Short grass, evenly spread over a flat, machine-leveled surface, flushed daily with water by an automated sprinkler and drainage system, mowed horizontally like World Cup fields every three days in the cool evening hours so that the freshly shorn grass wouldn't burn in daylight sun. A hillside provided ample spectator space and sheltered the field from the strongest breezes. There were even enough fields for separate men's and women's practice and game fields, a fact that never ceased to amaze me after my high school experience—the girls' team had played league games on the J.V. football team's practice field my freshman year in Portland.

Stepping onto the field each August was always the most incredible experience—grass springy beneath my cleats, familiar friendly (mostly) faces all around, sunlight warm on my bare arms and legs, new Adidas soccer ball at my feet—regulation size 5, FIFA approved, SDU logo embossed on multiple pentagons amidst the clean white leather hexagons. As the California breeze brushed my face and my teammates' chatter washed over me, I would rest one foot on top of the ball and think how lucky I was to be back for another season.

Preseason was a lifetime all its own. After the initial excitement came the hard work, when we pushed our bodies to do things they barely remembered, taught our muscles and minds to work in unison all over again. Ball at our feet, sweat soaking our hair and stinging our eyes, Coach yelling at us to, "Think, athletes! Play smart!" Anyone who hadn't followed the workout schedule he sent out mid-summer to all prospective and returning players knew even before that first practice they'd be hurting. And in August, the anticipation of pain was almost as sharp as the pain itself.

In the space of two hours that Sunday afternoon, the last weekend of summer, during timed runs, overlap drills, shooting practice, passing drills, each player invited to attend SDU's tryouts experienced frustration, satisfaction, self-loathing, egotism, exhaustion. And that was only the first day—we still had six and a half more days of preseason, which meant thirteen more practice sessions to run our butts off and push our bodies to their limits before Scrimmage Day.

Scrimmage Day fell on the Sunday before classes began. While the non-athletes at SDU were moving trunks into dorm rooms and unpacking, listening to CDs, sharing cigarettes and beers with the friends they hadn't seen in three months, we were playing three one-hour scrimmages, all before two in the afternoon, to determine who would stay on the team and who would go back to being a normal SDU student destined to look the other way anytime they ran into one of the rest of us on campus. By the time we left the locker room at the end of Scrimmage Day, Coach had posted the official team list on the Intercollegiate Bulletin Board. I never knew if he told the players he cut in person or left them to discover their names missing from the list. As a scholarship recruit, I had never had to worry about being cut. I hoped he told them in person. Holly always said that was the Oregonian in me talking. Probably she was right.

At four thirty in the afternoon on Scrimmage Day, Coach held the first official team meeting to hand out uniforms and have the official team picture taken, to be added eventually to the dozens of photos already adorning the Intercollegiate Wall on the second floor of the gym. Then he gave his usual "Welcome, athletes, these are my expectations" speech—which by now, year three, I could almost recite with him—and released us to catch a ride home, six people to a car, for an hour's nap before dinner. We had become well-versed in napping on the run, sleeping as we had the past week wherever and for as long as we could.

The following day, Monday, classes were due to start and the regular season practice schedule to begin. No more two-a-days now. With the rest of campus coming alive again, we would be settling into our dual student-athlete roles once more, preseason a steadily fading memory. But for tonight, there was only the deep untroubled sleep of the well-worked athlete, tryouts behind us and a bright, unwritten season full of hope and potential still ahead.

CHAPTER SIX

I didn't see Jess much those first few weeks back on campus. Soccer opened with a 2-0 win on the road at Irvine. I scored one of our goals on a penalty kick, which was good—Coach had told me during preseason that if I wanted to make All-American I would have to increase my offensive points. Meanwhile, tennis won their opening two matches easily, blanking their first opponent and nearly shutting out the next. Second week of September, the national singles' rankings came out. Jess, a preseason All-American selection, was ranked number one in Division II.

The Monday the tennis rankings came out, I stayed late after practice to talk to Coach about the defense. Our senior captains were a forward and a midfielder, and half the time they appeared to have no idea what was going on in the backfield. But Coach seemed distracted by the mountain of paperwork on his desk.

After a brief, unfulfilling conversation, I took the elevator down from the coach's office wing on the third floor to the lobby, where I stepped out directly into the path of someone exiting the nearby stairwell.

"Sorry," I said automatically before I realized it was Jess. Then, "Oh, hey! How's it going?"

Tiny frown lines faded from her forehead as she focused on me. "Cam! Hey."

We stood smiling at each other in the gym lobby, both dressed in practice gear, athletic bags slung over our shoulders. It was good to see her. I felt a sudden surge of energy.

"Are you going to dinner? Want to head up together?" I asked, picturing the two of us seated at a small table in the noisy student center, talking about our sports over a huge dinner befitting a couple of intercollegiate athletes.

"I can't, actually," she said, fiddling with the strap on her bag. "I'm on a limited meal plan this fall, and I already ate breakfast and lunch on campus today."

"Do you live on campus or off?" I started toward the door, aware that the ID booth attendant, a softball player whose name I couldn't remember, was openly eavesdropping on our conversation.

"Off." Jess reached the door first and held it open for me. We emerged into the evening and rounded the corner of the building, heading toward the parking lot.

"Where? If you don't mind my asking," I added, remembering how private she was.

"I rent the third floor of a house on Cistern, just off Ocean View."

We'd reached my car. I stopped next to the driver's door and looked at Jess, trying to think of some way to extend our conversation. The opportunity to hang out might not arise again anytime soon. With classes and the season approaching full swing, neither of us had much time to spend on extracurriculars like a social life.

She stopped on the sidewalk beside my little Tercel, looking off toward her Cabriolet a few spots away. Then she looked back at me, a trace of shyness in her eyes.

"I was just thinking, if you wanted you could come have dinner with me. It's only pasta and salad, carbo loading for Wednesday."

I was nodding before she finished. "That'd be cool. You want me to grab anything on the way? Soda or something?"

"That's okay, you can just follow me."

She toyed with the strap on her bag again. Was she about to change her mind? I held my breath.

"Okay then." She moved away.

I couldn't believe it—Jess Maxwell had just invited me to her apartment. Not at all what I had expected tonight. I slid into my car and tossed my bag on the seat. It was starting to get a little chilly. Not to mention, I smelled like dried sweat and the outdoors. While Jess started her car, I pulled on a relatively clean SDU soccer sweatshirt. Much better.

Jess waved as she backed out of her space, and I followed her from the lot. As we left the university behind, I found myself relaxing when I hadn't even realized I was tense. Soccer and school and team dynamics faded away, and all at once I was just a regular person driving through La Jolla as the sun drifted nearer the horizon.

On a tree-lined residential street a few minutes from campus, Jess pulled up in front of an enormous yellow Victorian house that looked like it belonged in San Francisco with its neat white trim and polished front porch swing. I stared at it in utter admiration. This was the kind of house I had always wanted to live in. The Northwest bungalow I'd grown up in was sweet and more than comfortable, of course. But this, this was my dream house.

I parked on the road behind Jess's car and got out as she walked toward me.

"You live here?" I asked.

"I know, I ask myself that almost daily. Come on," she added, touching my arm as she passed. "I'm starving."

"Me, too."

I followed her up the drive to a side door entrance. That was the first time she had ever touched me voluntarily. Maybe she was starting to feel more comfortable around me. I wondered again if she knew I was gay. How could she not? All anyone had to do was look at me, I'd always thought. Adolescent boy, or mostly grown woman? Must be a dyke.

Jess unlocked the side door and we headed up a long staircase that doubled back in the middle. There was a door on that landing too.

"That's the second floor," Jess said. "My landlords live on the first two floors and rent out the top."

"Cool." I had to stop saying that. No need to sound like a dumb jock.

I followed Jess through a locked door at the top of the stairs into a narrow hallway. A mountain bike leaned against one wall across from a closet with sliding wooden doors. Boots and worn cross trainers sat in front of the closet, while a poster of Gabriela Sabatini adorned the wall above the bike, a navy blue Trek.

"Nice wheels," I said as Jess led me toward the rest of the apartment.

"It's the reason I'm on a limited meal plan this semester," she said over her shoulder.

The main room of the apartment ran the length of the house. The front section served as a living room, complete with a brown paisley couch, an old black La-Z-Boy recliner, a low wooden coffee table, a small TV that perched in the middle of built-in floor-to-ceiling bookshelves, and windows that overlooked the front porch and yard. The back half of the room was the kitchen and dining area, with another pair of windows that overlooked the backyard. The floors were warm wood, walls painted cream, decorations worn but attractive. All of the posters, an eclectic collection of Impressionist and modern art, were framed.

"Your apartment is beautiful," I said.

Jess dropped her bag on the floor next to one of the mismatched dining room table chairs. "Thanks. I just cleaned yesterday. It's not usually this neat."

From the look of the place, messy to her probably meant a couple of books on the coffee table, an unwashed glass in the sink, maybe a jacket draped across a chair. Half the time I couldn't find the clothes I wanted because they were somewhere in the pile on my closet floor. I doubted Jess ever had that problem.

I wandered into the living room, stopping by the window.

The blinds were up, and I could see my car parked behind hers out on the street. Turning away, I walked from poster to poster in silver, brass and polished wooden frames. There were five total—four in here and one in the kitchen hanging over a small circular table that was covered with an Indian print sheet similar to the one in my dorm room. I recognized Monet's *Poplars*, brass frame and rose-colored matte bringing out the muted reds and golds. The only other work I knew was the kitchen poster, Picasso's *Dove*, green and blue and red flowers entwined about the bird's bodies.

The other three pieces were more abstract. I looked closer and realized they were paintings, not posters. I know nothing about art, but even I could tell these were good. One in particular I liked was a swirl of blues and grays and dots of white. It reminded me of a storm blowing in off the ocean, twisted clouds obscuring the lights that seemed to resemble stars and a misshapen crescent moon.

I headed back into the kitchen where Jess had filled a pot of water and set it to heat on the gas stove. She was washing her hands.

"I should do that too," I said, and moved in beside her. "Quite an art collection you have."

"Thanks." She wiped her hands on a clean dish towel.

"I don't recognize the paintings in there." I nodded toward the living room. "I really like the one of the storm."

She was staring at me, an odd look on her face, and I added, "It's supposed to be a storm, right? I mean, that's just what I thought when I saw it."

"No, you're right. It's supposed to be a storm." She turned away. "What kind of veggies do you want in your salad?"

The strange moment passed, and we set about fixing ourselves food, Janis Joplin's greatest hits playing on the living room stereo as we chopped green and red peppers, tomatoes, mushrooms and cucumbers to put in the tomato sauce and our salads. Jess warmed a loaf of French bread in the oven, her favorite bread from her favorite bakery in town, she said. Once a week she tried to cook a big dinner. Last week it was grilled chicken. For Thanksgiving, she was planning to cook a traditional turkey dinner downstairs for the couple she rented from, Sidney and Claire, and their friends.

"Wait." I paused in de-seeding a pepper. "You're staying here for Thanksgiving too?"

"Yeah." She concentrated on the tomato she was slicing. "I actually live here year-round. I've had this apartment for a couple of years already, since summer before freshman year." Turning away, she strode toward the refrigerator. "Anyway, what kind of dressing do you like?"

"Whatever. I'm not picky."

I watched her pull salad dressing from the fridge. No wonder her place was so different from other student apartments I'd visited. Those were usually cramped, a bunch of guys or girls sharing a house or a multiple bedroom apartment with raggedy furniture and cigarette-scorched rugs.

Then again, Jess was different herself from most other students I knew. She seemed like an adult already, a real person with a real life complete with walls to keep everyone out and a past I was dying to know. Why was this apartment her home? Where was her family? An image of the woman in the stands at the match the previous year popped into my head, but I didn't want to scare Jess off this early in the evening by grilling her about her family life. While we finished making dinner, I let her guide the conversation toward classes and sports and people we both knew. Safe subjects. Impersonal topics.

"I heard Cory Miller, the starting quarterback, is dating a guy on the swim team," Jess said as she pulled the bread from the oven and poked it with a finger. "This is ready. I think we're good to go."

"Awesome." I helped carry the food to the table. I was even more impressed now—the glasses and plates and silverware all matched, and the glasses were painted with the same sunflowers that adorned the heavy gray plates.

"Looks great," I said as we sat down.

"Let's hope it tastes that way," she said, tucking an errant strand of hair behind one ear.

She had disappeared into the room off the living room a few minutes earlier and reemerged clad in a gray Champion sweatshirt, dark hair freshly brushed and pulled back in a ponytail. We probably looked alike in our sweatshirts, faces flushed from practice still.

As she filled our plates, I asked casually, "Where did you hear about Cory Miller?"

I knew the swimmer in question was Jake Kim. If word got out, their relationship was destined to become the scandal of the sports world this semester, not only because they were both jocks but also because Cory was African-American and Jake was Korean and neither was out to his parents. Added to their familial issues was the fact that the university administration didn't typically look kindly upon gay boys who played football. I felt lucky sometimes to be a lesbian—at least we were expected to be high-performing athletes.

Jess handed me my plate, filled with mostaccioli noodles and vegetable sauce. "I heard from a friend on the football team, Chris Sanders. He actually said to keep it quiet."

I was pretty sure Chris Sanders was one of the beautiful gay boys I'd seen at dances and at Zodiac. What did it mean that he and Jess were friends? She seemed so casual, chatting about these gay folks. Interesting.

"I already knew, anyway," I admitted, swallowing a bite of pasta.

"I thought you would."

"You did?"

She shrugged, her face unreadable. "Well, yeah. I figured all the gay jocks would hear sooner or later."

In a way, I was relieved Jess was letting me know she knew I wasn't straight. But at the same time, I hoped she hadn't heard the gossip that Holly loved to report linking me with a handful of different women at a time. Flattering as the stories were, I hailed from Oregon, not California. Sleeping around wasn't really my style, no matter what the campus rumor mill claimed.

A moment later Jess asked me about our schedule this week. I told her we had two games, Wednesday and Saturday. It was our first full week of play, so Coach had scheduled a Wednesday game instead of the usual Tuesday-Thursday-Saturday lineup. In order to ease us into the swing of competition.

"Same with us. Maybe I'll check out one of your games next week."

"You're going to come to a soccer game?" I asked.

"Well, yeah. I always catch at least a couple."

"I didn't know that."

"You don't really notice what's going on off the field, do you? I always feel like I'm totally alone out there once the match starts. I don't even hear the crowd."

"That's because you're a tennis player. The crowd isn't allowed to make any noise," I teased, "or we get kicked out of the stands."

"Zip it," she said, and threw a mushroom at me.

I ducked, and the mushroom landed on the windowsill behind me. "Nice shot. I thought tennis players were supposed to have good hand-eye coordination." I picked up a pasta shell dripping with red sauce and raised it menacingly toward her.

"Cam!" She backed her chair away from the table.

I popped the shell into my mouth. Then I smiled at her, hoping I didn't have parsley stuck in my teeth.

"Don't worry," I said as she pulled her chair closer again. "I wouldn't trash your apartment. Otherwise you might never invite me back."

She smiled too, her eyes nearly golden in the sunlight angling in through the back window. "Don't worry. You'll be invited back."

We looked at each other until I felt color rise in my cheeks and glanced away. I was really here in Jess's kitchen, eating a dinner we had prepared together. How unexpected. I felt my life shifting, spinning out of control at her smile, at the look in her eyes. More than anything just then, I wanted to hold time, to stay there with Jess in her warm apartment, Janis Joplin crooning in the background. Then the CD ended, Jess got up to change the music, and time speeded up again.

Geez, what was my problem? I could be such a freak.

"By the way, do you like football?" I asked.

"It's okay. I haven't been to many games here. I'd rather watch NFL than college."

"Me, too. *Monday Night Football* should be on."

Her eyes lit up. "I love *Monday Night Football.*"

"The Bears and the Packers are playing. Do you want to watch a little?"

"I really should do some homework," she said, hesitating. Then she shrugged. "But I guess I can always catch up later."

We finished the meal and cleaned up together. She washed the dishes while I dried, putting them away by trial and error cupboard opening. She didn't have that many dishes, I learned. A couple of the shelves were empty, yellow contact paper dusty with disuse.

Grabbing a couple of bottles of Dos Equis—what was football without beer, we agreed—we headed into the living room. Jess dialed up the game on her small television and we sat back on the couch to watch. There was a local ad on for a car dealership on El Camino Real, the road that ran north-south nearly the length of the entire state of California.

I glanced sideways at Jess. "Do you speak Spanish?"

"I do."

"Say something, then."

"Like what?" She took a sip of beer.

"I don't know. Your choice."

Her eyes focused behind me for a moment on the painting of the storm. Her voice was soft. "*La luna brilla debajo del oceano.*"

"What did you say?"

We were sitting close together in the darkening room, faces lit by the flickering light from the television screen. She was staring at the painting, her eyes dark with an emotion I couldn't quite read.

Then she looked back at me, and the haunted look I'd glimpsed faded away. She smiled and knocked her bottle against mine. "I said the moon shines beneath the ocean. Go Bears!"

The game was already half over when we turned it on, but the score was only 7-3, Packers. As one might expect of an NFC Central showdown, it was a defensive battle. We cheered the players on rowdily, kicked back on the comfortable couch with our feet up on the coffee table. Whenever someone scored or made an impressive play, we slapped hands and Jess whistled between her teeth. She tried to teach me how but to no avail.

At the start of the fourth quarter, Jess glanced at her watch. "You didn't have anything planned tonight, did you? I mean, no one's expecting you?"

Was she asking if I had a girlfriend? "Not a one," I said. "What about you?"

"No way." She laughed a little and looked back at the TV. "Not me."

Undercurrents in the conversation. Again, if it had been anyone other than Jess Maxwell, I would have thought there was something more going on. But for some reason, I didn't want to be into her, as Holly had put it. There was something untouchable about Jess, something good and pure in the friendship growing between us. I didn't want to ruin it by making a pass at her. Anyway, she was probably straight. I would have heard if she wasn't. Wouldn't I?

It was after nine when the game finally ended. The Bears scraped by with a victory, thanks to a field goal in overtime.

"Have you ever thought about trying to play soccer after school?" Jess asked me. The postgame show had started, but neither of us moved from our places on the couch.

"I wish. Unfortunately, I'm not that good," I said, and stretched, arching my back, arms over my head. "I'm pretty sure I'd like to coach, though. That's part of why I want to be a teacher. That, and summers off would be pretty sweet. What about you? Any plans to join the pro tour?"

She frowned a little, hugging a cream-colored pillow to her chest. She even had throw pillows. "I don't know. I haven't really thought about it."

"Seriously? If anyone at SDU could go pro, it's you."

"I don't think so," she said, shaking her head. Still frowning.

But I didn't notice. I was too caught up in the thought of Jess playing the Acura Classic at nearby La Costa, the Sony Ericsson WTA tour, the U.S. Open even, eventually.

"Why not? God, I'd kill for the chance to play pro. You have so much talent, Jess."

She shook her head again. "No, I don't. I'm just lucky. It's not real."

Was she serious? "It's not luck. I've seen you play. You're really good. You're the real thing."

"No, I'm not. You don't know. I was never this good before, back in high school. It's not real." Her knuckles whitened as she nearly mangled the pillow.

"What do you mean?" I kept my voice soft, hoping she wasn't about to shut down again. Talking to Jess felt a little like walking into an unfamiliar body of water at night, aware that the bottom might drop off at any moment.

"Nothing." Staring at the painting of the storm again, she relinquished her grip on the pillow. "Forget it. I just don't want to live my whole life like that. It's okay for now. It's college. But I want a life someday. I want a normal life, you know?"

I nodded like I understood what she was talking about.

The theme song from *M.A.S.H.* blared out from the television just then, breaking the relative quiet. I looked up to see the credits roll over Alan Alda's face.

"I used to be able to play this song on the piano," I said conversationally, hoping to break the odd tension between us.

"Yeah?" Jess said, eyes on the TV.

"Can you believe it's called 'Suicide is Painless,'" I added, "not 'The M.A.S.H. Theme' or something else? Weird, huh?"

"That is weird."

A little while later I got up and rinsed my beer bottle out, even though she said I didn't have to. Then she walked me out to my car, though I said she didn't have to. The night air was warm, but I still felt chilled as a breeze blew down her street, mussing our hair.

"Thanks for dinner," I said, key in hand, watching her in the streetlight. We were standing on the pavement next to my car, looking at each other. Undercurrents, I thought again, and wanted to reach out and... And what? I wasn't sure.

"Thanks for coming." She hesitated, then touched the sleeve of my sweatshirt, just for a moment. "Don't worry, Cam. It's nothing."

She really could read my mind. I glanced toward the house, saw light shining at the edges of the third-floor windows, looked back at her.

"Okay." I unlocked the door, climbed in and rolled down the window. "I'll see you soon, won't I?"

She nodded and smiled, her fingertips trailing briefly across my windowsill. "I hope so."

Then she backed out of the lamplight and headed inside. I watched her go, an unfamiliar twist in my chest as she walked away, and waited until she had disappeared into her side door. Then I drove into the California night, replaying the evening in my mind. I couldn't shake the image of the blue-gray painting and the feeling that there was something there I should know, something I needed to understand.

I fell asleep that night still pondering the mystery of Jess Maxwell.

CHAPTER SEVEN

In the weeks that followed our impromptu dinner, I only saw Jess from a distance. During practice, I sometimes tried to catch a glimpse of her on the far-off tennis courts, certain I'd be able to identify the way she moved, fluid and lithe and strong. Whenever Holly caught me looking, she nailed me in the butt with a ball or ran past whispering, "How's your girlfriend?" At which point I would try to smack her back with a stray ball.

Soccer made the fall semester skip past as it always did, days slipping quickly into weeks. By the end of September, we were 5-0. I scored again in the fourth game, another penalty kick, and managed to add a couple of assists to my offensive total. The first week of October we had a Tuesday away game, Thursday home, and Saturday away. Tennis, I knew, was away Wednesday and home Saturday this week. Typical—with our opposing schedules, I hadn't attended even one tennis match yet.

But I didn't have time to worry about other sports, not when I was in-season myself. Our Thursday home game was against San Diego College, our big local rivals. They weren't that strong, but for some reason we always played poorly against them while they always played well against us, which made for some interesting games. We were 2-2 against them since I'd been on the scene. This time around, the stands on top of the hill were almost full, even though the men's soccer team was away. I checked the tennis courts while Holly and I warmed up together, practicing headers, volleys and passes, but the courts were empty. Maybe their coach had taken them off-site to practice.

Before every soccer game, the starting lineup was announced and the national anthem played. The day of the San Diego College game, I stood in the middle of the field with the rest of the team facing the American flag, humming under my breath. My hands felt shaky. This was an important game. If we lost this one, our national ranking, eighth in our division as of this week, would sink below the top ten, jeopardizing our chances at postseason play—only the top eight teams in the country went to nationals in November each year. Division II had only had a national tournament since 1988, and California teams had dominated the score line so far. We, naturally, believed we could take our place alongside the other Golden State teams who had won a National championship.

After the anthem, we jogged in for a quick pregame pep talk from Coach Eliot. Then we did our team cheer—"One-two-three-together!"—and the starting lineup took the field. As we jogged out to our places, Holly passed me, murmuring, "Are we having fun yet?"

The four of us in back put our hands together and shouted "Defense!" in unison while our keeper, a butch woman named Mel—short for Melissa, which suited her about as much as Camille suited me—executed her prewhistle ritual of pacing the goalmouth once, twice, counting her steps. Then she moved to the center of the six-yard goal box and spit into her gloves, rubbing them together. She was ready. At the top of the penalty box, eighteen yards from the goal line, I stretched in place and tried not to feel like I had to pee. I had just gone to the bathroom a half hour before, so I knew it was just pregame jitters pressing on my bladder. Then the whistle blew.

We had kickoff. For the first few minutes we controlled play, passing around the midfield and building an attack. Then an SDC defender stole the ball and cleared it up the field to one of their strikers for a quick counterattack. Jogging backward, I watched the SDC player dribbling down the field. She was good. She went right at our sophomore stopper, Jeni, who delayed, waiting for the forward to make a move. Suddenly an SDC midfielder burst forward, overlapping and leaving the player marking her behind. Now it was four versus four. Jeni tried to shut down the passing lane, but she was in a one-on-two situation. The SDC players were going to do a give-and-go, I could feel it, so I stepped up a bit, waiting, waiting, now! The forward touched the ball to the midfielder and sprinted forward. Jeni shifted over to take the midfielder who quickly laid off a through pass. The pass was almost perfect, the forward was almost there...

But so was I. I reached the ball first, faked left and dribbled right. The forward fell for my fake and ran past me, scrambling, unable to stop her momentum as I turned in the opposite direction. Dimly, from a distance, I heard laughter in the crowd. Then the overlapping midfielder was on me, all muscle and aggression and speed. I saw Jeni just to the right and passed her the ball with the outside of my foot. The midfielder slid me, trying to hit the ball. But I jumped, easily avoiding her leg, and yelled, "Up!" As a team, our defense pushed up to midfield, leaving the SDC strikers behind. Jeni passed the ball to Sara, our center midfielder, and we maintained possession for the next few minutes again. As the SDC forwards caught back up to us at the center line, the striker I had faked out brushed past me muttering, "Bitch." I grinned and felt adrenaline surging through my blood, sunshine on my neck and arms, leg muscles tingling with energy. This was what life was all about.

The game moved quickly, each team battling for possession. Though we had a couple of near misses up front, the score was still 0-0 with five minutes left in the half. We'd had the ball in their end most of the game, but their keeper saved shot after shot, even shutting down our senior All-American forward, Jamie Betz. I wasn't a fan of Jamie's, and the animosity was entirely mutual. She thought I was dirty because I played physical soccer while I thought she was mostly hype. We just never played any teams with decent defenders, I always told Holly. Not that I was complaining. If Jamie wanted to break the SDU scoring records, during this, her final year of college, I was all for it.

Finally, with five minutes left, the other team got a break. One of our freshman wing defenders gave up a corner kick, the first of the game in our end. We lined up in the box, marking players. My mark was the striker who had called me a bitch earlier. She lined up on Mel, trying to obstruct her view.

"Hey, ref, can you watch her?" I demanded. Goalkeepers enjoyed more protection than the rest of us. They were also a lot more vulnerable than anyone else on the field, frequently diving face-first into a swarm of kicking feet.

The ref nodded and blew his whistle. Play resumed.

The kick came in high and floating to the top of the six. Just as I stepped up to head it, I felt an elbow sharp in my ribs and faltered. The ball bounced once. Mel leapt on it screaming "Keeper" just as my mark snaked her foot out. The SDC player cracked Mel full in the side as I watched, still off balance, trying to scramble forward. The whistle screeched as Mel rolled over on her side, dropping the ball.

"You okay?" I knelt down next to her, touching her arm.

Her mouth was open, eyes squeezed tight in pain, both arms clutched to her ribcage. Finally she managed a gasp, sucking in breath. She'd had the wind knocked out of her. Our trainer appeared next to me, a little out of breath from her sprint across the field, and took over. On the sideline, our second-string keeper was already warming up.

Where was that bitch? I stood up abruptly, looking around. Adrenaline and rage bubbled in my veins. I was going to get her, and good. But the ref reached her first, shook a warning finger in her face and said a lot, quickly, in a low voice. The SDC forward didn't look even remotely contrite.

Then the ref reached for his pocket. Eject her, I thought, my fists clenched. But you usually aren't ejected until you've had a yellow, or warning, card, except for fighting or blatantly vicious fouls. This one was yellow card material because it had happened during a scramble. It was possible—though not likely, I thought darkly—that the collision had been an accident. The ref pulled his yellow card out and held it high in the air. The SDC coach pulled the forward off for the remainder of the half.

As the trainer and her student assistant helped Mel from the field, I turned away. This was my fault. I should have cleared the ball. If that striker hadn't clobbered me in mid-leap, none of this would have happened. We weren't going to lose this one, I decided at that moment. No way were we going to lose this game.

At halftime, I made a beeline for Mel. She was sitting on the bench, a bag of ice strapped to her side under her shirt with an Ace bandage.

"How you doin'?" I asked, my hand on her shoulder.

She shrugged, eyes red from crying. Mel never cried. "Win this one, Cam, will you?"

I nodded grimly and patted her head, feeling the softness of her short hair against my palm. "You got it."

More battling in the second half. Our offense couldn't seem to break through their defense and vice versa. Midway through the second half, I intercepted a long ball and dribbled forward. Anger and energy drove me. Jeni dropped back to cover and I turned on the speed I usually reserved for chasing down breakaways. The rest of the team got nervous when I dribbled up. They were used to having me in back. But I was in the mid-third of the field here. Even if I lost the ball, there probably wouldn't be that much damage.

SDC thought I was going to pass off. I dribbled around a surprised forward, avoided the hacking feet of an off-guard midfielder. I caught Jamie's eye where she stood in the middle of the field. We understood each other. I went straight at the center back, who left Jamie to head me off. Just as the SDC defender reached me, I sliced the ball off to Jamie, waiting at the top of the eighteen-yard box. She juked the SDC player collapsing to her and shot from twelve yards out, a rocket that was still rising when it hit the right upper corner of the net. Okay, so maybe she wasn't All-American for nothing.

The crowd cheered and screamed for us. The SDC keeper dug the ball out of the net and punted it angrily toward the midfield line. Holly and Laura both picked me up and twirled me around, separately. We were all laughing. Jamie slapped hands with the other forwards who mobbed her, but she was looking at me. I waited for her to catch up. We slapped hands then, holding on for a moment longer than necessary, eyes locked.

I nodded at her. "Sweet shot, Jamie."

She nodded back. "Nice ball, Cam."

We let go and jogged back toward our half for the post-score kickoff. We didn't like each other much, but on the field that didn't matter. This was a team, and we both understood what that meant. We both wanted to win.

Just before the whistle blew for kickoff, I glanced over at the bench and caught Mel's eye. She gave me a thumbs-up.

SDC was down. We ran all over them the last twenty minutes, pounding the goal with shot after shot. Their keeper kept them in, again, making incredible saves all over the penalty box. They only had a couple of shots on our net, desperation shots from twenty and thirty yards out. Our backup keeper, Anna, a true freshman, settled down and made the easy saves.

With five minutes left, one of SDC's midfielders juked ours and pounded down the left side of the field. I cheated over, ready to step up if I needed to. Then the midfielder wound up and chipped the ball down the far side of the field, kind of like a Hail Mary pass, hoping one of her strikers would win the foot race. I turned and ran back on an angle, ready to cover if Jodie, our outside defender, faltered. It was between Jodie and the striker who had taken Mel out. They were neck and neck, thirty yards out from the goal, almost to the ball, when Jodie stumbled. That was all it took. The forward sprinted past her on a breakaway.

She cut toward the goal, slowing just enough to control the ball. That gave me time to narrow the space. We were twenty yards out when she saw me coming from the side. She wound up, trying to get a quick shot off, but I slide-tackled her, hitting the ball square on and knocking it away for the save.

Only the SDC striker didn't avoid my tackle as I'd expected. Instead she lunged, a moment too late, into the spot where the ball had been. My follow-through carried all of my weight into her left leg, and I heard a sickening crunch as my foot connected fully with her ankle. We fell over each other in a heap.

At first I thought I'd broken my foot as hot pain shot up my leg. Then I heard a scream, close to my ear, and rolled away from the SDC player. She was sobbing and flopping around on the ground, hysterical, clutching her left leg. Her foot was twisted sickeningly, and I knew then that it was her bone cracking I had heard, not my own.

Her players and my players were there in an instant. Laura and Jeni helped me up as trainers from both schools sprinted onto the field. One of the SDC players knelt beside the injured striker, holding her hand and trying to calm her. Another player came toward me, eyes blazing.

"I hope you're satisfied, you fucking bitch," she spat at me.

A little ways away I saw their captain yelling at the head referee. He was shaking his head. Finally he said something to her and walked toward me. Jamie, our captain, followed him over, talking to him too. He ignored her.

"That was a fair tackle," he said to me. "You didn't mean to hurt her, did you?"

I shook my head, looking over at the sobbing girl. "No. She saw me coming. I know she did."

He nodded and walked over to the trainers to check on the SDC player.

Jamie touched my shoulder. "Nice hit," she said.

I looked at her quickly—was that sarcasm? But she seemed to mean it. I shook my head, turned to limp away. Jamie followed. My foot was killing me. There were tears sliding down my face, I noticed vaguely, though whether they were from pain or something else, I wasn't sure.

"She should have stopped," I said to Jamie. "I don't know why she didn't. You would have, right?"

She patted my shoulder. "You didn't mean it. I'm sure she knows that."

Holly caught up to me and slipped her arm around my neck. "You're limping. Are you hurt?"

"Yeah, I'm hurt."

She gave me a squeeze as we neared the edge of the field. "Take it easy. Don't worry about it. Shake it off, okay?"

I didn't answer. Head down, I made my way to the bench even before Coach waved me off. My foot hurt, but not as much as the other girl's ankle must have. The trainers were still working on her.

I could feel people in the stands staring at me in silence as I approached the bench. Then someone started to clap, and the rest of our fans joined in. I passed a hand over my face, swiping at the tears, and sat down at the far end of the bench. The clapping died away. I looked out at the field. No, she was still down. The clapping must have been for me. I wiped my face on my shirt sleeve, ignored my teammates' hesitant looks. She should have seen the slide coming. She should have pulled up. Shouldn't she? But as the moments dropped away one after another, my certainty began to ebb too, until I wasn't sure I hadn't hit her on purpose after all. Maybe Jamie was right. Maybe I was a dirty player.

Mel sat down next to me, wincing as the ice pack shifted, and slipped her arm around my shoulders.

"Don't worry yourself, little one," she said. "That was a clean slide. Just bad luck is all."

I shook my head and looked into Mel's dark eyes. She looked so mean, but she was really one of the kindest women I knew. She liked to talk about how many kids she was going to have, three or maybe four someday.

"I don't know." I sniffed. "She's the one who took you out. Maybe I meant it."

"Not your style," Mel said. "I appreciate the thought, though."

Coach Eliot approached, kneeling in front of me and looking up into my face. "You okay, champ?"

I nodded. "Just bruised." I looked at the clock. Four minutes left. "I'm sitting the rest?"

"You've done your part today. More than your part." He stood up and caught the eye of a student trainer. "Steve, a bag of ice for Cam here, please." Then he walked back to the other end of the bench to confer with his assistants.

They finally took the injured player off in an ambulance. Play resumed with an SDC throw-in where I had knocked it out. The final four minutes passed quickly. Our defense, guided by Jeni and Anna, shut down the deflated SDC team easily. The game ended 1-0.

My foot was bruised, the trainer agreed, so at the end of the game I got to ride back to the gym in a golf cart, foot swathed in ice. Before I took off, I limped over to the SDC bench, ignoring the glares some of the players shot me. I walked up to the coach, holding his gaze.

"I just wanted you to know I wasn't trying to hurt her, okay? Will you tell her that?"

He paused, eyeing me. Then he nodded once, sharply. "I'll tell her."

I walked away, head high, and climbed into the golf cart. Holly hopped in beside me. In the driver's seat, Steve started forward.

"I couldn't let you take this fun ride all alone," Holly said. "Anyway, I have your bag. And your sweats. And your shoe."

"Thanks." Suddenly I could barely hold my head up. The adrenaline was wearing off, and all that was left was a dull ache in my foot and a sharper pang of guilt. I had ended the SDC player's season, maybe even her soccer career. I stared down at my bare foot, where an Ace bandage held the ice in place against my heel. The ice hurt more than the actual injury.

Holly pulled me against her side. "Rough game, huh, Cam?"

"Yeah." I sighed and leaned against her shoulder, avoiding the curious looks of the spectators we passed leaving the field. "Rough game."

I was the last one to leave the gym that night. The trainer made me visit with her for a little while, just to make sure my foot was okay. Holly and Laura came into the training room to hear the verdict: just a bruise. Even though they were finished showering, they offered to drive me and my car up to the student center. They even insisted. But when I told them I just wanted to be alone, that I would meet them at dinner, they reluctantly left.

Alone in the locker room, I took a long, leisurely shower, then dressed in a pair of comfy Levi's and an SDU soccer T-shirt. I taped a piece of Dr. Shoal's tough skin in a crescent shape at the edge of my heel, as the trainer had directed, and pulled my Sambas on, leaving the right shoe mostly unlaced. The four Advil I had taken were kicking in. Now it just hurt to walk. I was supposed to use a crutch, so I tried it out in the locker room. It felt weird. I didn't think I liked being injured.

When I hobbled out of the locker room, I found, to my astonishment, Jess Maxwell curled up on a couch in the lounge reading a textbook.

She glanced up. "Hey, Cam."

"Hey." I was too tired to feel more than a flicker of happiness at seeing her. "What are you doing here?"

"I was at the game. Coach gave us practice off today." She closed her book, slid it into her athletic bag and stood up. "Are you okay?"

I ran a hand through my still-damp hair. "It's just a bruise. But thanks."

"Do you need a ride?"

I hesitated. I could always pick up my car tomorrow. "You going to the student center?"

"Yep."

"Okay, then. Thanks, Jess."

"De nada."

In the elevator she took my bag from me. I started to protest but thought better of it. My jock pride was misplaced now that I was temporarily disabled. We walked out to the car in silence. By the time I'd maneuvered into the car, my foot was throbbing again.

"Good thing you saw this game," I said. "The game where I manage to hurt myself breaking someone else's leg."

"I thought you played really well." She put the key in the ignition but didn't start the car. "You had the winning assist.

Everyone in the stands was saying how you guys could go all the way this year with you in back and Jamie Betz up front. When you and that woman collided at the end, mostly people were just scared you weren't going to get up."

We were still sitting in the parking lot, U2 rolling from the car stereo. Jess seemed so earnest. She was probably just being nice.

"We didn't collide. I took her out. You got to see someone carried off on a stretcher because of me, after all. Jamie's right, I am a dirty player. Not..." I stopped. I'd been about to say, *Not All-American material.*

Jess frowned, her brow furrowing. "I don't believe you," she said. "You wouldn't do that."

I shook my head again. "You don't know." The phrase reminded me of the words she had tossed out a few weeks before when I'd told her how talented she was. Did she remember, too?

She started the car. Out of the corner of my eye, I saw her hesitate before shifting into reverse and backing out of the parking space. The sun was setting behind the hill, streaking the sky pink. Sometimes I thought it was odd that we lived our lives just out of sight of the Pacific. Sometimes I imagined I could hear it late at night, breakers storming the beach. But you couldn't see the ocean from campus.

"What are you doing this Sunday?" Jess asked suddenly.

"I don't know. Nothing. I think I have a paper due sometime next week. Maybe I'll get started."

She turned in to the student center parking lot. "You're actually considering getting a paper done early?"

I had to smile. "Why, what are you doing Sunday?"

She shrugged and stopped the car near the door to the student center, letting the engine idle. "I was thinking of going down to Balboa Park for a bike ride." She paused. "You interested in coming along? Assuming your foot is okay by then."

Jess Maxwell, inviting me on an outing to the park? "A bike ride would probably be good for me."

"Okay, then. We could meet at my place, say, eleven? If that's not too early."

"Eleven is perfect." And all at once I felt better, now that I had something to look forward to. Maybe I'd even manage to forget about breaking that girl's ankle. "Are you coming inside?"

She shook her head. "That's Laura's Trooper, right?" she said, nodding at the Isuzu parked a few feet away. This late, the student center lot was almost empty. Most people had finished dinner long before now. Including, apparently, Jess.

"Yeah, but didn't you say you were on your way here?"

"I just said that so you'd let me drive you."

Was she flirting with me? She couldn't be. And if she was, I didn't think I could handle it just then.

I grabbed my crutch and bag from the backseat. "Good luck Saturday. Kick some butt."

"Same to you. Just don't kick any more legs, okay?"

"I don't think I'll be kicking much of anything until Monday, at least." I slid out of the car, pulling myself up with the crutch. "Thanks for the ride."

"No worries. See you Sunday." She pulled the door closed after me and drove off.

I hobbled toward the student center where the soccer team always ate together after home games. Inside, Holly and Laura saw me coming and jumped up to get the door. Holly took my bag and they escorted me to the tables the team had pushed together.

"Look who's here, everyone," Laura said, her voice rising easily over the others. "Our very own gimp."

They all started laughing and saying stuff. I tried not to blush.

"Everyone's afraid of you now, Cam," Jamie Betz said.

The other players went quiet, watching the two of us. It was no secret that she and I weren't exactly friends.

I looked into her light blue eyes, trying to figure out what hidden meaning lay beneath her words. But I couldn't detect even the slightest hostility there.

"Including my own body," I said wryly.

"I see that." She smiled, friendly in her sympathy.

Holly led me to an empty seat. "What do you want to eat?" she asked. "I'll grab it for you."

I shrugged, feeling tired again as I sat down. "I don't care.

Your choice. As long as it's got the four food groups," I added as she walked away. Holly sometimes picked food by color coordination rather than nutritional value. She just grinned over her shoulder at me.

Later that night, Holly walked me up to my room and stayed for a little while. We shared a bottle of Gatorade, one of the weekly dozen I bought and stored in my mini fridge, and lay on my bed talking.

"You know, this is the first time we've hung out like this in a while," Holly said, leaning against the Indian print wall, pillow at her back.

"That's 'cause you're always with your girlfriend."

I was tossing a tennis ball against the ceiling and catching it as an experiment to see how long it would take Holly to A) get annoyed or B) grab it for herself. She was a younger sister, like me, and not very good at sharing.

"You're just jealous," she said. "Remember, you're the one who said you wanted to be celibate. Although you couldn't tell tonight—accepting a ride from Jess Maxwell when you wouldn't take one from me and Laura."

"It's not like that and you know it."

"Do I? Seriously, she waited for you all that time, Cam."

"We're just friends." I hadn't given Holly any details of my dinner with Jess, mainly because I wasn't sure how to talk about it. Or even how to think about it. "I told you before I don't have the hots for her. It's different with her. I don't know how to explain it."

For once Holly didn't make a crack. "Okay. So you guys are friends."

"Exactly. We're friends." I tossed the ball again. "Anyway, how're things with you and Becca?"

Holly squinted up at the ceiling light. "You know."

I looked over at her. "Actually, I don't. What's up?"

She shrugged and grabbed the tennis ball from my hands, tossing it toward the ceiling. Not even five minutes. Typical.

"I don't know, Cam. It's like, one minute everything's cool, and the next, I don't even know her. She gets jealous for no reason. I don't get it."

Holly and I spoke the same lingo during soccer season. Each fall, the only words we used with any frequency were "cool" and "like" and "awesome." Sometimes all in the same sentence. But once soccer was over and we fell into the student habit again, our vocabularies improved. Immensely.

"She still gets jealous of you and me?" I asked.

"Totally." Holly shook her head. "Why does everyone you date and everyone I date always think you and I are sleeping together?"

"I have a theory on that one. Neither of us has ever dated a soccer player, right?"

"Thank God. Although people were wondering about you and Mel for a while."

"Mel and I are just buds. Besides, she's not my type and I'm definitely not hers. Anyway, she calls me kid."

"Everyone calls you kid," Holly pointed out. "You look about twelve."

"Do you want to hear my theory or not?"

"Go ahead." She tossed the ball.

"Anyway, so you and I are basically married to the team, right? I mean, in season it's all we think about, and off season, let's face it, soccer is pretty much all we talk about. So whoever we date resents the part that the team plays in our lives. Only sport is an inanimate, um, not object..."

"Entity?" she suggested, examining the stitching on the tennis ball.

"Exactly. Since soccer itself is an inanimate entity, our respective others view our soccer friends as the threat. It's easier to believe they've been dissed for some*one* else than some*thing* else."

"You know," Holly said, screwing up her face in supposed concentration, "I think that sports pysch class you took last year might have made you a little crazy there, champ."

I laughed. "Wouldn't be the first time that happened."

Leaning back on the bed, I folded my arms behind my head.

An image of Jess waiting for me in the lounge at the gym came to mind, unbidden. I quickly banished it.

"I thought you and Becca were doing better."

"So did I. Until I got home from dinner with the team last night to find a message on my voice mail saying she looked for me at the student center and where was I and she noticed you weren't there either."

"She did not!"

I didn't get Becca. She was this rich girl from San Francisco who had three or four different stepfamilies and a plethora of half-siblings. Her father was a famous surgeon who kept marrying younger and younger nurses every few years. Becca couldn't stand him. To my face, she was always really nice, even fun to hang out with. But there was always this tension just beneath the surface, like she wasn't pleased she had to share Holly with me. I just ignored it and went merrily along my way, which probably only made her more suspicious.

"I almost forwarded you the message," Holly said.

"That would have gone over well."

"That's why I didn't. Shit, Cam." She sighed and slid down on the bed next to me. "I don't know about this relationship stuff. It's hard enough finding time for soccer and classes."

"So I've noticed."

Holly had likely already skipped more classes than she'd attended this semester, which, for her, was par for the course.

"I'm serious, man." She looked at me sideways, tennis ball resting on her stomach. "I don't want to sound like a jerk, but I honestly don't need this. She gets annoyed when I won't come over the night before a game. What's up with that?"

"Wow," I said, not wanting to sway her one way or the other. Trying to be the objective friend.

"Maybe you're right," she said. "Maybe celibacy is the way to go."

"Come on, Hol. If neither one of us is dating anyone, then everyone will be convinced we're together. As it is, they probably already think I'm pining away, waiting for you to come back to me. Slut."

That got a smile. "Everyone thinks you're the slut, Cam, not me. Haven't you heard? You and Jess Maxwell are the hot new subject of gossip in the SDU sports world."

"Nuh-uh!"

"Gotcha."

As usual, our peaceful sojourn on my futon ended in a pillow fight. Eventually Holly headed back to her dorm, promising to call me when she got there. She always forgot, though. I didn't bother to wait. I limped down the hall to the bathroom and got ready for bed. When I returned to my room, the message light on my phone was blinking. Holly must have remembered for once. I dialed voice mail.

But it wasn't Holly. It was an off-campus call. I leaned back on my bed as Jess's voice sounded in my ear. She'd never called me before.

"Hi, Cam. Just called to see how you were feeling. Guess you're screening. Or maybe you're not there," she added quickly. "Um, if you get this, you can call me back. I was just watching the sports news and thought of you. I'll, um, talk to you soon." And she left her number.

I replayed the message, picturing her curled up in sweats on her couch, then hit save. I changed into the boxers and T-shirt I usually wore to bed and turned off the overhead light, leaving the bedside lamp on. The digital numbers on my clock read 11:23. I should really get to sleep. I reached for the bedside table, picked up the phone, dialed the number Jess had left.

She picked up on the second ring. "Hello?" Her voice was soft and sleepy.

"Jess? It's Cam."

I could hear the smile in her voice. "You got my message."

"I was just down the hall for a minute. I thought you were Holly, actually. She was supposed to call me when she got home. She always forgets." I slid lower in the sheets, wincing as the comforter pressed down on my sore foot. "What's up?"

"Not much. How's your foot?"

"Still sore. I don't think I'll be playing this weekend."

The thought depressed and relieved me at the same time. It wasn't a big game. We always beat Dominguez Hills soundly. Might actually be kind of nice to sit on the sidelines for a change, cheering my team on.

Just then the call waiting beeped. One beep meant on-campus.

"Sorry, Jess. My call waiting's going. Can you hold on for a sec?"

"Sure."

I clicked over. "Hello?"

"Who're you talking to?" Holly said.

"Um..." I didn't want to tell her. "Jess Maxwell." I was also a lousy liar.

"Couldn't wait to get rid of me, could you?"

"No, she called me," I said. "She just wanted to see if my foot was okay. You know."

"I do. Well, just thought you might want to know I made it home safely."

"What, like twenty minutes ago?"

"At least I remembered. Tell your tennis babe I said hello." The line went dead.

I clicked back. "Jess?"

"Still here."

"Sorry about that. Holly says hello."

"She remembered to call?"

"Finally." I settled into my bed again, reached out, and turned the lamp off. I wasn't going to click over if my call waiting beeped again. My room was dark and cozy now, lit only by the glowing red numbers on my digital clock.

"You were saying something about the weekend," she said. "Is it a big game?"

"Not really."

While we chatted, I closed my eyes and pictured her as I had seen her last in her low-slung Levi's, white T-shirt and the inevitable cross trainers. I was beginning to think she didn't own any regular shoes. Not that I had that many pairs of non-athletic shoes myself.

We talked about nothing for a long time. She told me what was on TV, which classes she had in the morning, what the score was in her last match. I told her what I'd had for dinner, which classes I had in the morning, what I was going to have for breakfast.

Then she asked, "Are you still upset about the game?"

I thought about it. "Not as much. Holly always knows how to make me laugh."

"Good quality in a friend."

"Seriously." I paused, hearing again the crack of bone splintering. I didn't think I'd ever forget that sound. "I never question what I'm doing out there, you know? I'm a soccer player. It's who I am. But tonight I actually wondered if it's worth it. I was sure she'd get out of the way. She just wanted to score so badly and I couldn't let her. It seems almost silly now."

Jess was quiet for a minute. "What did you decide? Is it worth it?"

"It has to be," I said. "At least for now. Without soccer, I probably wouldn't be at SDU."

"I know exactly what you mean."

In the dark, the sounds of other students audible through the thin dormitory walls, I knew she did.

A little while later, Jess said it was late, that she should go. I opened my eyes, surprised that the clock now read after midnight. As I set the receiver on the hook, I imagined her turning off her television and heading to bed. She wasn't far away, I knew, picturing her apartment from the street, light visible at the edge of the third-floor windows. For some reason, the image comforted me as I lay in bed alone listening to the faint thrum of my heart beating in time to the throbbing in my foot.

CHAPTER EIGHT

On Sunday morning, fall was in the air as much as it ever was in southern California, evident in cooler temperatures and a breeze off the ocean. I woke up at eight thirty and, still in bed, reached over and tugged on the window shade. It snapped up with a crack to reveal the perfect morning dawning in the courtyard. Yawning, I stretched my arms above my head, tightening all the muscles in my body and then releasing them. For once, waking up on a Sunday morning, I wasn't sore.

The day before at Dominguez Hills I had sat the bench in street clothes. Coach made us dress up for away games. For me, that meant khakis, collared shirt and Sambas. During the game, I sat as far from Coach Eliot as possible and listened to the talk on the bench. Coach had a habit of playing the same eleven starters throughout the entire game with very few substitutions, which left seven players on the bench watching game after game.

Turned out the younger kids I had never paid much attention to, the players I'd thought were quiet and retiring, were funny as hell. We were winning, and they kept the jokes and cracks flying, making fun of the referee and the other team and even our teammates. Each time Jamie Betz got the ball, a sophomore forward named Toni would begin a mock sportscaster's voiceover, holding a water cup up to her mouth as a microphone, speaking just quietly enough that Coach Eliot, Jamie's biggest fan, wouldn't hear.

"And it's SDU's star forward, All-American Jamie Betz, with the ball. She fakes left, she fakes right, she fakes the defense right out of their sports bras. What do you think, Bert? Will it be another sparkling performance out of the SDU senior, All-American and Big Eight record holder? Or will she choke?"

A freshman whose last name was Whittaker and whose first name I thought might be Lisa leaned in with her own cup. "Well, John, it's hard to say. My vote is, she chokes."

Then they would look out on the field, follow the play, and finish, "And you're absolutely right, Bert. She choked. But we can rest easy. Teammate Sara Alexander, All Region midfielder and team assist leader—all to Betz, I might add—doesn't seem to realize there are nine other teammates out there! Betz should get the ball back for yet another attempt any moment now."

"And speak of the devil," Whittaker would chime in, "there she goes!"

The first time they did this, about ten minutes into the game, I pulled my baseball cap low over my eyes and slouched in my seat. What did they say about me? Probably called me SDU's vicious center back who liked to literally bulldoze the other team's offense.

Anna, the freshman backup keeper, was sitting next to me. "Don't worry," she said. "They think you're cool because you don't kiss Jamie's ass."

Good to know.

Watching the game from the bench, I felt tension and pressure easing from my shoulders. It was just a game, after all, and no one at our level was infallible. Even Mel, who had been all-conference for two years, let in an easy goal every once in a while. Jamie only converted one out of every ten shots. But when you were on defense and you messed up, the other team scored. If you were on offense and you made a mistake, the other team just got the ball back.

As the game progressed, I laughed at the bench players' jokes and cheered with them when we scored, which we did four times that day. And I enjoyed myself. I remembered why I loved the game as I watched our team outplay their team, the sound of the whistle and the slap of leather on leather echoing across the wide field, mid-afternoon sunlight warming the air.

Coach put the second-string in with fifteen minutes left. They all made sarcastic comments about being excited as they shed their warm-ups, but I could tell they wanted to play. They loved soccer as much as the starters did. Otherwise, they wouldn't ride the bench every game and still show up on time to every practice and put in the same amount of work the rest of us did.

Personally, I couldn't imagine it. I might be low-key in the rest of my life, but not on the soccer field. I had played on only one team where the coach hadn't started me, a spring select team in the high school off-season. The coach, a college guy named Tom, had never coached girls before. I was sixteen years old, burnt out from playing soccer ten months a year for ten years. My timing was lousy, my clears worse, and Tom benched me.

One night after practice in the middle of the season, I stayed late intending to ask him how I could improve my game and regain my starting position. To our mutual chagrin, I burst into tears and demanded to know why I wasn't playing, why I was sitting the bench, why he thought I wasn't good enough. He reassured me as best he could, promising that I would see more playing time in the near future. Then we both practically ran to our cars. From that day on, I started and played the majority of every game at midfielder, where I couldn't do much harm. My level of play was still lousy, but Tom didn't bench me again.

At the end of the season my mother suggested I take a break from soccer. I resisted, so she packed me off to my aunt's ranch in Colorado for six weeks, timing the trip so that I would miss tryouts and half the summer travel team season. At the time I hated her. Now I knew she'd been right. The next time I took the field, that August just before high school preseason, I was back. My skills and my timing and, most importantly, my love of the game were all stronger than before. Plus I had met a girl in Colorado who worked with my aunt's horses, and fallen in love for the first time. Not a bad summer, really, even if the girl in question had ditched me for someone else shortly after I went home to Oregon.

Now, once again, I was taking a well-needed break from soccer, from the pressure and stress of the whole thing. Today, Sunday, I intended to relax and have fun hanging out with Jess Maxwell. I wasn't going to think about soccer at all.

Which almost happened.

At eleven fifteen I pulled up in front of Jess's house. Birds were singing and I could hear children screaming in play somewhere nearby as I walked up the driveway. The side door was open slightly, so I pushed it open and walked up the stairs, careful not to put pressure on my heel. The bruise was healing, but it still hurt to put all my weight on it. At the top of the stairs, I knocked on Jess's door.

She opened it immediately. Like me, she was wearing a T-shirt and cut-offs, her hair trapped in its usual ponytail.

"Hey," she said, smiling. "What's up?"

"Not much. You ready to hit the park?"

"Definitely. Let me grab my bag."

Down on the street, we strapped our bikes to her bike rack. No need to take two cars, we'd agreed. I snagged my backpack from my car and slid into her front seat. Sunglasses masking our eyes, we drove off.

"No crutch?" Jess asked.

"I only used it one day. My foot's a lot better."

"That's good. You barely look like you're limping. How was the game?"

We talked about our Saturday matchups and listened to the

Some Kind of Wonderful soundtrack as we headed down I-5 south to the city. The album was one of my favorites, I had confessed to Jess when I saw it in her glove compartment.

"Me, too," she'd said. "Put it in."

We drove down the freeway, singing along with The Furniture (*You must be out of your brilliant mind*). It was Sunday, our day of rest. I munched on the bagel with cream cheese I'd picked up on my way over, and offered Jess a sip of sports drink. But she had her own beverage, a bottle of iced tea. This was the life, I decided as we sped along the packed freeway.

The San Diego skyline appeared around a curve that passed between two hills. The airport lay at the western edge of town on a mass of land that bordered the bay. Huge jets, gliding beside the handful of skyscrapers that made up the San Diego skyline, hung momentarily suspended over the bay before touching down. They crossed over the city every ten or fifteen minutes. Slightly disconcerting, I always thought.

We took the Balboa Park exit north of downtown and parked on Sixth Avenue, just up the hill from the park entrance. To the north lay University Avenue and the queer-friendly district, chock full of progressive bars and bookstores and theatres that occasionally showed queer films. In the off-season, I made it into the city a couple of times a month. San Diego couldn't compare to San Francisco or L.A., but with the local LGBT community, made up of mostly college students, ex-hippies and recent post-college adults, the city had a friendly feel despite the conservative bent to the broader community.

On Sixth, we lifted the bikes down from the rack, tightened the straps on our backpacks and pedaled into the park. Paved paths led under trees and along the edge of a wooded cliff that dropped onto the highway far below. Mounted on our matching Treks, we circled the zoo, then stopped near the San Diego Lawn Bowling Association field where a group of elderly women, all dressed in white, were in the middle of a game. I explained the rules to Jess, who had never witnessed anything like it. We watched for a few minutes and then rode on. A little while later, Jess waved at an open green near Cabrillo Bridge.

"You want to lay out for a while?"

I nodded. "Sure."

We dropped our bikes on the grass and spread out an old sheet Jess had brought along. Warm from the sun and exertion, I pulled my sweatshirt off and made it into a pillow. Kicking my running shoes off, I lay down on the sheet and watched Jess take her own sweatshirt off. Her shirt crawled up, momentarily revealing her back and a purple sports bra. I tried not to stare too obviously at her impressive tennis player muscles. She was ripped.

I pushed my short sleeves up, tucking the extra cloth under the strap of my own sports bra. Time to get rid of that farmer's tan. My legs were the worst—shin guards kept the front of both legs completely covered and left the back exposed, except where the strap circled the calf just below the knee. You could always tell a soccer player by her tan lines.

We lay on the sheet talking idly as the early autumn sun tracked across the sky. Jess kept sitting up to watch dogs and their owners playing on the green. A couple of times a dog came over to visit. Then I would sit up too and watch Jess play with the animal, scratching its head and rubbing its tummy and talking to it in a low, sweet voice. Eventually the owner would whistle and the dog would take off, with one last kiss for Jess and barely a sneeze in my direction. "You're a real animal person," I said at one point as a boxer she had been visiting with scampered off across the green.

"I love dogs," she said, smiling as the boxer nearly tripped over the tennis ball its owner had thrown. "Sidney and Claire have a chocolate Lab named Duncan. I take him running every day in the summer, early in the morning before anyone else is up. They said I could have a dog upstairs, but I don't have time. Once I graduate, maybe then." She glanced over at me. "What about you? Do you like animals?"

"I do, but my mom is allergic to anything with fur. My brother and I always wanted a dog, but it wasn't meant to be." I shrugged and lay back down.

"Too bad." Jess plucked a strand of grass to chew on and watched me. "Wasn't meant to be—does that mean you believe in fate?"

A question like that usually precipitated the kind of deep conversation I liked to engage in with my dorm friends in the off-season, late at night over coffee and an occasional cigarette. I couldn't remember ever talking like that with a jock before, though, not even with Holly. Maybe especially not with Holly.

I faced Jess, cradling my head on one hand. "I guess. I think there's luck, too, like the kind of family you're born into. But the choices you make on a daily basis are what lead you to a particular fate."

She tilted her head sideways. "It almost sounds like you believe we're responsible for everything bad that happens to us."

Did I? I frowned. "No, I'm just saying there are certain decisions we make that lead to specific outcomes. Like getting in a car wreck. You make so many small decisions—the time you left, how fast you drove, the route you picked. If you get in a wreck, it's lousy luck, but it's a fate you've sort of made for yourself."

"Got it. I think. So are you religious?"

"Not really. My parents are both Unitarians and believe in Christ as a historical figure, not as the literal Son of God. But I guess I'm more of an agnostic myself. My brother too. What about you?"

"Organized religion is at the root of so much evil in the world, it isn't something I'm interested in participating in. Besides, I don't believe in God." She said it firmly, as if there were no doubt in her mind.

An atheist, then—I wasn't sure I had ever met one, though I knew I must have. Maybe atheists were like gays and lesbians, closeted for fear of how other people would react to the truth. We talked religion for a while, oblivious to the people around us—soul versus the body, mind versus spirit, heaven versus hell. Zen Buddhism and the practice of meditation. Hindu beliefs about gods and bovines. It turned out we shared a lot of the same views, not to mention a lot of the same unanswered questions about life and death.

"I kind of believe in reincarnation," she said at one point, watching me out of the corner of her eye. "I think there are old and young souls. The old souls are the ones who have been a bunch of different animals and people. Like, they were a centipede and then they were a person who lived to be a hundred and then they were a cat."

"Hmm," I offered. "Interesting."

I wasn't sure what else to say. I had spent time thinking about such matters, of course, but not enough apparently to formulate my own hypothesis on the nature of souls.

Jess didn't seem to hold this against me. "This friend of mine," she continued, "used to say she thought the ultimate state of being was a tree." She paused. "That probably sounds bizarre. You think I'm crazy, don't you?"

We were so close I could see myself reflected in her sunglasses, light a halo behind me. "I kinda thought you were crazy already, Maxwell."

"Nice." She plucked a handful of grass and threw it at me.

I almost told her to stop killing all those souls, but decided I didn't know her well enough yet to be truly obnoxious.

"Seriously," I said, "I love hearing what other people think about this stuff. Sometimes it feels like I'm the only one who lays awake at night trying to figure it all out."

"You're definitely not the only one." She fell silent, resting her cheek on her sweatshirt.

"So what about you?" I asked. "What religion did you grow up in?"

I held my breath, waiting to see how she would react to my probing into her past.

"Lutheran," she said, unsmiling. "Until high school."

"In Bakersfield?"

"Yeah. And back in Chicago."

I watched the shadow of a small cloud creeping toward us across the green. "I didn't know you lived in Chicago."

"I was born there. My mom and I moved out here when I was seven so we could be close to her family." Her voice was so low I almost didn't hear the question: "You're wondering about my father, right?"

"Um." I was starting to get that floundering sensation I'd

had that night at her apartment when we were talking about tennis and her future. "Yes," I hazarded, unsure what the correct answer was.

"He killed himself." Her voice was tight like the muscle I could see pulsing in her jaw. "He hung himself in our basement when I was in first grade. He was a musician, a jazz pianist, and I guess his career wasn't going well. I don't remember much about him. My mom and I were visiting her parents here at the time, so we just stayed."

"God, Jess. I'm so sorry. That's awful."

How traumatic for a little kid. A piece of the puzzle slipped into place. Now I could begin to understand the distancing, the walls, the shyness. Almost.

The cloud enveloped us. Jess gazed up at the sky. "The thing is, for the longest time I thought he was killed in a car wreck. My mom didn't tell me the truth until I was a senior in high school."

"Why not?"

"I don't know. She never said."

We were both quiet. I was trying to imagine Jess's father, a Spaniard with wavy dark hair and golden eyes. Her mother, the Scandinavian, I pictured as a cool, patrician blonde with remote blue eyes. I really was beginning to understand. And with that inkling of comprehension, I wanted to reach out and smooth the frown lines from her forehead.

The cloud inched away, leaving the sun exposed again. Jess plucked at thick shoots of grass.

"I don't know why I told you all of that," she said. "You're the first person I've told in a while."

"I am?" Not that that should surprise me. "That's cool. I'm glad you did."

"I don't know what it is about you. It just feels—I don't know." She stopped and shook her head, looking back at her hands. "Just don't tell anyone, okay? The last thing I need is the student paper breathing down my neck, trying to get a feature. 'Local Athlete Triumphs Over Personal Tragedy.'"

I smiled a little. "Don't worry." I wanted to say, *What is it about me?* But I didn't. Instead I reached out and squeezed her shoulder. "You can trust me."

She flashed me a speculative look. "Yeah? To hear it told, you're not exactly the most trustworthy woman on campus."

I pulled my hand back quickly. "I don't know what you're talking about."

"I think you do." She was openly grinning now, enjoying my discomfiture. "Wait, are you speechless? I thought you always had the perfect comeback."

I turned over on my stomach. About time I worked on the tan lines on the backs of my legs.

"You're just jealous. You wish you could be me."

"That's totally it," she said, and I could hear the smile in her voice.

A little while later, we walked our bikes across the bridge toward the Plaza de Panama where a beautiful ceramic-tiled fountain drew local visitors and tourists alike. This section of the park contained the zoo, several museums and an arts and crafts village. We locked up our bikes near the Art Institute and went for a stroll, making our way eventually to the Spanish Village Art Center where working artists kept their studios open to visitors. Jess seemed excited as we wandered the old-fashioned village watching metalsmiths, basket makers and sculptors at work. She lingered longest at a demonstration of paint-mixing using a variety of plants and roots harvested from the wild.

"Some day I'm going to try this," she murmured almost to herself, watching the Village Paint Master dip a crushed root into a small container of water to produce a rich brown watercolor.

"You paint?" I looked at her with interest. I knew she was taking a studio art class this semester, but I'd gotten the impression that her interest in art was mainly academic.

She smiled her shy smile. "A little. Come on. Let's go check out the pottery demo."

Hooking her arm through mine, she pulled me along gently, mindful of my sore foot. Somehow the world seemed right and SDU very far away as we wandered the art center together. We kept smiling at each other, exclaiming at the smallest things, enjoying everything we saw. When we'd had our arts and crafts fill, we left the village and crossed a cement bridge that led over a four-laned, divided street to a cactus garden. To the right was a sprawling maze-like gazebo, vines growing in and around the wooden structure. We headed for the center, where a fat cactus grew beside a bench.

I dropped onto the bench, slipped my shoe off and rubbed the sole of my right foot. I hoped the bruise would heal soon. I wanted to be able to play in Tuesday's game.

"Are you doing okay?" Jess asked, touching my foot hesitantly.

"Fine," I said, continuing to massage my foot. "Just a little sore."

"Do you want to head back soon?"

I checked my watch, a Timex Ironman my parents had given me for my eighteenth birthday. Best sports watch on the market, they had said proudly.

"It's four thirty. Do you want to go?"

She shrugged. "It's up to you."

An idea occurred to me. "Why don't we eat at that café near the gate? Then we can head back to the car and maybe check out University Ave."

"Perfect," Jess said.

We walked back to the café and ordered sandwiches that we carried to a covered veranda at a wrought iron table. A comfortable silence reigned as we dug into our sandwiches and chips, trying to satisfy our sports-trained appetites. Sparrows fluttered around the sidewalk just beyond the eating area, cleaning up stray crumbs. Jess tore tiny pieces from her crust and started to feed the hungry birds. She tossed the bread closer and closer to her chair, until eventually the bravest sparrows were eating from her hand. I watched, thinking that she could have crushed any one of the little brown birds in her racket hand. But she just held the food out to them, her eyes glowing with pleasure.

The scene reminded me of what she'd said earlier about reincarnation and old souls.

"So which are you, Maxwell? An old soul or a young one?"

She tossed a final crumb. "Old." She sounded very sure.

I brushed my napkin across my mouth, hearing the sparrows cheeping at our feet. "What do you think I am?"

She tilted her head. "Middle-aged, I'd say. Not very young but not terribly old, either. What do you think?"

"You're probably right. Although my body feels pretty old right now," I added lightly. "Guess that's what fifteen years of playing a contact sport will do."

Later, as we rode our bikes back to the car, I wondered what she thought made her an old soul. She enjoyed life, you could tell by the way she leaned forward over her handlebars and rode into the wind, ponytail flying behind her. Then there was the way she played tennis, fierce and barely contained and driven, almost. But sometimes, when her eyes darkened and her jaw tightened and her walls sprang up, fully formed, setting her apart from everyone and everything, she looked as if she had never been happy. As if she never would be.

A half hour later we were perched on stools at a coffee shop on University, watching people pass on the street. I had ordered my cappuccino in typical L.A. fashion to amuse Jess: "Single tall half caf half decaf cap with skim milk, chocolate, and cinnamon. For here, please." Meanwhile, she'd ordered a pot of raspberry herbal tea because, she said, she was trying to limit her caffeine intake. This reminded me of Jake Kim and his obsessive dietary constraints. Plenty of SDU students had eating disorders. The cult of beauty seemed particularly powerful in Southern California, where conservative politics combined with a long swimsuit season to afflict even the most secure of women—and some men—with pangs of self-doubt. During my sophomore year, a freshman on the volleyball team had died suddenly. The autopsy had determined that her heart had been severely damaged by starvation. After that there was a flurry of eating disorder workshops and support groups, but now, a year later, the issue had faded to the back burner of campus politics.

"Everyone has dogs," Jess said, interrupting my depressing reverie.

I focused on the Jeep Wrangler stopped at the light just outside the café window, cute woman driving, cuter pit bull hanging out in the passenger seat watching pedestrians walk by. There had been an inordinate number of attractive women in cool cars with animals at their sides today. Maybe I would have to move to the city once I graduated.

"That'll be you in a couple of years," I said, sliding a glance at Jess. She wasn't looking too bad herself, hair tucked under her white Nike cap, eyes bright from our bike ride.

"I'd have to get a bigger car if I want a dog like that."

Dangerous territory, but I couldn't resist asking, "Do you think you'll stay in the area after graduation? Or are you going to take off for grad school or something?"

Frowning a little, she looked down into the swirling red of her tea. "I don't know. I like the area, I like Sidney and Claire. This is perfect for now. I'm just not sure about later."

"Sometimes I get scared, thinking about The Future. You know, after we graduate and they send us packing."

"You get scared?" she repeated. "I thought you had it all worked out."

I shrugged. "I've always thought I would like to be a teacher, like my dad. But sometimes I wonder if there might not be something else, something better. There's just so much to choose from. It would be easy to get lost."

"I know what you mean," she said. "My mother used to say that when she was growing up she was told she could be a teacher, a nurse or a housewife. She always said how lucky I was to have so many options. But for us, we don't know what it was like to live in such a narrow time, and we still have to figure out what to do when college ends."

I sipped my cappuccino. This was the first time I had heard Jess voluntarily mention her mother. An image of the woman in the white hat who had shown up at the tennis match the previous spring flashed into my mind.

"Your mother must be pretty proud of you now, with the rankings and everything."

Jess shrugged. "I don't actually know."

"You aren't close to her, are you?" I pressed, making my voice casual, pretending to watch people pass by beyond the coffee shop window.

"No. I'm not." Her words were clipped. "My mom and I got in a fight my senior year. I moved out. I haven't spoken to her since."

More pieces to the puzzle. "Must have been a pretty major fight."

Her fists were clenched, her breathing quick, twin spots of color tingeing her cheekbones. As I watched, she unfurled her fists and took a deep breath. "It was." When she looked at me, her eyes were almost black.

I reached out and touched her hand. I didn't know what to say, so I didn't say anything. We just looked at each other over our warm beverages there in the coffee shop, emotions passing unspoken between us. I remembered again what she'd said about souls. Had we known each other in another life, another time? But that was ridiculous, I thought, catching myself. I didn't believe in that past lives stuff. This was the only life I knew.

"What kind of dog would you get?" I asked finally, looking out at the sidewalk and taking a sip of my cooling cappuccino. "You know, hypothetically speaking."

"Probably a mutt," she said, voice calm again, "from the pound. They put so many animals to sleep every year, it seems crazy not to take one."

We talked about dogs some more while we finished our drinks. Then we strolled back to the car, stopping at a couple of bookstores along the way. Neither shop we browsed through was strictly gay, but they both had decent LGBT sections. In the second store, Jess lingered in the art section while I thumbed through psychology books. Psych was my minor. I'd first started taking it because I thought it might help to understand the workings of the human mind if I was going to be a teacher. The more psych classes I took, though, the more I interested I got.

"Find any good twelve-step guides?" Jess asked, looking over my shoulder at the book I was leafing through.

I started. I hadn't heard her approach. Trying not to blush, I showed her the cover—*The Psychology of Homosexuality*. "Not exactly."

"Oh. Oops." She smiled at me, seemingly not embarrassed in the least.

The sun was setting as we headed back to the car. The days were getting shorter. Soon we would have to set the clocks back. Glancing over at Jess, I watched her walking beside me. Her eyes were light again, her brow unfurrowed, the corners of her mouth turned up as if she were going to smile at any moment. I had to know suddenly.

"So what's your story, anyway, Maxwell? Are you, like, straight but not narrow or what?" I held my breath waiting for her answer.

Squinting a little, she shrugged. "I don't know. I don't think of it in terms of labels."

In other words, a fence-sitter, as Mel liked to put it. I had nothing against fence-sitters. Holly was one. I just wished they'd be upfront about their uncertainty.

Then she said, looking at me with her shy look, "If you called me anything, you'd probably call me asexual. I haven't dated in a while."

"Define a while."

"Well, the last person I dated was this guy Sean in high school, junior year. We were really good friends. He ran track and taught me how to lift when I was a freshman and he was a sophomore."

I tried to ignore a pang of what felt like—but couldn't be— jealousy. "What happened?"

"We dated for a few months, nothing all that serious. My mom was so happy that I was finally dating someone, anyone, she didn't make a big deal about him being black. Which is surprising for her," she added, voice slightly bitter. "Then he left for college and that was pretty much it. He was a really good guy. Good to me, anyway."

"Got it." So while I was dating Cara, a female basketball player, Jess had been dating Sean, a male track star. Kind of funny. I wondered if they'd slept together. That, I wasn't about to ask.

We took I-5 back toward La Jolla, both of us quiet, listening to the stereo. The sun was a ball of orange hovering over the ocean in the distance. At the exit before SDU, Jess glanced over at me.

"Want to hit Seal Beach?" she asked.

"Totally."

Seal Beach was an enclosed cove where seals slept almost

every night. No one knew when the tradition had started, but most nights there were a couple dozen seals sleeping piled together on the sand, ignoring the curious humans who came to observe them.

Jess parked a few blocks off Prospect Street, the Rodeo Drive of La Jolla, which, in turn, was the Beverly Hills of San Diego. We walked a block down to the ocean, around a small white public beach house and down a flight of stone steps to a walkway that led out along the top of a concrete wall. The wall jutted out thirty or forty yards into the ocean, parallel to shore. The surf pounded against it, the spray dousing unwary passersby. We were careful not to get drenched as we watched the final moments of the sunset. Then we turned our backs to the horizon and watched as the seals began their nightly sojourn in the dying light of early evening.

"They're so cute," Jess said, watching as the seals flopped their way onto shore, dragging their plump bodies out of the water with difficulty.

Their fins were too small to be of any use. Not the most graceful of creatures out of water, just like I was a nightmare to behold in the water.

"They are cute," I agreed, laughing as one dragged itself over the unmoving body of another.

"That would be you on the bottom," Jess said, "not even concerned as your buddy climbs over you."

I leaned against the iron rail. "You trying to say I'm fat? Or just lazy?"

"I wouldn't say lazy, exactly," she teased, leaning against the rail next to me, our arms nearly touching.

"What're you trying to do, wreck my body image?" I held my hand across my heart, mock wounded.

"Puh-lease." She rolled her eyes. "You know you think you're hot."

The question was, did she? I turned back to the beach, watching as a couple of more seals crawled up on shore.

"Want to go down there?" I asked.

"Sure."

We retraced our steps along the top of the wall and climbed

down a steep sand bank onto the beach. There were other people down here, a family with two young children, a couple holding hands, three guys who looked our age. As we approached, they checked Jess out and even gave me a passing onceover. We ignored them and walked closer to the seals, stopping just behind a thin rope people weren't supposed to go beyond.

Jess crouched down, looking intently at a couple of seals only a few feet away. They stared back, brown eyes wide and thoughtful, almost.

"Whenever I feel down, I come here and hang out with these guys," she said, smiling at the nearest one. It wiggled its whiskers.

"Yeah?" I knelt beside her and took up a handful of sand, letting the grains slip through my open fingers.

"There's something so peaceful about them. They're so trusting," she explained, still watching the same seal. "I mean, they come here every night, right up on shore, no matter how many people are on the beach waiting for them. They could be attacked so easily, killed by anyone at any time during the night. People still kill seals for their fur, you know? But they come back every night and nothing happens to them. I don't know. It's just cool."

I nodded. "It's almost like they trust we won't hurt them, so we don't. Like a self-fulfilling prophecy."

"Spoken like a true psych major."

"Minor," I corrected her, slightly embarrassed.

Holly would have made fun of me for lapsing into psych language too. Decent of Jess to pick up the slack.

We stayed on the beach as the sky darkened and the wind picked up. When it got too cold, we climbed up the bank to the concrete stairway. As we neared the top, I glanced back for one more look at the ocean and noticed that the three guys had followed us.

"Hey!" one of them called, jogging up next to us.

Jess and I stopped, watching them. All three were tall and dressed like we were in shorts, sweatshirts and baseball caps.

"What's up?" I asked. Jess, I noted, hung back behind me.

The same guy spoke again. He was clean-cut and good-looking, his eyes friendly. "We were just wondering if you wanted to grab a drink with us. We're about to head up to Hard Rock on Prospect."

I was always amazed when guys thought I was straight. For some reason, I thought they should just know. Often they did figure it out pretty quickly, more often than women, anyway.

"Hey, thanks," I said, flashing my social smile, "but we took the whole day off. I really have to get back and hit the books."

Jess still didn't say anything. Out of the corner of my eye, I could tell she wasn't smiling.

"Come on," a second guy said, blond hair poking out from under his navy blue Adidas cap. "Just one drink. Then you can do your homework."

Keeping my smile firmly in place, I shook my head. "Sorry. Maybe some other time."

The third guy spoke up then, his eyes on Jess. "I thought you looked familiar. You play tennis, right? I'm Dave Seaver, Julie's brother," he added when she stared at him blankly.

"Oh, Dave." The ice in her eyes thawed a bit. "How're you doing?"

"Great. Julie tells me you're not doing too bad yourself. This is Jess Maxwell, guys," he added. "She's ranked number one in Division II singles. Pretty awesome."

His friends made impressed noises. There were introductions all around. I shook hands with the guys and thought they seemed cool. The first one, Chet, and I chatted about how we'd spent the day. They'd gone roller-blading along Mission Bay before heading in to La Jolla for dinner. We all agreed that Sundays were divinely intended for play.

"We should really get going," Jess said as a short lull fell over the conversation.

I looked at her, surprised, and remembered suddenly that everyone on campus thought she was something of a bitch. *Just chill*, I thought, flashing her a quizzical look.

She ignored the look. "It was good seeing you again, Dave. I'll tell Julie you said hi."

The guys waved and headed toward Prospect Street while Jess and I walked in silence back to where we'd left the car.

Before she could start the engine, I put my hand over hers. "Are you okay?"

"I'm fine." She hesitated, looking at my hand covering hers. Her shoulders relaxed slightly. "I guess it just made me nervous when they came up behind us."

I laughed a little, trying to get her to relax. "I don't think they had any clue how it would seem to us. Typical guys."

"I know. They don't get it. If three girls came up to them in the middle of a dark street, they'd be psyched."

"Seriously. Thanks for suggesting this," I added, purposely changing the subject. "I never think to come down here. The seals are so cute."

It worked. Her head lifted a little. "Aren't they?"

She started the engine and guided the car inland, back toward campus. I watched the houses speed past, window shades still open to the early evening. Sometimes I felt overwhelmed by the sheer number of people living along the coastline of Southern California. Oregon was much more sparsely populated. There, you could go for a walk on a beach and not run into anyone. But here, there were people everywhere, houses built nearly one on top of another in the hills overlooking the ocean. So many people, so much money, so much ceaseless sunshine. Life didn't seem real here sometimes.

Soon Jess was pulling up behind my Tercel. Downstairs, through the front window of her house, I could see a woman playing a baby grand piano, her back to us.

"That's Claire," Jess said, following my gaze. "She's a music professor at SDU. She likes to practice on Sunday evenings."

I nodded and looked over at Jess. "So."

"So." She paused. "Want to come up? Claire made zucchini bread yesterday."

"That'd be cool. I'm starting to get hungry again."

"Me, too!"

We laughed at our in-season bottomless pit stomachs as we took our bikes from the rack. I removed the front wheel from mine and locked everything in my car trunk. Then Jess shouldered her bike and led the way inside.

Soon we were settled on the living room couch munching

zucchini bread, the room warm with lamplight. Jess had opened the front window so that we could hear the sounds of Claire's music floating up.

"She's really good," I said, pausing in my hunger to appreciate the classical music. I closed my eyes, intent on the music. "That's Haydn, I think. I love Haydn."

When I opened my eyes, Jess was watching me.

She looked away. "That's right. You said you used to play piano, right?"

"Until I was fifteen. I was pretty good," I said matter-of-factly.

"Why'd you stop?"

I shrugged. "I thought I had to pick between soccer and music. I didn't have enough time for all the practices and performances and lessons and games. Something had to give."

"You might have been able to do both. It just would have taken some serious scheduling."

"That's what my parents said. I'm not sure they ever forgave me for picking soccer over music."

"But they have to be proud of you," she said, echoing what I had said about her mother earlier. "You're here on a soccer scholarship. You're a wonderful player."

I rubbed my neck, self-conscious at her praise. "I'm good, or I wouldn't be here. But my mom at least would have been happier if I had stuck with music and gone to school closer to home, like my brother. I think my dad is proud of me, though he did grow up in eastern Oregon, so he's more of a baseball-football guy. Speaking of which," I added, checking my watch, "Sunday night football should be on. Want to see who's playing?"

She chewed her lip. "I really do need to study."

"Study while you watch," I said persuasively, flashing her the same smile I'd bestowed on our beach stalkers.

"Well, okay." She rolled her eyes. "Like I'm really going to study." She grabbed the remote and switched the TV on. "Want a beer?"

"Sure." I watched her cross the room and disappear momentarily behind the refrigerator door. I really should get some studying done too. I had a ten-page paper due in my abnormal psych class on Thursday morning. But knowing me, I probably wouldn't start it until Wednesday night around, oh, eleven or so. If I left now, I would only sit around my room listening to music and wondering what Jess was doing.

She returned, handing me a bottle of Dos Equis. "You staying?" she asked.

Our hands brushed as I took the beer. "Is that okay? Don't let me talk you into doing anything you don't want to do."

"Don't worry," she said with a slow smile that warmed her eyes. "I wouldn't."

"You wouldn't, would you?"

"Watch the game."

"Yes, ma'am."

We watched the game.

CHAPTER NINE

Jess and I got to be a pretty good team in the kitchen that fall. Most Mondays after practice I would head over to her place for dinner and *Monday Night Football*. Since we were both in season, our conversations revolved around our coaches and teammates as we ranted to each other and made one another laugh. Whenever I could manage it, I attended tennis matches, always dragging soccer players with me. In return, Jess made it to the soccer games she could, bringing along her teammates too.

In mid-October, on the Monday after tennis hosted and won Big Eights, I finally met Sidney and Claire. When I pulled up in the driveway, Jess was sitting on the front steps, athletic bag at her feet. She waved when I pulled up, but otherwise stayed where she was. Behind her, I noted, her landlords were sitting on their front porch swing, one partially hidden behind a newspaper.

I grabbed my bag out of the backseat and headed up the front walk. Claire I recognized from the night I'd seen her through the window playing piano. As I drew closer, the person beside her on the swing lowered the newspaper, and I got my first look at Sidney. Turned out he was a she. Sidney and Claire were a middle-aged lesbian couple.

Trying to hide my surprise, I came forward to shake hands with Jess's landlords. Claire was thin, her forearms muscular, long brown hair peppered with gray. Sidney's short hair was graying too, her smile brisk, handshake firm. We chatted for a few minutes. They asked about my team and my studies while I complimented them on their house and garden. And wondered why exactly it felt like I was meeting Jess's family.

As we headed upstairs a few minutes later, I said, "They really look out for you, don't they?"

Jess shot me a questioning look as we reached the third floor. "What do you mean?"

I dropped my bag next to hers in the hall and followed her into the kitchen. "Dude, they acted like they were your parents determining my suitability as your friend. I'm not actually sure I passed."

"Don't be paranoid. They were just being friendly. Want a soda?"

"Sure." I waited until she'd handed me a can of Sprite. "Why didn't you tell me they were both women? They are together, aren't they?"

"Yes, they're together." She hesitated. "I guess I just wanted to get to know you before I introduced you. That's all."

"You think you know me, then?" I grinned crookedly.

"Maybe." She smiled back. "Now, come on. Let's get dinner going. I'm—"

"I know, you're starving. What's on the menu?" And we set to work dividing up tasks.

Later, after dinner, I asked Jess if I could borrow a pair of sweats. She was reading a novel for an English class and barely looked up. "There's a pair in the bottom drawer of the dresser." She waved toward her bedroom.

"Sure I'm allowed in there?" I asked, only half joking.

"You're allowed."

I pushed the door open, blinked at the darkness, and felt for the switch. As light flooded the room, I looked around curiously. The ceiling was peaked, and a window lay directly ahead on the far wall. Jess had pushed her double bed up beneath it, pillows just fitting under the sill. A real mattress and box springs and everything, I noticed enviously. She'd told me the place came fully furnished. Lucky duck. The dresser was just inside the door. I opened the bottom drawer and pulled out a pair of sweats, then flicked off the light and shut the door.

"Nice room," I said.

"Thanks." She watched me pull her sweats on over my shorts. "You look cute in my clothes."

My heart speeded up a little. I wasn't sure what to say to this, though, so I pretended I hadn't heard and went back to reading my calculus textbook. Jess thought I was cute, and Sidney and Claire were lesbos.

Life, I thought, was good.

Not so much on the field, though. Late in the season, tensions began to run high on the soccer team. Most people believed that this was our year to go further than we'd ever gone before. It was generally accepted that we might even have a shot at a national championship—if we could only play to our full potential. As a result, the pressure mounted throughout the season. By late October, with only two regular season games and the conference tournament left, we were ranked seventh in the country and first in our conference. All we had to do was keep our ranking and we would go to the opening round of nationals, the finals of which were set this year to be played in Seattle.

As the pressure intensified, certain personalities on the team clashed. Specifically, mine and Jamie's. Our conflict splintered the team off the field—her buddies Sara Alexander and Kate Bzrezewicz, nicknamed Breezeway because no one could pronounce her last name, and the other four seniors except Mel took her side against me, while Holly and Laura and most of the underclasswomen took my side. I could see the divide widening between the two factions, but I couldn't seem to figure out a way to stop it. It wasn't that I didn't like Jamie Betz. It was that she didn't like me.

The Monday before our next-to-last game, a rematch against SDC set for Tuesday afternoon, Coach ended practice with a hard scrimmage, starting defense against starting offense. He matched individual players against each other. My mark was Jamie. I liked marking her. She was always a bit more of a challenge than anyone else, even Holly, who was a finesse player and easily muscled off the ball. Jamie combined speed, skill and, most importantly, strength.

Coach ordered us to play hard—we wouldn't be helping our teammates prepare if we didn't play all out. So I did. At one point, Jamie was on a near breakaway. I slide-tackled her, careful not to hit her very hard, and sent the ball out of bounds. I even let her land on top of me, cushioning her fall. She sprang back up immediately.

"What the fuck, Cam?" she said, face red as she loomed over me. I was still picking myself up. "Are you trying to break my fucking ankle too?"

I felt my own face grow hot. "Jesus, Jamie. Take a chill." And I started to turn away. But she grabbed me by the arm and whipped me around. Fortunately, Coach jogged up just then and stepped smoothly between us.

"Take it easy, Betz," he said. "Cam's just playing hard. You both were. That's the level of emotion I like to see, but save it for the game." And he walked her away, trying to calm her down. "Wallace, mark Holly." He winked at me, but I was the only one who saw it.

Holly jogged over and tugged on my smelly blue pinny to annoy me. Somehow defense always ended up with the pinnies that hadn't been washed in years and could practically run around on their own.

"Nice All-American temper," she commented.

"No shit." I was still off-balance. "Was it me, or was she totally out of line?"

"Completely," Holly agreed.

Then Coach punted the ball into the middle of the field—a free-for-all. Holly pushed off me and headed for the ball.

It was already past six. We scrimmaged for another ten minutes, and then Coach gave us a quick pep talk, reminding us to save our intensity for the other team. Practice over, I pulled off the pinny and headed for the field house where we kept our bags, keeping an eye out for Jess. But the tennis courts were already empty.

I was almost to the field house when Jamie brushed against my shoulder from behind, hard, growling in a low voice, "Sometimes I'd like to kick your ass, Wallace."

Momentarily speechless, I watched her walk away. Then I half-laughed. "I'd like to see you try."

She turned and faced me, and our eyes locked, hers burning and angry, mine defiant.

"After the season," she said. "After nationals."

"Anytime, Betz." I watched her walk away, then glanced over my shoulder as Holly drew near. "Did you hear any of that?"

"Any of what?"

I filled her in.

Holly whistled. "You're shitting me. Doesn't she know not to mess with you?"

"Guess she missed that part of my personal history."

Even my mother didn't know about the self-defense lessons her younger brother had given me whenever we visited him in Seattle. Uncle Alex was cool. A former Air Force engineer, he lived on Lake Washington in a sun-filled condo and worked at Microsoft. When I was a teenager, he'd taught me how to fight because, he said, a girl like me should know how to defend herself. I'd only recently realized that he actually meant a big ole dyke like me. Being a military engineer had helped him develop advanced gaydar, I liked to joke.

In reality, I didn't want to fight Jamie. I wanted everyone to like me. Whenever someone didn't, I tried to figure out what it was about me that irked them. To no avail, usually.

"Don't worry about it," Holly said, slinging her arm over my shoulder. "She probably just wants you. Kidding! She's an ass, that's all. Come on. You don't want to be late to your girlfriend's, do you?"

I shoved her away. "Watch it, or it'll be your ass I kick."

"Ooh, I'm shaking." But she danced out of my reach, just in case.

It was Jess who trotted out the psychoanalysis over dinner that night and told me that Jamie didn't hate me, per se. She was under a lot of pressure to score goals and was taking it out on me because I was handy.

"I'm under pressure too," I said, frowning at Jess across the kitchen table.

"Yeah," she agreed, "but it's not in your nature to take it out on the people around you. Anyway, you said yourself that Jamie stuck up for you during the game against SDC. Doesn't sound like she hates you."

"She even joked around with me that night."

"See? It isn't you. Maybe she just gets annoyed when you trip her. Can't blame her, really."

"It's called a slide tackle," I corrected her. "A trip is illegal."

"You know what I mean." She took a sip of Gatorade. "Just don't take it personally, okay? She's frustrated and acting out, and you happen to be a pretty good target. It's not like you'd react. What'd you do, laugh at her?"

I bit my lip. "Not exactly. I might have said I'd fight her whenever she wanted, something like that." At her raised eyebrows, I added, "What? It's not like I could just back down."

"No, of course not. That would be the mature thing to do." Her eyes darkened, and she looked away.

I hated it when she got like that, cold and supercilious like the Jess everyone else thought was the real her. I tried to change the mood. "Not like it'll ever happen. Can you see it, me and Jamie throwing down? She's such a closet case. That's why she's pissed at me, because I'm out and people still treat me the same."

"You think? Everyone knows she's seeing that basketball player. What's her name?" Jess asked, spearing a tomato with her fork.

"Joy Lassiter, who is totally cute, by the way. What she sees in Jamie I'll never know."

"Sounds like someone's jealous."

"Hardly." Not when I was here with—I cut off the thought. Dangerous territory. "Who's playing on *MNF* tonight, anyway?"

On to more immediate matters.

Despite the drama leading up to our last conference match of the season, we ended up winning 2-0 in fairly straightforward fashion on the road at SDC, thereby securing top seed in the upcoming conference tournament. Holly scored both goals on assists from Laura and Kate, and we carried her from the field on our shoulders when the final whistle blew. I was psyched someone other than Jamie was getting recognition. Didn't hurt that it was my best friend.

We celebrated briefly with friends and family on the sidelines, but we weren't on our home field so the win was a bit anticlimactic. Coach said a few words, and then we headed back to the SDC gym where the bus was parked.

The girl whose ankle I had broken had been on the sidelines during the game in street clothes, a cast poking out from under the cuff of her pants. As we walked back to the gym, I saw her maneuvering on her crutches ahead of me and jogged to catch up.

"Hey," I said as I drew near.

She glanced back, and her face grew serious. She recognized me. "Yeah?"

"I just wanted to say I'm sorry about…" I waved at the cast.

"Breaking my ankle?" she challenged.

"Well, yeah. I wasn't trying to hurt you." I squirmed under her hard gaze.

After a minute, she relented. "I know. I've gone over it in my head a million times. You thought I'd pull up, right?"

"Totally," I said. "Otherwise I wouldn't have gone in so hard."

She nodded, and we looked at each other. Then she leaned on one crutch and held a hand out. "Consider yourself forgiven," she said, and even smiled a little. "I'm Kelly, by the way."

"Cam." I shook her hand. I was pretty sure she was gay. Not bad looking either.

We ended up walking back to the gym together talking about soccer and our college experiences. Members of both teams passed us, eyeing us strangely. No one expected to see the two of us making friends. But that was sport. If our positions had been reversed, if she had injured me and I believed it was unintentional, I would have accepted her apology too. Maybe not right away, but it had been five weeks. In fact, Kelly said, she was getting her cast off soon. Which was good because her foot itched like crazy.

At the gym, we stopped and slapped hands.

"Good luck with rehab and everything," I said.

"Thanks. Good luck with nationals. I hope you guys kick butt. It'll make us look good," she added, smiling.

"We'll do our best. See you next year?" She was a junior, like me.

"Definitely."

I jogged away, feeling like a weight had been lifted. One fewer person who hated me, I thought, rolling my eyes at my own insecurity. I could be such a dork sometimes. But just then, I was a happy dork.

Two days later, we won our last regular season game, finishing up with an overall record of nineteen wins and two losses, the latter both to teams ranked in the top twenty nationally. The conference tournament started that weekend. We took a charter bus up to San Francisco on Friday night, rolled over CSU-Pomona in the semifinals Saturday, and met Fullerton State in the finals on Sunday for the second year in a row. To cement our nationals bid, we needed a win. We got it in emphatic fashion, 3-0.

That night, when we got back to SDU, Coach called a team meeting in the downstairs lounge at the athletic building. He stood with Terry and Mark, his two grad assistants, up near the chalkboard while the team, still clad in dress clothes, sprawled on the couches and chairs strewn about the lounge. Coach was a tall man, in his mid-forties, with a wife who had once been a beach volleyball star and two cute, tow-headed little kids who came to most of our home games. As he stood before us in shirt sleeves and a loose tie, I could sense the tension in the room. While the rest of us had been eating dinner at a Mexican restaurant near L.A. a couple of hours earlier, he'd been on the phone with his NCAA committee contact.

"Athletes," he began, his face and voice unreadable, "I learned earlier tonight that the NCAA Division II coaches' poll was announced this afternoon." He paused, and we all looked at each other, wondering what the news would be.

"It came as no surprise to us," he said, waving toward his assistants, "that we're currently ranked number six in the nation. On Thursday we play Texas State College here at home in the regional finals. If we win, we go to nationals in Seattle next weekend. Congratulations, athletes! You should be proud of yourselves tonight. I know I am."

We erupted into cheers, hugging each other and exchanging high fives. It was what we had expected, of course, but there was always room for politics and favoritism when it came to the coaches' poll. The teams who deserved home field advantage in regionals didn't always get it. That was just part of the game.

Coach held up his hand. "Hold on, there's more." We quieted down. "The All-Regional team was also announced today. We have three members: Congratulations to Jamie Betz, Sara Alexander and Cam Wallace, all first team."

More applause sounded. Cool, I thought, grinning.

Holly elbowed me in the ribs. "Way to go, dude," she said in my ear. We were sitting together on one of the couches.

Coach held his hand up again. "One more thing. The national committee also voted on All-American honors today. We have among us two All-Americans." He paused, and my smile faded a little. No doubt he had plugged Jamie and Sara, his favorites. "Let's give it up for second time All-American Jamie Betz, first team, and our own first timer, Cam Wallace, second team All-American!" And he smiled broadly at me.

Coach had come through, after all. I couldn't believe it.

Judging from Sara's forced smile, she couldn't either. She was a senior; this season had been her last shot at All-American. But I didn't have time to feel sorry for her. I grinned and slapped hands with my teammates and coaches, only too happy to accept their congratulations. I had done it—I was an All-American. And as a junior, no less. Now all we had to do was win nationals and life would be downright perfect. I couldn't wait to call my parents in the morning, and Nate up in the wilds of Alaska. Even my mom, the non-sports fan, would be impressed by the honor conveyed in the award.

The meeting wound down after Coach announced he was giving us the next day's practice off. We lingered a little after the coaches took off, all of us reluctant to leave the air of achievement permeating the lounge. There's a reason people like to win. It feels awesome. But it was already after ten on a Sunday night, and several people on the team had early classes in the morning.

At last we filed out of the athletic building and piled into our cars. I dropped off a trio of freshmen who all insisted on giving me hugs, even a particularly straight girl who sometimes seemed leery of me in the locker room. As if, I'd always wanted to tell her—it wasn't like she was all that and a bag of chips, to tell the truth.

Drop-offs complete, I parked in a nearly full student lot, and Holly and I headed toward our dorms. She threw an arm across my shoulders as we walked.

"Congrats, buddy. I totally knew you could do it."

"Thanks, Holl." For a moment I wondered if I caught a glimpse of envy in her eyes. "But you know it's all political."

She punched me. "Doesn't mean you don't deserve it. I'll see you tomorrow, okay?"

"Okay. Goodnight, Holl."

"G'night, Cam."

Goodnight, John Boy, I thought, trying to gauge how many times Holly had been the last person I talked to at night, the first person I talked to in the morning. And here I was getting all of these honors while she had to play in the shadow of Jamie Betz, senior all-star and queen bitch. Next year, I thought, everyone would see that Jamie wasn't the only quality striker in the SDU program.

Twenty minutes later I lay under my sheets, smiling away and trying to sleep. I was so happy I was almost scared. Something had to give, right? No one could have it this good. I closed my eyes, but I wasn't sleepy in the least. I was physically exhausted but my mind was executing cartwheels. I glanced at the clock: eleven p.m. I reached for the phone, dialed in the dark, hoped I had hit the right buttons.

Jess picked up on the second ring. I could hear the sound of the TV in the background.

"What're you doing?" I sat up and leaned against the wall.

"Just trying to write a paper for tomorrow."

"Is that why the TV's on?"

She laughed. "I was taking a break to see if the local news had anything about you guys. How'd it go? Did you win?"

"Yep." I grinned in the darkness, remembering the winner's ceremony that afternoon when we'd been presented with the Big Eight trophy for the third year in a row. "We beat Fullerton 3-0. It was awesome."

"Congratulations! You guys rock."

"There's more," I added, trying not to brag. But I couldn't keep the pride out of my voice as I told her about the coaches' poll and our upcoming home match against Texas State College.

"That's great, Cam! Way to go!"

"But wait, there's more." I heard her laugh and continued. "Jamie and Sara and I got All-Region first team. And Jamie got All-American first team and I got All-American second team! Can you believe it?"

"Of course I can." Her voice was warm. "That is so great. Congrats, girl. I wish I was there to give you a hug."

"Me, too." I smiled into the phone. "I'm glad you're still awake. I couldn't wait to tell you."

"I'm glad too."

We talked a little while longer. I told her about the two games, and that Holly, Sara, Jamie and I had also gotten all-conference. Holly was the second leading scorer in Big Eights behind Jamie. Next year, I said, she was going to kick some butt. When I finally piped down, Jess rehashed her match from the day before, the last in the fall season. Nationals in tennis weren't until spring. Jess had lost a match earlier in October against the top seed from a Division I team. Her new winning streak finished at ten.

"It's strange the season's already over," she said, "but in tennis the season's never really over. I'm ready for a break, though."

"I know what you mean."

Time was doing what it does, inexorably dragging us forward into the recent future. In a week, my junior season would be over, one way or another. Then I would only have one more season left in my college soccer career.

We wound down, finally. Since neither of us had practice the next day, we agreed to meet early for dinner, at my place for once. Then we could figure out where to go from there.

After I hung up, I lay in the dark staring up at the ceiling. Thoughts skipped through my mind, fragments of ideas and emotions and memories chasing each other in circles. I'd made All-American. Did it feel like I'd expected? I thought about the coming days when I would walk across campus, this new title appended behind my name for all my professors, fellow students and student-athletes to see. Yes, I decided, grinning in the dark. It felt pretty damn amazing.

Was this how Jess always felt? For some reason, I doubted the recognition she'd received for her tennis abilities meant as much to her as this meant to me. Maybe that proved I was shallow. Narcissistic, even. If so, there were worse things to be, I told myself, planning the phone calls I would make to relatives and friends in the morning.

CHAPTER TEN

For national quarterfinals, regional finals, at home on Thursday, a huge crowd took over the hillside. Jess was there, I knew, along with half the school it seemed. Starting lineups were announced, the national anthem blared over the loudspeaker, both teams took the field. We were playing Texas State College, who we'd beaten my sophomore year 2-0 on a road trip through the Lone Star State. We were confident as we kicked off—in ninety minutes, we would surely be Seattle-bound.

But perhaps too confident, too certain of ourselves and our destiny. TSC was the underdog; they had nothing to lose, while we were already thinking of Seattle. I was looking forward to playing in front of my parents, my aunt and uncle and younger cousins, friends from high school. Looking beyond the game we would have to win to punch our ticket to the Emerald City.

Ten minutes in, TSC stole the ball in the midfield and caught us napping. They popped it over the top to their right wing, who dribbled past Jodie, one of our outside defenders. I shifted over to cover, but the TSC striker unexpectedly took a quick shot from twenty-five yards out. It was a lucky shot—lucky for TSC, anyway. The ball curved upward, heading unerringly for the far upper corner of the goal. Mel, caught off her line, backpedaled furiously. At the last moment she dove into the air and tipped the ball up and over the crossbar. Whew—a save. But we weren't out of danger yet: a corner kick for TSC. Both teams lined up, eighteen players within the eighteen-yard box. The kick, a scramble inside the six, a shot, and a hand snaked out to make another save. Only it wasn't Mel's hand this time. It was Jeni's, ungloved, uniform sleeve pushed up her forearm, Jeni who had knocked away a certain goal. Screech of the whistle, moment of silence, moment of stillness.

Then time speeded up again. The referee pulled a red card from his pocket and motioned Jeni toward the sideline—rightfully so, we knew, even as Jamie, our captain, argued with him. An intentional handball in the box is an automatic red card. Jeni knew this too, and stumbled from the field crying. Meanwhile, a penalty kick had been awarded to TSC, a free shot from twelve yards out with only the keeper to beat. Coach Eliot stepped onto the field, shouting at the ref. Coach Eliot was shown a yellow card. Coach Eliot was pulled back to the bench by one of his assistants while the rest of us gathered helplessly at the edge of the penalty box, hoping, praying for a miss, a rebound, a save. The whistle blew again, the TSC center midfielder took the penalty kick—and scored.

Fifteen minutes into the game and we were down both a goal and a player—because of Jeni's red card, we would have to play ten versus eleven the rest of the game. Under pressure, our nationals trip suddenly at risk, we floundered. Our passes missed their targets, our runs were ill-timed, our confidence nonexistent. We couldn't seem to trap or head a ball to save our lives. The crowd on the hill was eerily quiet, our stunned spectators as unsure as we were how to react.

The whistle at halftime came as a relief. Maybe now we

could take a breath and regroup, I thought, heading with the rest of the team for the goal nearest the home bench for our traditional team talk. But our captains seemed to have a different objective in mind. Midway down the field, Jamie and Sara caught up to Jeni.

"What were you thinking?" Jamie demanded. "Were you trying to lose this game? You just fucked it up for the entire team!"

She and Sara were seniors. If we lost this game, their soccer careers would be over.

Coach Eliot was deep in conference with his assistants and didn't appear to notice the captains' sneak attack on Jeni, who was rubbing the back of her hand against her nose, head down. Somebody clearly needed to do something. I dropped my water bottle and headed for the threesome.

"Hey," I said as I approached. Ten yards away, the rest of the team was looking now, all except for our clueless coaches. Or maybe they just didn't want to see. "Leave her alone," I said. "It's not her fault we're sucking it up." And I smiled reassuringly at Jeni, my little sophomore defender. She nodded at me gratefully through her tears.

"Stay out of this, Cam," Jamie said, glaring at me. "It's your fucking defense that got us in this mess to begin with."

My eyes narrowed slightly. I was aware of the team only ten yards away, of the sun pounding on the back of my neck, of the ground solid and green beneath my feet. I swallowed my anger.

"Grow up, Jamie," I said, taking Jeni by the arm and pulling her toward the rest of the team. "I don't see you working any miracles out there." I turned away.

But Jamie grabbed me and spun me around as she had done once before the day she threatened to kick my ass. "Fuck you, Cam." Tension and possibly fear pounding in her blood, Jamie forgot the crowd, shook Sara off and actually threw a punch at my face.

Fortunately I too was in soccer mode, adrenaline flooding my system. I dodged her swing easily and trapped her arm against my side. In a low voice I said, "We're on the same team, jackass. Get your fucking head together."

Sara grabbed Jamie and dragged her aside, whispering angrily. I took Jeni's arm again and made her sit near me in the goalmouth, while Jamie and Sara took up positions as far away from us as possible during Coach's halftime talk. But I knew the rest of the team had seen the exchange. Dread pooled in my stomach as the minutes ticked by. We were crumbling, no bones about it. We were on the verge of self-destruction.

In the second half, TSC came out strong, pounding up and down the field tirelessly. With an extra player, they dominated, while we continued to fade. Our passes were still off, our runs entirely without purpose. My legs felt heavy, as if I were running through mud, and I could tell I wasn't the only one afflicted by this malaise. TSC had chance after chance while we were lucky to get it across the half line.

Then, with twenty minutes left in the game, Jamie crossed a beautiful pass in front of the goal just out of reach of the keeper. But no one was there. No one made the run. Jamie screamed, words carrying on the wind: "What the fuck? Am I alone out here?"

And suddenly, I understood what the phrase *seeing red* meant.

"Shut up!" I shouted at Jamie as TSC got ready for a goal kick. Everyone looked around at me in shock, including Jamie. "Just shut up, Betz, and play the fucking game!"

Apparently that was one too many curses—the whistle blew and the referee gave Jamie and me each a warning. Swearing isn't generally permitted on the field, though male soccer players curse themselves and each other up one side and down the other with little objection from the officials. But we weren't male.

"One more outburst like that," the gray-haired referee lectured us, "and you'll both be looking at yellow cards."

As he glared at us, I wondered if he knew that we were both lesbians, if he was looking at us thinking, *Fucking militant dykes.* I nodded sullenly and paced away, wishing I had maintained better control. Jamie and I had embarrassed ourselves and our team. What was more, we had behaved in a distinctly un-All-American fashion. No one would quite look at me as I shifted back into position for the goal kick. Not even Laura, who disliked Jamie as much as I did.

The seconds continued to tick down while we flailed about on our home field, unable to believe that this was how our best-ever season could end. When the final whistle blew, the TSC players screamed and jumped around the field, our field, as we watched in silence. Our seniors started to cry as they headed for the bench. We shook hands mechanically, quietly, grabbed our gear and headed for the gym in twos and threes, heads down, stunned, ashamed. Our loyal fans stayed where they were on the hill, watching us trail away across the field.

Holly, Laura and I walked toward the gym together. We were shell-shocked. This was not supposed to happen. We weren't supposed to lose at home to a team we had easily dispatched the year before. We were supposed to go to Seattle. We were supposed to have a shot at winning the whole thing.

Inside, Coach Eliot met us in the classroom near the women's locker room. In a clipped voice entirely different from Sunday night, he told us we would have a team meeting the following day, Friday, at four. *Instead of practice*, he didn't have to say. We already knew all about the end-of-season meeting to turn in our gear and figure out a date and location for our team banquet. None of us had expected to have such a meeting so soon.

In the same voice, Coach directed us not to be too hard on ourselves. This was just the way of sport, of soccer, as we all knew—any given team could beat any other team on any given day. Unfortunately, someone always had to lose. A 19-3 record was nothing to be ashamed of, and he hoped we could be as proud of ourselves as he was. True, we didn't fulfill our potential, but that was his fault more than it was ours. We should just be proud that we'd made it this far. He was. And with that final pronouncement, he nodded at us and left the room, silent assistants in tow.

This was usually the moment when the captains held the floor and declared that just because the season was over didn't mean we weren't still a team, what with intramurals to look forward to and important off-the-field bonding the rest of the year. Instead, Jamie stalked out, slamming the classroom door behind her. Sara, her co-captain, touched her hair nervously. Everyone was looking to her now.

"Um, we'll talk tomorrow after the meeting, okay?" she said. "Don't worry about it, you guys. We'll talk tomorrow." And she slipped out the door too.

In the locker room, no one showered. We stripped off our uniforms one last time as the rookies hefted the laundry bags, not bothering to grumble as they usually did. Everyone was deathly quiet until Mel, whose eyes were red from crying for the second time this season, sighed dramatically and said, "Well, I don't know about the rest of you, but I intend to get completely wasted this weekend. Like, puking my guts out wasted. Anyone else up for that?"

Tension broken, everyone laughed, the younger kids looking at the juniors and seniors cautiously.

"Count me in," Laura said, and slapped Mel's upraised hand.

We rode to the student center packed five and six to a car, and pushed our usual tables together in a corner of the cafeteria—everyone but Jamie and Sara. Silence forgotten, we talked about the game, then the season, then, finally, our non-soccer lives. Our daily bond had broken, and suddenly we were just a group of friends whose reason for getting together every day had unexpectedly ended. We lingered over dinner, reluctant to let go. After tomorrow, we would have to make an effort to see each other.

Eventually the team dwindled, soccer players leaving to ice sore joints, study at the library, write papers and lab reports, sleep, until only Holly, Mel, Laura, Jeni and I remained. We sat close about a cafeteria table laughing and slapping hands, growing quiet again whenever anyone mentioned the game. It was after eight when we finally rose from our seats, embraced one another, and left the cafeteria as teammates one last time.

Back at Laura's dorm, Holly and Laura and I sat out on her balcony drinking beer and smoking cigarettes and talking until one in the morning. As far as soccer was concerned, we were seniors now. Only one season left to strive for that elusive championship title. None of us could quite believe it, and no one said what we were probably all thinking: This year was it. Without Jamie and Sara, we probably wouldn't ever come this close to a national championship again.

Later, back at my dorm, I found a message on my voice mail from Jess. She had been at the game and wanted to tell me how sorry she was about everything and to make sure I was okay. Wanted me to call her when I got in. I listened to the message twice, but I didn't call her. I couldn't talk to her, knowing she had seen the game. Had seen me and Jamie take the team down in our personal war.

Room spinning slightly around me, I lay down on my bed and waited. Sleep, I knew, would be long in coming.

CHAPTER ELEVEN

I almost didn't recognize Jess when she stopped next to my table the next day at lunch—beneath her baseball cap, her hair was down.

"Hey," she said, tray in hand. "Anyone sitting here?"

I waved at the chair in question. "All yours."

As she sat down across from me, I noticed that she looked cute as usual in her low-slung jeans and a white shirt, gray Nike hat pulled low on her forehead, dark hair curling around her shoulders. Meanwhile I was feeling slightly hungover. Not to mention depressed.

"Sorry I didn't call you last night," I said. "I didn't get in until late."

"That's okay. I figured you might not be in the mood to talk. Tough game, huh?"

"You could say that." I hadn't been able to think about anything else. I'd skipped both of my morning classes, which was not good. The dread and shame were still twisting in my stomach. I almost wished Jess hadn't been there. "Did you see the whole thing?"

"I did. That poor girl, Jeni. Everyone in the stands felt bad for her, especially when Jamie lit into her." She took a bite of her sandwich, looking at me consideringly.

"You saw that?"

She nodded and touched my hand. "Did Jamie really try to hit you? Because that's what it looked like from where I was sitting."

I looked down at my plate, embarrassed. "Yeah," I said, my voice low. "I was hoping no one on the hill saw that."

"I don't think most people did," she assured me. "But what happened?"

"Jamie totally lost it. She was reaming Jeni so I stepped between them and she got all pissed off and told me it was my fault we were losing. I told her to grow up and started to walk away, and the next thing I know she's taking a swing at me."

"That's crazy." She paused. "What was up with the referee in the second half? When he stopped the game, I mean. We couldn't tell what was going on from the hill."

Picking at the remnants of my potato salad, I explained my exchange with Jamie and the warning the ref had given us. "Basically we both freaked out and took the team down with us. Jamie and I fucked up. That's all there is to it."

"You don't blame yourself for losing, do you?"

"I don't know." I sighed. "I guess I do. If I'd been more alert, they never would have gotten that first shot off, or the corner kick, and then Jeni wouldn't have had to save the goal herself."

"No one else thinks it's your fault." She shook her head, smiling a little. "You weren't the only one on that field yesterday, Cam. There were eleven other players out there with you."

"Actually, only ten."

"You know what I mean." She threw a grape at me.

I caught the grape. "Thanks for the pep talk, but I still feel like shit. This is the second year in a row we've lost at regionals."

"I'm sorry. That really sucks." She paused. "Want to come over and have dinner with me and Sidney and Claire this weekend? You know, take your mind off soccer?"

"That would be good. Saturday night or something?" I stopped. We would probably have a soccer party this weekend— get together and get good and drunk and try not to feel too sorry for ourselves.

"Can we make it Sunday?" she asked. "We're having a tennis party on Saturday."

Jess was one of the captains of the tennis team. She never let them party at her apartment, though, she'd told me, mainly because she knew they'd trash the place. Rich girls weren't good with other people's property.

"We'll probably have a soccer party that night, too. You know what?" I added. "We should all hang out together. Soccer could drink your team under the table."

She lifted an eyebrow. "Oh, yeah? Even with a game of Chandeliers?"

Chandeliers was a particularly nasty drinking game involving quarters and shot glasses. I nodded boldly. "Totally. We'd kick your butt."

"No pun intended?"

"Good one. How about it? You guys want to take us on?"

"I'll talk to the team and get back to you, but I can't see them saying no." She stuck her hand across the table. "Looks like I might be seeing you Saturday night after all."

I took her hand and smiled across the narrow cafeteria table as college students passed us on all sides. I could already feel my soccer-induced depression receding. Had nothing to do with the fact that I liked the feel of Jess's palm against mine.

That weekend, Mel let the soccer team invade the on-campus apartment she shared with two other seniors. Laura, Holly and I were the first to arrive. We opened a case of Rolling Rock and stocked the refrigerator, then sprawled on the couch, chatting as we watched Mel finish her last-minute cleaning. The apartment complex belonged to the university. Each apartment was its own two-floor building with a kitchen and living/dining room downstairs, bedrooms and bathroom upstairs. Mel said it would probably be the nicest apartment she would live in this millennium.

Soon after we got there, the doorbell rang again. Sara, Kate and Jamie came in and stood in the entryway, hands deep in their jeans pockets, all three in the navy blue team jackets we'd bought the year before.

After a minute, I cleared my throat. "Beer's in the fridge."

The tension in the room eased a bit. Jamie and Mel put their heads together at the stereo in the corner of the living room, lining up CDs for the evening, while Kate and Sara left the beer they'd brought in the kitchen and grabbed bottles from the fridge. The doorbell rang again and a whole mess of freshmen and sophomores wandered in, almost unfamiliar to me in street clothes. We got everyone beer, except for a couple of freshmen who'd brought wine coolers. They didn't like beer.

Jamie grinned malevolently. "We'll have to take care of that, won't we, Mel?"

Mel nodded, unsmiling, playing the mean butch. "We certainly will."

The two freshmen exchanged a wide-eyed look and cradled their wine coolers closer to their chests. They were probably afraid of Mel. Then again, even I had been intimidated when I first met her. Mel caught my eye and turned away, hiding a smile.

It might seem strange, but I always felt like I really got to know my teammates during the off-season. At this point in the semester, we'd spent countless hours together on buses, at practice and in locker rooms, but we were basically a group of strangers still. We knew who could chest trap the ball well and who was good at crosses or volleys, who was on scholarship and who was a walk-on, who had bad ankles and how long most of us had played soccer. But beyond the neat rectangle of the soccer field, we didn't know each other that well.

At off-season parties, I finally got to know the teammates I hadn't talked to much at practice. The cliques were still obvious, but as soon as everyone gathered around the table for a game of quarters, the barriers dropped and laughter bonded everyone. Seniors learned the names of freshmen. Juniors and sophomores cemented friendships. And freshmen forgot to be shy as they tried to catch their teammates with a quarter in a shot glass.

When the doorbell rang half an hour after the last soccer player had arrived, Mel and I exchanged a look. I went to open the door and discovered Jess and a dozen or so of her teammates waiting outside. Judging from their bright eyes and the tall plastic cups they nearly all carried, they had pre-partied somewhere along the way. My bet was on a frat party.

"Hey," Jess said, smiling at me.

"Come on in," I said, holding the door wide. This was going to be interesting.

At first the tennis players were more reserved than we were, accustomed as they were to a sport in which any display of emotion resulted in point penalties. The drunker they got, though, the rowdier they were and the more fun everyone seemed to have. As I'd predicted, the soccer team drank the tennis team under the table. But it took a while, and most of the beer in the apartment was gone before the tennis team finally folded.

Unlike the rest of her team, Jess didn't drink much. She had to drive home, she said. Mel told her she was welcome to stay in one of the rooms upstairs—her fourth roommate had dropped out of school, and friends were always staying over in the empty room. At this suggestion, though, Jess just shook her head and got all quiet. Then she excused herself and went upstairs to the bathroom, and I got caught up in my turn in the drinking game. By the time I noticed she was back a little later, everything seemed normal again. Well on my way to getting drunk, I couldn't be sure I hadn't imagined the odd look in her eyes at Mel's suggestion.

The party was more fun than I'd expected. The music was good, and people from disparate social strata actually got along. The one bummer was that Holly left early. She'd promised Becca she would meet her for a drink at midnight—*booty call*, we all razzed her as she pulled on her team jacket and resolutely headed for the door. The party raged on for another hour before soccer players and tennis players began to stagger off toward central campus in twos and threes.

Finally it was only Mel, Jeni, Anna, Jess and me left. Jess and I were sitting on the orange couch in the living room talking about nothing. The other three were at the dining table doing the same. The stereo was crooning the Eagles' *Greatest Hits*.

"Awesome party," Jess said. "Even if you did kick our butts."

"Told you so."

I wasn't quite drunk, more like happily buzzed. The buzz was beginning to wear off, though, and I was starting to get sleepy. I leaned my head against the back of the couch and squinted down at our feet. We were sitting close together in the middle of the wide couch, our jeaned legs barely touching, sneakered feet up on the wooden coffee table.

Jess was watching me. "You're so cute," she murmured, and reached out to touch my cheek, her fingers gliding gently over my alcohol-flushed skin.

That woke me up. I looked over at her quickly. "Jess," I said, my voice low. Then I stopped. My hand caught hers, our fingers interlacing almost of their own accord. Our eyes held, an unspoken undercurrent passing between us.

Then, blinking, she looked away, glanced at her watch. "It's late. I should go." She released my hand with a quick squeeze and leaned forward, resting her elbows on her knees.

I sat where I was, wondering what had just happened. Had she really touched my cheek and called me cute and looked at me with that rare wide open look? I stared at her back, muscles visible beneath her long-sleeved shirt, and had to resist an urge to slip my arms around her from behind. I drained the last of my beer and closed my eyes. Maybe I was drunk after all. Or maybe I had just been celibate for too long. Five months felt like a lifetime.

Beside me, Jess started humming along to "I Can't Tell You Why," one of my all-time favorite Eagles songs. Her voice was good, I could tell. I felt her lean back next to me again, our thighs touching. I was afraid that if I opened my eyes, she would move away.

When the song was over, she touched my leg briefly, her

hand warm through the denim of my jeans. "Hey, champ. You awake?"

Reluctantly I opened my eyes and blinked in the lamplight. Jeni and Anna were standing up now, looking over at us and laughing at something Mel had said. Jess was watching me, her eyes shuttered again.

"Unfortunately," I said.

The party was over. We walked out together—Anna, Jeni, Jess and me. Jess's car was parked on a nearby street, so I walked her to it while Anna and Jeni waited for me under a streetlamp. At the Volkswagen, Jess turned to me and held up her hand. I slapped it automatically even though I would rather have given her a hug. Jess wasn't the hugging type.

"You know," I said, "you could stay at my place tonight if you don't want to drive."

As soon as the words were out, I regretted them. I hadn't intended to say that.

She looked down at the keys in her hand and shook her head. "Thanks anyway, but I should go."

I cleared my throat quickly. "That's cool." Why had I said anything? All at once I felt like a lecherous lesbian, though I hadn't meant anything by the invitation. At least I didn't think I had. I stepped back. "Okay, well, drive safely."

"I will." She watched me backing away. I spun on my heel and headed toward my teammates. Behind me, I heard Jess get into her car and start the engine. I didn't look back as she drove away.

Anna, Jeni and I walked quickly through the cooling California night, chatting and gossiping about the party. Jeni kept talking about Mel. I would have to remember to tell Mel that, I thought. Jeni didn't look gay. With Anna, though, it was obvious. Her hair was cropped short except in front where it was bleached blonde. She wore a black triangle earring in her left ear and walked with this cocky, jock-dyke walk. She actually reminded me of myself back in my radical days, as Holly liked to call them. I sighed a little and looked up at the faint stars, nearly blotted out by the San Diego lights. I must be getting old. The thought of dating practically any attractive woman who showed interest, as I'd done my first two years of college, no longer appealed to me in the least.

"What's up with you and that tennis player, Cam?" Anna asked as we neared central campus.

Bold little baby dyke. I could almost respect that. "What's it to you?"

She smiled disarmingly at me. "I was just going to say you guys look good together."

"Right." I recognized that smile too. "We're just friends. But as long as we're on the topic of dating girls, I'm going to give you two a few tips passed along to me by another soccer player my first year at SDU. Number one, never date anyone on your team. At least, not anyone who will be on your team next season," I amended, catching Jeni's frown out of the corner of my eye. "Number two, try to date people who are about your size. That way you can share clothes." They giggled. "Number three, never date anyone who lives on your hall. If you break up, bathroom scenes can get pretty ugly. And last, don't date straight girls. It only gets you into trouble." A tip I would do well to remember, apparently.

"Cool," Anna said, and held out her hand for a fist bump.

I complied. We'd reached my dorm, and I fished in my jeans pocket for my keys. "Be safe, you two. Watch out for scary frat boys."

A couple of gay guys had been beaten up the month before walking home from a party, not to mention the usual date-rapes and random rapes that plagued a university this size. The administration had installed extra security lights and phones, but you still had to be careful.

Jeni and Anna waved and strode off down the sidewalk, bellowing a song so out of tune I didn't recognize it.

On my hall, I stopped in the bathroom to get ready for bed. I lived in a women-only dorm so there weren't any football players puking in the stalls, fortunately, not like in Laura's dorm. Even the bathrooms on Laura's floor were co-ed. I wasn't sure she'd ever mentioned this fact to her parents, conservative Republican types from Orange County.

As I brushed my teeth, I stared at my mirrored reflection. No wonder Jess had opted to go home alone. I looked terrible—my face was flushed, hair a mess, T-shirt disheveled. I raked a hand through my hair. No use. I still looked like shit.

Scowling, I filled a plastic cup with water and took it down the hall to bed with me. In my room I stripped down to my underwear, leaving my clothes where they fell. Then I flicked the light off and crawled into bed. In the dark, I made myself drink all of the water in the cup before I rolled over and burrowed into the sheets. My mouth was still dry when I fell asleep.

I didn't sleep well that night. By five a.m. I was lying in bed noting the varied symptoms of my hangover. For the second time in three days, I stared at the ceiling through bleary eyes and tried to quiet the rumbling acid in my unhappy stomach. I'd been awake for less than a minute when the scene with Jess reasserted itself. Groaning, I rolled over on my side and buried my face in a pillow. My only hope was that she hadn't thought I was hitting on her. But why would she? As far as she was concerned, we were buddies, the same as Holly and me. And buds didn't hit on each other.

Once my stomach had calmed somewhat, I met Holly and Becca at the cafeteria for brunch. They were happier together than I'd seen in a while, and kept exchanging sugary smiles and furtive hand squeezes they thought no one would notice. Like, duh. Anyone who knew there were lesbians thriving on the SDU campus knew that Holly and Becca were together.

Despite my best intentions, their bliss irritated me. When Becca got up to top off her coffee, casting a last secretive smile back at Holly, I had to bite back a sarcastic comment. Instead I went for mildly supportive: "Looks like you guys are doing better."

Holly smiled, watching her girlfriend walk away. "Have I mentioned she's really good in bed?"

"Dude," I said, making a face. "I totally don't need to hear that."

Holly focused fully on me for the first time. "What's up with you? Didn't you have a good time last night? You and Jess were looking pretty tight when I left."

"Shows how much you know," I said, and told her about my inadvertent semi-proposition the night before.

Holly seemed surprised. "You got dissed? That's gotta be a first."

I stared at her across the table. "I told you, I wasn't hitting on her. And anyway, you know none of that gossip is true. Jesus, Holly."

She held up a placating hand. "Take it easy. Calm down, Cam."

"Why should I?" I stopped. I rarely called Holly on anything she did that annoyed me. I rarely called anyone on anything. Except Jamie Betz, maybe. I stood up as Becca returned to the table. "I gotta go. I'll see you guys later."

"Fine," Holly said shortly, her scowl matching mine.

Outside the student center, I pulled on my fleece, hopped on my bike and took off. When I got to my dorm, though, I didn't stop. Instead, I veered onto a road that led off-campus. I needed to get away. Thoughts of soccer and Holly and Jamie and Jess were all swirling through my mind, one unresolved problem after another. I wasn't used to this. Usually I just let things happen as they might and didn't worry about the end result. But nothing was working out the way it should. I was sick about soccer, uninterested in most of my classes, worried about the whole Jamie Betz thing, and now I wasn't sure if the friendship I had going with Jess was really what I wanted. I'd thought it could be enough, but after the previous night, I wasn't so sure anymore.

I ended up at Seal Beach, standing on the wall at the end of the walkway letting the surf crash at my feet and splash me with spray. The ocean soothed me, its wildness something tangible I could taste in the salty dampness of my skin. It was a windy day, the waves high, gray clouds moving quickly overhead and blocking the sun. It probably wouldn't rain, though. Southern California was in the grip of a drought that felt permanent. Not like lush Oregon. Or rainy Seattle.

Seattle. I checked my watch. National finals would be underway right now. At this moment, I should have been heading a cross out of the air, or tracking down a breakaway. I should have been saving a certain goal in front of a crowd that included my family and friends. Instead I was standing on a concrete walkway staring out at the dark, gray Pacific, pondering my plethora of recent failures.

My life really was amazingly good, I knew. I was healthy and playing my way through school, my future wide open and waiting for me to discover it. I loved my family and they loved me. They had even accepted my sexual orientation as natural and somewhat unavoidable, probably because I'd always been a tomboy and good at sports—the stereotypical lesbian. I was lucky, I knew. I just didn't feel like it right now.

I made my way down to the beach and lay in the sand near the rocky cliff wall, watching the low-flying clouds pass overhead. I emptied my mind of everything but the worry eating me up inside and let it have its way. After a little while, the anxiety began to turn on itself and the world didn't seem so gray anymore. I started to notice colors again—dark green seaweed, red and blue plastic remains of a child's toy strewn across the rocks at the bottom of the cliff, brown vines that snaked up the cliff, blue sky just visible through the racing clouds.

Gradually my tension eased. The puzzle pieces in my mind felt like they were falling back into place. Holly was still my best friend; it was only natural that we would get sick of each other every once in a while. And I hadn't lost the game for my team. If anyone felt guilty for our loss on Thursday, it had to be Jeni. As head of defense, I would have to remember to call and check in on her. As for Jamie, not everyone I met would like me. That was just a fact I would have to deal with, preferably in a mature fashion rather than a junior high brawl.

The only thought that still made my head hurt had to do with Jess. For one thing, I wasn't sure why I had asked her to stay over after the party. Holly and I had spent the night in the same bed before, and it had always been completely innocent. Nothing but friendship had ever occurred to either of us. But with Jess, I wasn't so sure of my motivation. I kept seeing her look down and shake her head as we stood beside her car outside Mel's. That was reality, I told myself—Jess turning away, rejecting me. But what about earlier when she touched my cheek and told me I was cute in a voice that sounded more than friendly? What did those two separate incidents, linked together, mean?

When I was tired of thinking, I walked my bike back to the road and headed out to Mission Bay. Not many people were out. *Wimps*, I thought, turning my bike into the wind and pedaling hard into the salty breeze along the bay.

I must have ridden twenty miles that day, pushing my body until the adrenaline flooded my system and drove out the anxiety and self-pity and doubt. When I finally returned to my dorm late in the afternoon, my mind and body had been cleansed by exertion. Whatever reality was waiting for me, I would deal.

Back in my room, I checked my phone and found my voice mail full—a couple of old messages I hadn't deleted plus five new ones. I flopped on my bed, flushed and sweaty, my face wind-burned from the ride, and listened to the messages. One was from Mel, who wanted to know what I was doing, to take her mind off the finals, to ask me about something. Jeni, I thought, smiling a little, and deleted the message. The next was from my parents, who were just calling to say hi and that they hoped I wasn't feeling too badly today, what with the tournament and all. Sweet, I thought, and hit delete. The next message was Holly, who was going to study in the library but just wanted to say she was sorry if she'd upset me and that today sucked and that I should call her later. Another delete.

The last two messages were from Jess. In the first, she was calling to see if I had a hangover and if I was still coming over for dinner. In the second, she wondered where I was, anyway, and why I hadn't called yet. She sounded completely normal, as if nothing untoward had happened. Apparently the angst wasn't mutual. Maybe she had forgotten that she'd touched my face and called me cute. Or maybe it just hadn't meant to her what it had to me.

She picked up on the second ring. "Hello?"

"Hey, it's me." My heart rate picked up at the sound of her voice. Traitor.

"What's up? Where've you been all day?"

"I went for a bike ride." So far she didn't sound any different. "I was feeling restless so I headed over to Mission Bay."

"You must not have a hangover, then," she said.

"I drank a lot of water before bed and slept in."

"Good thinking. So are you still up for dinner tonight?" she asked. "I told Sidney and Claire we would make them pasta."

I hesitated. "Do you still want me to come over?"

"Of course." She sounded puzzled. "Why wouldn't I?"

"I'm just not in a very good mood," I hedged.

Now was my chance to put distance between Jess and me, to protect myself from an inevitable future rejection that would hurt significantly more than last night's had. But I could picture Jess in her upstairs apartment in Claire and Sidney's house, her eyes warm and open. She trusted me. Jess didn't trust many people.

"We'll cheer you up," she promised. "It'll be good for you to get away from campus. I mean, if you still want to come over."

"Of course I do." And it was true. I couldn't wait to see her, which was what worried me.

We hung up a moment later. I shed my clothes, pulled on my bathrobe and stepped into my soccer sandals. Jess was acting as if she had never looked at me in that particular way and I had never invited her to come home with me. Everything was apparently fine—as long as I didn't examine my feelings for her too closely. Totally fine, I told myself as I padded down the hall to the showers. Now if I could just catch up in my classes and forget about the way soccer season had ended, life would be perfect again. Or almost perfect, anyway.

I turned the shower on and stepped in, closing my eyes as the warm water washed away the afternoon chill.

CHAPTER TWELVE

The week before Thanksgiving break, the soccer team had our formal end-of-season banquet. There, Jamie offered an olive branch of sorts, pulling me aside and saying she hoped I had never taken her too seriously, that sometimes she just liked to blow off steam, that she knew I cared about SDU soccer as much as she did. I paused, then smiled at her and said, no, I'd never taken her seriously; I knew soccer was her world the same as it was mine. We shook hands, the rest of the team looking on. She even half-hugged me.

After the meal, Holly and I were voted co-captains for the following year. Laura said she didn't mind not being picked, but her eyes seemed over-bright after Coach announced the results. Jackie, the only other junior, was second-string, but Laura was a starter. After the banquet, she took off by herself, claiming she had to study. Meanwhile, Holly and Mel and I went for a drink at a gay-friendly bar in the city, Holly and I flashing our fake IDs as usual. Mine was my older cousin from Colorado's "lost" license. She'd sent it to me right after she turned legal, suggesting I might have greater need of it than she did. I'd assured her I would put it to good use.

We sat at a booth in the back, pint glasses on the table before us. We even shared a few cigarettes. Mel, it seemed, was falling for Jeni and wanted to ask us what we thought she should do. Holly and I told her to go for it. Jeni, we informed her, was totally crushing on her.

"Really?" Mel asked hopefully, cigarette in one hand, beer bottle in the other.

"Really." Holly and I both nodded.

You would never have known we were scholarship athletes, I thought, with our cigarettes and beer bottles, the practiced way we inhaled the smoke and drank the alcohol. At least we could be sure Coach Eliot would never stumble across us at a gay bar. Anyway, our season was officially over now, which meant the usual in-season team rules—limited alcohol intake, no smoking, and self-enforced curfews the night before each game—no longer applied.

"Enough about me. What's up with you and Jess Maxwell?" Mel asked suddenly, pinning me down with her hawkish gaze.

I shrugged, frowning down at the heavily battered table that had probably seen thousands of patrons in its many years of service.

"She claims they're just friends," Holly announced.

"Huh. Looked to me like something was brewing at the party last weekend," Mel said. "Jess and I had a pretty interesting conversation in my kitchen before you left."

I looked up quickly. "You did? What about?"

"She asked me if you were dating anyone. I said not that I knew of. Then she asked if all those rumors about you were really true, and I told her of course they were."

I gasped out loud. "You did not!"

Holly snickered, taking a pull on her beer and looking from me to Mel and back again.

Mel's tough look crumpled when she smiled. "Don't get your panties in a bunch, Wallace. I told her people just like to gossip, that's all. I said they even had you and me together at one point, but you usually go for girlier women than me and vice versa."

Jess had been asking about my love life? That cast our interaction at the party in a different light, didn't it? But frankly, I hadn't gotten laid in so long that my judgment when it came to attractive women was most definitely suspect.

I glanced sideways at Mel. "You're saying I'm not girly enough for you but Jeni is?"

"Um, yeah."

"Did I tell you guys that Becca thinks I'm kind of butch?" Holly put in.

"You're kidding," I said.

"No, seriously."

Mel took a swallow of beer. "You tell that girl there's a big difference between athletic and butch. You aren't a true butch until you get called 'sir' to your face more than a handful of times."

Holly and I had been with Mel on several such occasions. It always amazed us that people could overlook her rather ample chest. She got a kick out of correcting them, though, she said. Otherwise she would have grown out her hair.

Late that night Holly and I walked back to our dorms together. When our paths diverged, we slapped hands and then hugged.

"I'm glad we're captains," she said, "for our last season."

"That sounds so crazy."

"Tell me about it. I can't believe we'll be seniors next time we take the field."

"It seems way too soon for that."

We stood staring at each other beneath the warm sky, clothes and hair smelling like the bar. Then Holly moved away.

"See you at lunch tomorrow," she said over her shoulder.

"Goodnight, Holly."

"Goodnight, Cam."

Goodnight, John Boy.

After Thanksgiving, there were only two and a half weeks to get ready for exams. I'd gone home with Holly as usual, while Jess had stayed and celebrated with Claire and Sidney. Now we were back and racing to finish papers and projects and cram for the dreaded blue book exams. Surprisingly, I usually did better grade-wise during first semester, probably because playing soccer forced me to budget my time. I had to keep a 2.75 average for scholarship and eligibility purposes, so I didn't have much choice—I needed to do well in my classes if I wanted to stay on the team.

This semester didn't seem any different. As I handed in my last blue book for a 400-level literacy class, I was pretty sure I'd done okay on my tests. At least one part of my SDU life was under control. I wasn't sorry to see the end of this semester. Despite being named All-American, I was leaving campus feeling more unsettled than I usually did, and not only because of the way soccer season had ended.

Jess gave me a ride to the airport to catch my flight to Portland. I'd left my car parked outside her house where she could keep an eye on it. My parents didn't want me driving home alone in the winter. The mountain passes on the California-Oregon border could get testy.

At the terminal, we hugged each other beside the car, briefly, awkwardly. This was the most intimate we'd been since the night of the party. I was careful not to hold on too long.

"Give me a call if you want," she said as I pulled my suitcase from the backseat. "I'll be around."

Her high school art teacher from Bakersfield, an old friend of Sidney and Claire's, was coming up to La Jolla for a few days. Jess hadn't mentioned plans to see her mother during either holiday.

"You, too," I said, backpack slung over one shoulder, suitcase at my feet. "I gave you my number, right?"

"You did." She was watching me. "You know, I'm going to miss you. Kind of got used to having you around."

"I'll miss you too."

I reached out and hugged her again, whether she wanted me to or not. We'd exchanged gifts at her apartment earlier. I was wearing the silver chain she'd given me with a small sunshine pendant, and she was wearing the moon earrings I'd given her. Kind of funny, I'd thought but hadn't pointed out—we'd given each other the sun and the moon. Doh…

She pulled away just enough to kiss my cheek, her lips soft against my skin. "Have a happy new year, okay?"

I backed away. Just a friendly kiss, I told myself, like people exchanged all the time in France and other foreign locales. "You too. I'll probably be hanging out with a bunch of guys from high school, getting drunk and playing video games. You know, the usual." I was rambling, which was ridiculous. It hadn't even been a real kiss.

She lifted an eyebrow. "You hang out with guys in Portland?"

"Sure," I said. "They're more fun."

"Depends on what kind of fun you're talking about." She turned away to close the car door. "Anyway."

"Anyway," I echoed, willing the blush I could feel building not to spread past my neck. If I wasn't mistaken, Jess had just alluded to lesbian sex. First the kiss, now this—was she trying to tell me something? "See you next month."

"The sixth, right?" She had offered to meet me at the airport when I got back in January.

"Right."

"Okay. Well, talk to you later."

"Right," I repeated.

She finally stopped staring at me and slid back into her car. I watched her pull away and check over her shoulder before easing the Cabriolet into the nearest lane. She waved at me and I waved back, fingering the pendant at my neck. I would see her in three weeks, I reminded myself as I headed into the airport, trying to ignore the ache in my chest that had started as I watched her little red car pull away from the curb.

Back at home, I settled into my usual winter break routine: staying up late at night reading science fiction novels and watching Letterman, sleeping until noon, gorging on junk food, and generally bumming around. A few days in, I told my mom that one of my friends didn't have any family to spend Christmas with, so she helped me wrap a few gifts to send to Jess—a couple of ornaments, a small wreath of cedar boughs from a tree in our backyard, a mix of music I knew she liked, a Wallace family Christmas card and one of the wool sweaters my father's family was always bringing back from trips to Scotland. La Jolla never got that cold, but maybe she would need it someday.

Jess called on Christmas Day to thank me for the box. Her grandmother and her aunt had sent packages too, she said, but none of her friends at school had ever done anything like that. She sounded really happy. We talked for a long time before she said she had to go downstairs to help Sidney and Claire and Barbara, her art teacher, with dinner.

My father officially had Christmas vacation too. But he still had to meet with his students' parents and plan for the coming semester, so he was busy as usual. This was the second Christmas in a row without my brother—winter was nearly as busy a season as summer for his guide company up in Fairbanks, and Nate couldn't get enough time off to make traveling down to Portland worth it. Without him around to distract me with day trips to snow fields and sci-fi marathons late into the night, I mostly passed the time with the same group of friends I hung around with in the summers, five guys I'd known since elementary school. Home for the holidays from various West and East Coast colleges, we had a long-standing tradition of spending New Year's Eve together down by the river watching the city fireworks and drinking beer. They all knew I was gay, but we rarely talked about it. In the summer we were usually too busy hiking and camping out to dwell on such matters, while at winter break we filled the time playing video games and watching more than our share of football.

But we were getting older now, and a couple of the guys in our group were overseas on junior year abroad programs. The rest of us didn't hang out as much as we normally did, which left me on my own much of the time. As usual, I was ready to go back to school—back to my real life—after only a couple of weeks of break. Decompression, Holly called the post-finals, pre-January term period. A necessary evil, but sometimes it lasted longer than I needed or wanted.

At the end of the third week, my parents took me to the airport. At the departure gate, we sat together in molded plastic airport chairs, the two of them flanking my bags and me.

"Well, Cam," my dad said, "I suppose you're ready to get back to your friends."

He and I shared the same auburn hair and hazel eyes, the same interest in teaching and education. Still, despite our similarities, his favorite sport was baseball. How he could stand watching the most boring game ever invented, I would never understand.

"I guess so," I said, feeling a little guilty. "I'll miss you guys, but it'll be nice to be back at school."

My mother smiled and squeezed my hand. "I remember what it was like getting back after a vacation. You can't wait to see your friends."

My parents had met in college in Eugene. When I'd told them I was going to SDU, I think they were both disappointed I was going so far away. But they just congratulated me on Coach Eliot's scholarship offer and said they would support whatever decision I made. They were amazing that way. When I told them my senior year of high school that I was dating Cara, they thanked me for trusting them enough to share the truth. Of all my friends, I had the easiest coming out story of the bunch. Then again, I was also the only one whose parents had lived together in Eugene in the sixties before they were married.

I left them to guard my suitcase while I bought a bottle of soda at a nearby newsstand. They were a funny couple, I thought as I stood in line watching them: my mild-mannered father with his receding hairline and a penchant for flannel shirts leftover from his childhood in eastern Oregon, my mother with her brisk manner and immaculate business suits. She was the driving force in their relationship, the one who did the taxes and paid the bills while my father focused on ways to help his students' families adapt to life with a mentally or physically impaired child. My mom and dad were so different, yet I couldn't imagine one without the other.

I also couldn't imagine never speaking to them again because of a single fight, like Jess and her mother. I had argued with my parents, of course, like any kid, especially during junior high and early on in high school. But my brother had broken them in—he'd always been a wild child, breaking curfew and coming home drunk and crashing multiple cars in his legendary pursuit of speed. After him, I'd probably seemed easy despite the gay thing.

Besides, no one in our family was particularly confrontational. Wallaces preferred to pretend a problem didn't exist rather than cause a disagreement or hurt someone's feelings. Eventually the issue either took care of itself or we all forgot about it. Not exactly the healthiest way of resolving conflict, I realized when I took my first psychology class at SDU. But at least we didn't fight that often. I couldn't imagine the level of disagreement it would take for me to cut my parents out of my life. What unforgivable act had Jess's mother committed? Or was Jess the responsible party?

I paid for a bottle of Diet Coke with a twenty my dad had slipped me on the way out of the house, and headed back to the gate. My mother frowned when she saw the bottle.

"You're not on a diet, honey, are you?"

"No, I just like the taste better than regular."

As a soccer player, I'd always burned enough calories that I didn't have to watch my weight. The only diets I believed in were ones that improved muscle tone and overall health.

"I'm glad to hear that," she said. "I was reading an article recently in the *Chronicle* about college athletes and eating disorders. Apparently many more women athletes suffer from these disorders than you might think."

My mother was always quoting articles from the *Chronicle of Higher Education*, her all-time favorite print publication. A university administrator, she loved academia. In a way, I would be following in her footsteps too when I became a teacher.

A few minutes later, my flight started to board.

"Gotta go," I said, fumbling with my boarding pass. In only

a few hours, I would see Jess. Classes didn't start for a couple of weeks, so we should have some time to hang around together. Maybe I would check out an indoor tennis tournament or two.

"Take care, Cammie," my father said, hugging me. "Don't eat any snozzcumbers."

This was a reference to *The BFG*, one of my favorite childhood storybooks. I'd always thought my father accustomed as he was to the limited mental capacity of his students, I'd always thought my father liked Nate and me best when we were still young enough to laugh at words like "snozzcumber" and "whizzpopper." Whenever we said our goodbyes now, he still trotted out this old line.

"I won't." I hugged him back. We were almost the same height. Was I still growing or was he shrinking? "Bye, Dad. Good luck with school." I kissed his cheek, his stubble scratchy against my chin.

"You too, sweetheart," he said. "I love you."

"I love you, too." I turned to my mom. "I'll call when I get there," I promised before she could say anything, hugging her in turn.

She held me tightly, her arms surprisingly strong. Neither of my parents worked out, but they tried to walk a couple of miles together around the neighborhood every night after dinner.

"Have a safe trip, honey," she said, and kissed my cheek. "Love you. Give Holly and your friend Jess our love."

The way she said it, I could tell my mom thought Jess was my girlfriend. It would have taken time and effort to correct her, so I just nodded and shouldered my bags and headed for the jetway.

As I passed through the doorway, I glanced back at my parents, noticing all at once that they didn't look nearly as young as they used to. They had both turned fifty the previous year. When they'd told me they were old enough for AARP, it had freaked me out. Now I waved and they waved back, standing close together, arms around each other. I turned again and strode down the jetway.

Back to life, back to reality, I thought as I waited in line near the entrance to the plane. Only which was my real life, which my reality? Oregon and the family I'd lived with for eighteen years? Or Southern California and the friends I'd made there? It was hard to say. That was the thing about school. All of this leaving, friends graduating, new people taking their place, all in preparation for your own eventual leave-taking. Commencement, they called it, but I always thought it was more like an end to life as you knew it. You couldn't really go back to who you were before college, and you couldn't just hang out in your college town after you graduated. After commencement you had to be a responsible person with a job and an apartment and plants, even. No more afternoon naps, no more food waiting for you beneath the plastic bubble in the cafeteria, no more aimless hanging out. Suddenly you were expected to have a purpose in life.

Holly called it the plants-to-children progression. First you had to get some greenery, see if you could remember to water it and give it the proper amount of sunlight. If your plants survived more than a year, then you could get a dog or a cat. Pets, of course, were a little more complicated, but also easier in a way. While pets had to be fed, watered, exercised and played with, if you forgot to do any of these things animals didn't sit quietly on the windowsill wilting, dying a slow, silent death. Wisely, a pet would piddle on the floor or crap in your shoe or chew a hole through the cupboard door where you kept the biscuits.

If your pet survived for more than a year, then, assuming you were in a long-term committed relationship of some kind (though nowadays that part wasn't necessary), you could procure a child by whatever technology was appropriate—that is, if you had a job, insurance and a roof over your head.

Which brings us back to a purpose and a direction in life. If you had that, the rest would fall into place. Or so I had been told.

"Welcome aboard," a flight attendant said, smiling brightly at me as I reached the plane.

I nodded at her and went to find my seat.

CHAPTER THIRTEEN

Without a daily soccer commitment around which to schedule my time, second semester always seemed less orderly than first. Classes started the second week of January, and I settled in and managed not to skip very many right off the bat. I even bought all the books I was supposed to buy, possibly a first for me. This semester I was taking a teaching history methods class, a seminar on American involvement in World War II, Philosophy and Women with Holly—very cool—and Macroeconomics. Laura, a business major, had convinced me that macro might come in handy someday. I bet Holly over lunch our first week back that since I was taking Macro on a pass/ fail basis, I could successfully complete the class without ever opening the textbook, relying solely on lecture notes. She accepted the wager, crowing almost giddily as Laura stalked out of the student center muttering about the juvenile nature of education majors.

Outside of class, Holly and I settled into our off-season workout routine: running or biking most days, lifting three times a week to keep our muscles sleek and strong. Intramural soccer had us playing six on six throughout January and February. After that we would meet weekly for pickup games, sometimes scrimmaging with the men's team, sometimes competing against other eligible opponents. As the upcoming season's captains, Holly and I were expected to organize these sessions. Seniors weren't required to participate, which was fine with me. Despite our truce, the less I saw of Jamie Betz, the better.

Jess and I resumed our Monday night dinners the first week of classes, even though the pro football season was winding down. We were good enough friends by now that we didn't need an excuse to hang out. I never brought up the night of Mel's party, and she didn't either. I attended all of her home indoor tennis tournaments and the ones within driving distance from La Jolla, accompanied by Holly and Laura. We watched in something akin to awe as Jess pulverized her opponents. She was on a definite roll, playing better, if that was possible, from match to match. Not that I was biased.

At the end of January, I convinced Jess to host a Super Bowl party at her apartment. The Washington Redskins were taking on the Buffalo Bills, neither of whom we particularly cared about. But it was the Super Bowl, so Jess agreed and I invited Holly, Becca, Laura and a handful of other soccer players while Jess invited a couple of friends from the tennis team. Only Becca declined the invite—she wasn't into "ritualized male violence," Holly told me privately, trying loyally not to laugh.

The day of the Super Bowl, I swung by Jess's early to see if I could help. She had left her downstairs door unlocked, so I jogged up the stairs and knocked on the third-floor door. No answer. I could hear Melissa Etheridge echoing through the apartment. I tried the door and found it, too, unlocked. Usually she was so careful.

I pushed the door open and called, "Jess!"

No answer. I could hear her singing along to the music,

or shouting, anyway. I tracked her voice to the kitchen, where I found her cleaning the sink, yellow gloves pulled up to her elbows, stereo blasting on the kitchen table.

"Jess," I tried again, reaching out to turn the music down.

She spun around suddenly, eyes wide, rubber gloves dripping soap on the floor. "Cam! What the fuck?"

"Sorry." I froze where I was. "I just came by to see if I could help."

She stared at me, brow furrowed. "Did I leave my door unlocked?"

"Yeah. I knocked, but I don't think you could hear anything over Melissa."

She turned back to the sink. "Sidney and Claire are away for the weekend, so I turned it up."

"Gotcha."

I stood where I was a moment longer, watching her lean both hands against the sink edge, her chin lowered. I could almost sense her heart pounding from across the room. I wanted to go to her, rub her shoulders, smooth the lines from her forehead. But touching her, I was pretty sure, would only exacerbate matters.

I forced my voice to sound cheerful. "So. Can I help?"

"You could vacuum if you wanted," she said, her back to me, voice as tight as her shoulders.

It was like I wasn't even there—or, more accurately, like she was no longer there. She'd done this before, withdrawn into some private place where no one else could follow. From experience, I knew if I left her alone she'd reemerge at some point. I was only hoping it'd be before our friends invaded her personal space.

I vacuumed while she finished up the kitchen and tackled the seemingly spotless bathroom. Everything looked pristine to me, as usual. Jess had told me that she enjoyed cleaning, which I had no trouble believing—the apartment nearly always looked freshly scrubbed, even when she was in season.

By the time I put the vacuum away, Jess was making eye contact again and even smiling a little at my lame jokes. We made a quick trip to the convenience store to stock up on chips, dip, cheese, crackers and beverages. We forked over more money than either of us could really afford, but after all, this was the first—and only, she insisted—party Jess had ever hosted at her apartment.

On our way back in, we stopped downstairs to let Duncan, Sidney and Claire's chocolate Lab, pee in the backyard. Then we headed back upstairs, Duncan trailing happily after us.

Mel, Jeni and Anna arrived first in Mel's father's old Mercedes, followed by Jess's tennis pals Taylor and Julie in a brand-new BMW. Laura and Holly showed up last.

"Where do you want these?" Holly asked as she came through the door. She and Laura were each carrying two large pizza boxes.

"Over here." I motioned them to the kitchen table. "Good call, you guys."

"It isn't the Super Bowl without pizza," Laura declared.

"You got some without meat, didn't you?" I asked. I'd recently decided to embrace vegetarianism.

"Of course," Laura said, rolling her eyes.

Everyone grabbed a piece of pizza and settled into the living room for the Super Bowl, keeping an eye on the pregame show to see which new commercials would make television history this Super Bowl Sunday. Duncan sat on the floor glancing eagerly from one to the other of us, waiting for dropped chips or pizza crust, his tail thumping the furniture whenever anyone laughed.

As the game got going, beverages flowed freely, food was munched continuously, and conversation—about sports, campus politics, food, families—frequently drowned out the sounds from the TV as Jess's friends and mine mingled easily. I liked seeing the apartment full of people chatting amiably. I thought she might too. The game wasn't very close—Buffalo managed to lose their second Super Bowl in a row in embarrassing fashion—but the creative advertisements provoked the usual giggles and groans. All in all, a fun time appeared to be had by everyone.

Shortly after the game ended, Taylor and Julie announced that they had to get some studying done. Mel, Jeni and Anna left with them. Jess and I had been a little surprised that the two tennis players, both of whom had boyfriends, had bonded so easily with Mel and Jeni, officially a couple now, and Anna the bold baby dyke.

"Guess they're straight but not narrow," Jess said to me in the kitchen with a slight smile, reminding me of the previous fall when I'd asked her what her deal was.

Holly and Laura stayed to help pick up. There had only been one accident, a beer knocked over on the rug under the coffee table. We'd cleaned it up immediately. Fortunately, the threads of the Persian rug were dark maroon and navy blue, so the stain didn't show. The rug was old anyway, Jess had said, mopping up the amber liquid with a dish towel.

Holly and I had just finished the dishes when Jess's phone rang. She grabbed it and walked into the living room.

"You sticking around?" Holly asked me, wiggling her eyebrows suggestively.

Laura caught the look and glanced from me to Jess, who was frowning into the phone on the other side of the room. "Wait. You don't mean..."

I patted Laura's arm. "No, she doesn't. She's just messing with you."

"That was a perfectly innocent question," Holly protested.

"Tell Jess thanks for the party," Laura said, dragging Holly toward the hall. "Later, Cam."

"Later."

I locked the door behind them and wandered back down the hall. Jess was still talking on the portable phone, looking out the window in the living room, one hand on her hip. Trying not to eavesdrop, I started to put the dishes away, but the apartment wasn't exactly huge.

"I know," she was saying. "I know you mean well, Nana, but you and Aunt Sara don't know the whole story." She was quiet for a long time, listening to the voice at the other end. "Good, I'm glad. But it doesn't change anything... No, it's not like that. You should ask her... I appreciate that, but it's something she and I have to figure out, okay? Okay, Nana? I have to go. There are people here... I know. I love you too. Give Sara and the boys my love. I'll come see you soon. Bye." She turned off the phone and stayed where she was, still staring out the front window.

I lifted a glass from the white plastic dish drainer on the counter, then paused. Was that a sniffle I'd heard coming from the living room? Duncan was leaning against Jess's leg, and as I hesitated, he gave a low whine.

"Jess?" I asked.

She swiped at her face but didn't turn around. "Did Holly and Laura leave?"

"Yeah. They said thanks for the party." I wiped my hands on a dish towel. "Are you okay?"

Abruptly she pulled the wooden blinds down, shutting out the night. She turned and I could see faint traces of the tears she'd wiped from her cheeks. "I'm fine," she said, not quite looking at me as she crossed the apartment. "I have to take Duncan for a walk. You coming?"

"Um, okay," I said, uncertain if I'd actually been invited along or not. "Are you sure you're all right?"

"I'm fine."

Her voice was firm, her eyes dark even in the warm, bright kitchen. Brushing past me, she headed down the hall and grabbed her SDU Tennis jacket from the closet, Duncan's leash and her house key from the hook beside the door. I followed, tugging my navy blue fleece over my head.

Jess ran down the steep stairs at full speed. "Come on," she said over her shoulder. I wasn't sure if she was talking to me or the dog. We both hurried after her.

She led the way quickly through the residential neighborhood, her face in shadows most of the time. Duncan and I trailed her. He stopped to pee frequently. Marking his territory, Jess had told me the first time we'd borrowed Duncan for an after-dinner walk the previous fall. That was what male dogs did. Typical, I had said, and we'd both laughed.

But she wasn't laughing now. I could feel her tension, see it in her clenched jaw, the set of her shoulders. I walked quietly, letting her work it out on her own. I knew her well enough to understand that Jess didn't like to talk through her feelings. She preferred to pin them down and crush them before they could get loose. I didn't know why she maintained such rigid control over her emotions. I wondered if anyone else did. Maybe her mother. Probably not her grandmother, judging from what I'd heard of their phone conversation.

We walked a few blocks to a small overgrown lot where Jess let Duncan off-leash. Then we stood silent, watching as he bounded happily into the bushes, a dark blot moving among darker shadows. I could hear him snuffling and clambering about through the brush. Soon he careened out again, tongue lolling in a pant of satisfaction, and stumbled to a halt at our feet. Jess pulled a dog biscuit from her jacket pocket and tossed it to him.

"Good boy," she said, her voice low. She hooked the leash to his collar and we turned back toward the house.

The silence was beginning to unnerve me. Finally I couldn't stand it any longer.

"Look, Jess, what's up?" I asked, taking the plunge I usually avoided. "You're obviously upset about something. Why don't you talk about it? Might make you feel better."

She laughed, only it came out short, bitter. "You're hardly the queen of communication, Cam."

Frowning, I caught a glimpse of her face as we passed under a streetlamp. There was that haunted look I remembered seeing the first night I'd been to her apartment.

"I never said I was," I pointed out. "But we're not talking about me. What's up?"

She was quiet for a long time, so long that I thought she didn't intend to answer. We passed spacious houses with well-tended lawns and neat fences that Duncan stopped to pee on. We paced the narrow sidewalk lit by streetlamps and porch lights, side by side but not touching. We were on the walkway to Sidney and Claire's front door before she stopped abruptly, surprising both me and Duncan.

"Look," she said in the same low voice. With her face in shadows, I couldn't make out her features. "There are some things you just can't talk about. Some things that if you even think about them, they suck you in and it's like a whirlpool, and you might never get free. Do you know what I mean?"

"Uh-huh." I nodded, a little scared of the intensity in her voice. Honestly, I didn't have a clue what she was talking about.

She made a fist with one hand. "Talking doesn't fix anything.

It doesn't help. Nothing does, except maybe time. And even then, even when you're sure you've got everything under control, it comes back. It always comes back, and then you just try to get through it. That's all. You just get through it because really, it's not like there's any other choice." She shook her head, took a few paces away from me, unfurled her fist and flexed her fingers. "Come on. It's getting late."

I waited outside while she let herself into Sidney and Claire's part of the house to turn off lights and close curtains. Then we returned upstairs in silence, Duncan trailing at our heels. She slipped her keys onto the hook near the door and hung her jacket back in the closet. When she headed into the kitchen, Duncan and I both followed. I wasn't sure what came next.

"I'm making tea," she said, filling the kettle. "Want some?"

I hesitated. I should really head home and try to get a little reading done before I hit the sack, but I didn't want to leave yet, not like this. I wouldn't be able to sleep thinking about her all alone in this big house.

"Decaf?"

"Raspberry patch."

"Okay."

I pulled off my fleece and hung it over a chair. Duncan lay down on the cool tile floor with a deep dog sigh. I watched as Jess moved deliberately about the kitchen, pulling two cups with mismatched saucers from the cupboard, two teabags from a metal tea box, two spoons from the squeaky old silverware drawer. When the kettle whistled, she poured boiling water into the cups and carried them over to the table. She set a mug in front of me.

"Did this come with the place, too?" I asked, gesturing at the mug. A picture of Garfield in tennis gear adorned one side.

She almost smiled. "No, it was willed to me by a senior on the team last year. Beth Jackson. Do you remember her?"

An image of a petite blonde woman with the inevitable tennis tan flashed into my mind. "Vaguely."

"She was pretty cool. She kind of looked out for me when I was a freshman." Jess blew on her tea, steam rising about her face.

"Are Sidney and Claire coming home tomorrow?"

She nodded, cupping her hands about her mug, decorated with a picture of the San Diego bay at sunset.

I tried again. "I can't believe football season is over."

"I know."

"Only a month until March Madness."

"Yep."

Obviously, she wasn't in the mood to talk. I set my teabag on my saucer and picked up my cup, blowing on the surface. I wanted to shake her. I wanted to hug her. Let's face it, I thought, staring into the crimson tea, I wanted to kiss her. I sighed noisily.

Jess glanced up. "You okay?"

"I don't know," I said, letting some of my frustration into my voice. "You shut everyone out. It's hard sometimes, you know?"

She toyed with the wet teabag on her saucer. "I'm fine. Honestly."

"Great. Awesome."

It wasn't, though. I wanted her to need me. I even thought I might need her to need me.

We drank our tea in silence, listening to the CD that was playing in the living room—Peter Gabriel. When "In Your Eyes" came on, I gazed into my tea. All Jess would have to do was look at me and she would know I cared about her more than any mere friend had a right to.

The tea made me sleepy. When I'd finished my cup, I looked across the table at her. "I think I'm too tired to drive. Mind if I crash on your couch?"

She glanced from me to her living room. "Of course not."

Was that relief in her eyes? Apparently she didn't want to think of herself alone in this big old house tonight, either.

We got ready for bed as soon as we'd rinsed out our tea mugs, even though it wasn't quite eleven, still early by college student standards. She loaned me a T-shirt and boxers, a spare contact case. I used the bathroom before she did, washing my face and brushing my teeth with a toothpaste-smeared finger. I also opened the mirrored medicine chest and examined its contents. Advil, dental floss, contact solution, moisturizer, a box of Tampax, zit cream and Band-Aids. Feeling slightly guilty, I closed the mirror, wincing as the hinges squealed. No medications, no questionable drugs and no condoms. Or dental dams, for that matter.

In the living room, Jess had set out a pillow and some bedding.

"Are you sure you'll be okay out here?" she asked, watching me tuck the sheet and blanket under an end cushion.

"I'll be fine. It's not like I haven't fallen asleep out here before," I assured her.

We had each dozed off more than once watching football, especially back in October when we'd been in-season and exhausted all the time.

"Well, if you need anything," she waved at her room, "just let me know."

"I will." I stood looking at her in the lamplit living room. Her hair hung loose about her shoulders, and she was dressed like me in boxers and a T-shirt. She looked beautiful. And nervous. But why?

"Thanks for letting me stay," I said.

Her eyes rested on mine. "Thanks for staying."

"De nada." I smiled and turned away. "Wake me up when you get up, okay?" We both had a ten o'clock class in the morning.

"I will."

She left the bathroom light on so that I could find my way if I needed to, her door partially open. I lay on the couch listening to her move around her room. Pretty soon she turned off the light and settled into bed. Duncan gave me a kiss and headed into the bedroom, where I heard the springs squeak as he jumped up on the bed. Jess's voice sounded through the wall soft and affectionate, and for just a minute, I envied Sidney and Claire's dog.

The grumbling of the old house kept me awake for a little while. Wood shifting, floorboards creaking, window panes rattling. And then those same noises grew familiar and lulled me, put me at ease. Until finally, there on the lumpy brown couch in Jess Maxwell's third-floor apartment, I slept.

CHAPTER FOURTEEN

Freshman year at SDU, I took a sociology class that required us to spend a day asking strangers their opinion on the meaning of life. "To be happy" was the most common answer I heard the afternoon I wandered La Jolla trying to get up my nerve to approach perfect strangers. When I would ask for an explanation of "happiness," most people's eyes glazed over and they would shrug, get defensive, walk away.

Only an older woman I met in a park feeding pigeons gave me more than a pat answer. I sat down beside her, told her I was a college student conducting sociological research, and popped the question: "What do you believe is the meaning of life?"

She looked over at me, brown eyes watery with age, and said, "That's easy: love. When we can love everyone and everything around us equally, then we've achieved a life of value."

"Everything?" I repeated, wondering if she was about to get all Christian on me as she scattered bread crumbs for the softly mewling birds.

She nodded. "Everyone needs to be loved."

As I rode my bike back to campus at the end of the experiment, I wondered if I would ever achieve such a state of unconditional love. It was hard to love strangers when so many claimed to hate me. Men in passing cars had yelled profanities at me more than once as I walked down a city sidewalk hand-in-hand with another woman. Male students from other schools routinely called me "dyke" from the soccer sidelines because they thought their yelled slurs would throw me off my game. Sophomore year a woman on another team had even called me a "fucking dyke" to my face when we were jostling for a ball deep in the corner of the field. I cleared the ball toward the half, then glared at her, momentarily speechless. After the game she'd tracked me down to apologize, but I'd ignored her and turned away. I wasn't sure how to handle these strangers who hated me because I wasn't like them. I certainly didn't think I would ever love any of them.

When you're gay, sometimes you wonder not only why you love a particular person, but why you love a person of a particular gender. Why her and not him? But it's not like it's a choice, no matter what Fox News and the Catholic Church—both such reliable sources of information about the modern world and human nature—say.

There's a Bonnie Raitt song I like, "You," that asks if it isn't love that we're sent here for. In "Mystery," the Indigo Girls wonder whether love is dictated or chosen. And in "Circle," Sarah McLachlan ponders the value of a love that keeps her hanging on despite the fact it isn't good for her. All good questions. Ones, in fact, that I found myself coming back to again and again in the weeks that followed Jess's Super Bowl party.

That semester, alone at night in my white-walled dorm room, I lay awake for hours, illicit candles flickering on the bedside table, red power light glowing on my stereo. I should have been studying but instead I was listening to sappy, romantic music and trying to figure out what to do about Jess. I knew I loved her. I knew it when I woke up on her couch in the middle of the night after the Super Bowl party and listened for her breathing on the other side of the wall. It was a truth I could no longer ignore.

Once I acknowledged that truth, though, I was in a quandary. What to do? Should I tell her and risk driving her away? Should I pretend nothing had changed, that I was still happy just being friends? Alone in my room on Valentine's Day, I wrote down a list of pros and cons for either action. For telling her, of course, there were more cons than pros. She might never talk to me again, which would ruin everything because I felt happiest when I was with her. Or thinking about her. Or talking about her. None of which I could do happily if she were no longer speaking to me. The pros side of the list was measly: Resolution. And who really wanted resolution if it turned out to be the opposite of what you wanted most in life?

The cons had it, I decided that night. I would say nothing and seek solace in the notion that the feeling of love alone was enough. Jess didn't have to return my sentiment or even know that I felt it. Love was good, wasn't it? And this love would remain pure.

I soon learned that I wasn't the only one suffering from unrequited love at SDU. A couple of weeks after Valentine's Day, Alicia Ramirez sat down next to me in Philosophy and Women. I'd noticed her before. I noticed all of the attractive women in my classes, more out of habit than anything else.

"Hi," Alicia said as she slid into the empty seat beside me.

Holly was skipping class that morning. I'd promised to take copious notes, as was our arrangement.

"Hi," I returned, waking up more fully as I noticed Alicia's smile, her long dark hair, her warm brown eyes. Superficially, she reminded me of Jess. But the fleeting impression passed as she regarded me with a forthright smile. Jess's smiles usually had a sideways quality, as if she'd rather not look at you straight on.

"You're on the soccer team, aren't you?" Alicia asked.

I refrained from glancing down at the "SDU Soccer" emblem on my T-shirt. "I am."

"I was just wondering, do you have a partner for the essay yet?"

Our professor had assigned a collaborative essay—very

Women's Studies of her, Holly and I had agreed—due just before spring break. The idea was that each pair of students would choose one of the philosophers we'd been studying to write a paper about. While one student researched the philosopher's life, the other would analyze the subject's body of work. Then together the students would take what they'd found and shape it into a cohesive essay. Or at least, that was the theory.

"I'm actually paired up already," I admitted.

Holly would kill me if I dumped her for a cute girl. Besides, while Alicia was indeed attractive, I wasn't looking. That was one of the cons of being in love with Jess—I couldn't seem to generate an interest in other women. Not for lack of trying, either.

"I thought you probably would be." Alicia paused as our professor strode into the classroom juggling a leather bag and travel mug. "Well, do you maybe want to go for coffee sometime?"

I looked down at her hand lying on top of her notebook. A silver ring with a women's symbol adorned one of her fingers.

"Um," I hedged.

"Don't worry," she said, "I'm not hitting on you."

And why exactly was that? But even going out for coffee with someone who announced up front they weren't interested in me was preferable to moping around by myself yet another night listening to songs about lost love.

"Coffee sounds like fun. I'm Cam," I added, extending my hand.

"Alicia," she said, her ring cool against my palm.

The very next night we walked off-campus to a coffee shop on Main for cappuccinos and dessert. It didn't take long for Alicia to get to the point: "Are you friends with Anna Sampson?"

Anna, the bold baby dyke backup goalkeeper? This was definitely a first. "Yeah, I know Anna. *She's* the reason you asked me to hang out?"

"Maybe," Alicia said, ducking her head over her mug.

"You know she's dating someone, don't you?"

"She is?" Her face fell almost comically.

"She's been seeing this girl on her floor for a couple of weeks now." Which was completely against my rules of same-sex dating, I only just refrained from pointing out.

"On her floor?" Alicia repeated. "But that's just stupid. What was she thinking?"

"I know, right?"

Alicia, I decided that night, was pretty cool in spite of her questionable taste in women. We lingered over coffee, procrastinating from the homework that beckoned us both, talking about race and gender and class, philosophy and education and sociology, her major. We described our families and our histories and what we hoped would be our futures, and I watched her smile and laugh at the things I said, noticed how easily she answered even when I asked her a personal question, and all at once I wished that I could put Jess out of my mind and fall instead for someone like Alicia. Someone who didn't flinch away whenever I got too close.

And yet…

And yet, I also found myself remembering the first time I'd gotten coffee with Jess in the fall. I found myself missing her as I sat with Alicia drinking coffee at the small ceramic table, chatting about our older siblings. And that night, back in my dorm room, I lay in bed alone thinking of Jess, who was probably at that moment on a bus home from a match up in Fresno. The next morning, Jess was still the first thing I thought of when I woke up, even before I tugged on the window shade to see what kind of day waited.

The worst thing was knowing I was hopelessly in love for the first time as a reasonably mature adult but unable to admit that love to anyone. Literally the love that dare not speak its name, damn it. And yet, it was also the best thing to wake in the morning thinking of her, to feel my heart literally, physically leap at the sight of her across the cafeteria or the tennis courts. The best thing of all to watch Sunday afternoon NBA double-headers with Jess and Holly at Jess's apartment, the three of us sprawled across the couch, our books stacked on the coffee table.

A few days after our coffee date, I ran into Alicia outside the cafeteria. No heart leap, but a pleasant surprise nonetheless.

"*Hola*," she said, smiling. "Want to grab lunch?"

"Sure," I said, surreptitiously checking the vicinity as I followed her inside. Jess usually ate lunch on campus on Fridays after her ten o'clock studio art class, and I was hoping to run into her. We had been playing phone tag all week, and the tennis team was due to leave that afternoon for a weekend tournament in San Francisco. They wouldn't be back on campus until Sunday night.

Alicia and I took our food out onto the patio. Almost March, the day was warm enough for shorts.

"What a perfect soccer day," Alicia said, sighing wistfully.

Was she thinking about Anna? "Do you play?"

"A little. My high school didn't have a girls' varsity team until I was a junior, though, and anyway, my parents didn't exactly encourage me to play sports. Not the thing in our culture."

Her parents had immigrated to the United States from Mexico in the seventies, Alicia had told me during our coffee date. They were progressive in a lot of ways, but old school in others. She wasn't out to them, wasn't sure if or when she would be. Definitely not until after college—she'd had friends whose parents had withdrawn financial support when they found out their kids were queer.

"That's too bad," I said. "But you're a fan of the beautiful game?"

"I love soccer. My brothers all grew up playing, and my entire family always gets together to watch the World Cup on the Mexican TV stations."

"No way! Mine, too."

"You get Mexican TV up in Oregon?"

"Dude, everyone gets Mexican TV."

"We are everywhere, kind of like the gays. Though admittedly less reproductively challenged."

I didn't think I knew her well enough yet to rip on the Catholic drive for procreation, considered among the Protestant Wallaces to be a blatant, cynical attempt to spread their religion.

We chatted some more about families and school and collaborative essays. Then she said, "So I have a question. Are you seeing anyone right now?"

I paused. Seeing someone in my head probably didn't count. "Nope. Totally single."

"Really? I heard you were dating some tennis chick."

"I wish." It just slipped out, and I stared at Alicia. "I mean, no, I'm not dating her."

"But you want to," she said, eyes narrowed.

"I didn't say that."

"No, you kind of did."

I sighed and tugged my baseball cap lower. "Don't tell anyone, okay? You and Holly are the only ones who know. I'd kind of like to keep it that way."

"You do have a reputation to protect," she said. "But I'd say we're even in the secret crush department. What's the deal? Do you have a crush on this girl, or are you, like, actually in love?"

Squinting across the lawn, I watched a couple of long-haired, shirtless guys tossing a Frisbee. "I've had crushes before, but this is different." I looked back at her. "Honestly, I think she's probably straight and I'm wasting my time waiting around for her to magically feel the same way."

Alicia nodded slowly. "I did that scene for a while. Gets pretty old."

"So I've noticed."

We both bit into our sandwiches and chewed in silence. Then she took a sip of juice and said, "You're cooler than I thought you would be. You seem like you have a clue, Cam."

"Thanks, I think. You're not so bad yourself."

"Now, if you could just convince Anna of that fact…" But she smiled like she knew her crush was doomed to remain forever unconsummated.

Later, as we carried our trays back inside, I looked around the cafeteria again. Still no Jess. Maybe I'd catch her at the gym.

Outside, Alicia and I stopped near the bike rack.

"Give me a call sometime," I said as I unlocked my bike, "and we'll hang out."

"Do you mean that? Or is it some insincere jock line?"

"No line." I paused. "Actually, a bunch of us are going to a party before the LGBA dance tomorrow night. Anna won't be around but some other fun people will. Think you could handle hanging with a bunch of jocks?" I held out my hand.

She took it and held onto it, smiling at me flirtatiously.

"Maybe for a little while." Her eyes focused over my shoulder for a moment, and her voice dropped. "Okay, are you sure you're not seeing anyone? Because there's this woman behind you—don't look, idiot—glaring at us. Anyway, call me about the dance, okay?"

I nodded, wondering who was watching us. Some random freshman with a crush? I'd gotten my fair share of crank calls as well as the inevitable anonymous Valentine in my campus mailbox.

"I'll call you tomorrow," I said, releasing her hand.

"*Hasta luego*, Cam." She waved and strode off, confident in her faded jeans and Doc Martens, her dark hair flowing from beneath a purple Lakers cap.

I glanced casually over my shoulder toward the entrance of the student center, but all I saw was a straight couple on the steps. No single women shooting daggers in my direction.

I didn't see Jess before she left for the weekend. I left a message on her machine but she never called back. By the time I made it down to the gym that afternoon, the bus had already left for San Fran. Disappointed, I jogged out to the track and warmed up. Jess was always going away and I was always missing her. Then again, I missed her even when we were together sometimes. I concentrated on running, feeling my muscles loosen and my mind clear as I pushed my body around the track. Sometimes I wondered what I would do without endorphins, to which I was most certainly, happily addicted.

On Saturday, without Jess and the tennis team around to distract me, I studied all day. I even kind of enjoyed it, especially the analysis of the feminist philosopher Holly and I had selected for our Philosophy and Women project—Angela Davis, author of *Women, Culture and Politics*. I know, a couple of privileged whitey-whites (as my Portland Parks friend John would call us) trying to engage with the writings of a black, Communist champion of the working class. But she was a ton more interesting than Catherine Mackinnon or Andrea Dworkin, I thought, and her work was infinitely more thought-provoking than my other classes. I still hadn't cracked my Macro textbook. Midterms were coming up, so I'd know soon enough if I would have to end my economics experiment to keep my soccer eligibility.

After a day of studying, Alicia came over and we headed out with Holly and Becca to an off-campus house for a party before the big LGBA dance. Alicia got along well with Holly and Becca, which was a relief. We'd talked about coming from middle class families and being surrounded by rich, mostly straight, L.A. college students—like my best friend and her girlfriend. For Alicia, being Hispanic and a woman and a lesbian, those three strikes often made her wish she would have picked a less white school, she'd said. And what school would that have been, I'd asked her. Fortunately, she'd laughed at the joke.

I warned her ahead of time that Holly and Becca were both from Orange County and semi-closeted to boot. But she said that if they were friends of mine then she would reserve judgment. Holly and Becca, meanwhile, weren't completely clueless. Though they had both grown up with Mexican housekeepers, they treated Alicia as they would any new person I introduced to our circle of friends.

Scary that I was even worried about it, but it was Southern California, after all. SoCal, where there were random car-checks, kind of like truck weigh stations where if the lights were blinking, you had to stop. Signs near those road stops that said "Caution" in English, with a picture of a man, woman and child with obviously Mexican features fleeing. Other signs with the same picture that bore the Spanish word "*Prohibido*." Immigration was a regional hot-button issue, and even supposedly liberal Californians sometimes espoused blatantly racist views, I had found.

At the party, several people did double-takes when Alicia and I walked in together. No doubt it would be around campus by the end of the weekend that she and I were a couple, I thought, rolling my eyes at Holly as people watched us walk by. We hung out with Jeni, Mel and Mel's roommates, a couple of field hockey players. One of the roommates liked Alicia, I noted right off the bat as we grabbed a couple of beers from the keg in the kitchen.

Jake, Brad and Cory, the football player, stopped to chat. Alicia and Cory seemed to know each other already, so while they talked, Jake and Brad worked on me.

"Who's the girl?" Jake asked.

"Subtle," I said. "She's just a friend. You know I'd tell you otherwise."

"So you say." Brad lifted an eyebrow. "You never told us about Jess Maxwell. We had to hear about her through the grapevine."

"I definitely would have told you if anything was up there. Anyway, I've taken a vow of chastity this year."

"Like one of those lesbian nuns," Jake said. "Only we all know you're not in it for religious reasons."

Cory moved closer. "What are you guys talking about? Or should I ask?"

Jake smiled at him from under his eyelashes. "Just hassling Cam."

"Not that I can't take it," I said, and punched him in the bicep. He was looking good in tight jeans and a leather vest. Being in love with the star quarterback suited him.

"Brute. Let's get out of here before she hurts me. You going to the dance later?" he added, glancing back at me.

"Wouldn't miss it. We'll see you there."

They wandered away, and back came the field hockey roommate. The three of us hung out for a little while. Definite flirting going on there—Alicia appeared to have clued in to the other woman's attraction and was casually encouraging it. Nothing major though, her look told me. Mel's roommate would strike out tonight. I tried not to feel self-righteous, but it was good to know I wouldn't be the only one going home alone.

Once we were suitably tipsy, Holly, Becca, Alicia and I headed out to the LGBA dance at the student center. There, in a darkened ballroom with music pulsing from giant speakers, I managed to forget about Jess, at least for a little while. Mostly the music was fast, and I danced in a group with Holly, Becca, Alicia and some of Alicia's friends. A couple were exes, she told me as we danced. Her friends eyed me curiously. Judging from the looks being cast our way, they didn't realize Alicia and I were both harboring feelings for other people.

As we danced to the fast songs under the twirling lights, surrounded by beautiful young queer people, I scoped openly, happy to be in a safe, all-gay environment. Being out in the straight world could be frightening at times. It was nice to be able to let down my defenses for an evening.

The slow songs, though—I couldn't pretend to myself then that I didn't miss Jess. The DJ played the usual crooner classics, Madonna and Sinead and Prince. I sat the first few out while Alicia danced with a group of her friends, laughing and touching each other flirtatiously. When one last slow song came on as the dance was winding down, "Damn Wish I was Your Lover," she drifted over and caught my hand.

"Want to?" she asked, her palm soft against mine.

"Um." What could it hurt? "Sure."

At first we moved awkwardly together. Then we laughed, relaxed, and our bodies flowed more smoothly, breasts lightly touching, my hand on her hip, hers on mine as we moved slowly around the room in time to the music. Our cheeks brushed, and I could smell her perfume. I closed my eyes, letting my cheek rest against her sleek hair. But she didn't smell delicate or floral. I opened my eyes and pulled away a little. She wasn't Jess.

She smiled a little sheepishly and I knew she'd been doing the same pretending. Still, it felt nice to be close to someone I was starting to think of as a friend, and I moved in again, shutting my eyes and enjoying the moment. If I couldn't be with Jess, at least I could be out among people who knew and accepted me for me.

Later, as we walked back across campus, Alicia slipped her arm through mine. Holly and Becca walked just ahead of us, careful not to touch as we passed frat houses blasting rock music and overflowing with Greek boys and girls.

"I wish we'd met each other first," Alicia said.

"I know. Me, too."

"Why are the people who don't want us so much more attractive than the people who could?"

"Human nature?" I suggested. "Or maybe it's internalized homophobia. You know, we don't really think we're worth real love so we fall for unattainable women." As she looked at me sideways, one eyebrow raised skeptically, I added, "Or maybe it's just bad timing."

"Think I'll go with bad timing," she said as we reached her dorm. She leaned in and kissed my cheek, her lips brushing my skin tantalizingly. "Thanks for a fun night, Cam. Give me a call, okay?"

"You got it," I said, and turned away.

As Alicia entered her building, I jogged after Holly and Becca. Holly glanced at me, eyebrows raised as I fell into step beside them.

"You're sticking to this celibacy thing better than I expected," she said.

"Too bad no one else believes it," I said, shoving my hands in my jeans pockets. "By this time tomorrow it'll be around campus that Alicia and I are sleeping together."

"But you know you're not," Holly said, sliding an arm across my shoulder, "and that's what counts."

They walked me home, holding hands once the houses on Fraternity Row were safely out of sight.

"I'll call you tomorrow," Holly promised with a look that meant we'd talk more when Becca wasn't around. I'd made her swear not to tell anyone I was in love with Jess, not even Becca. As far as I knew, she'd kept her word.

"Cool." I waved at them and tried not to feel envious as they strolled away, an established couple by now, well past the honeymoon and into that comfortably symbiotic stage where you shared clothes and everyone around you began confusing your names even when you looked nothing alike.

In my room, I lay in bed in the dark, thinking about the evening. Dancing with Alicia had reminded me how much I enjoyed being close to another woman. I wanted to have that closeness again. I wanted to have sex, damn it. After dating fairly consistently the past few years, it still felt strange not to have someone to spend the night with. But then I thought of Jess sharing a hotel room with one of her teammates, and suddenly I was glad I was alone in my bed. Hooking up with someone else now would only complicate matters. Still, resolution was looming increasingly importantly in my world view, threatening to overtake the cons list I'd drawn up on Valentine's Day. Sometime soon, I told myself, I would have to move on from this ridiculous state of limbo. One way or the other.

CHAPTER FIFTEEN

On Sunday night after dinner I met Holly at the library, supposedly to work on our paper. As usual, though, we ended up chatting and generally annoying the people around us. Particularly one woman with thick glasses and a broad center part—Holly called it the butthead look—who kept leaning around the edge of her carrel to glare at us and whisper, "*Shhhhh*," which only succeeded in bringing us to near hysterical laughter. We could be such dumb jocks without even trying.

Eventually we left the library to wander campus aimlessly. We ended up on the steps to the new science center, a multi-million dollar project with a sophisticated astronomy deck built into the roof. Holly pulled out a pack of cigarettes and we shared a couple. We had convinced ourselves that if we only smoked a couple of cigarettes at a time, and only occasionally, our health wouldn't be harmed.

She listened to me trying to figure out my love life as the stars flickered and grew brighter in the evening sky. When I grew tired of rehashing significant moments with Jess, Holly blew a cloud of smoke into the air and said, "I think you should just tell her. That way, if it works out, then great. But if not, you can just get the hell on with your life."

I frowned a little, looking up at the wide night sky. She had a point. If Jess wasn't interested, shouldn't I know now and get over her? I just wasn't sure I could. This was something I didn't want to let go of. Then again, a one-sided relationship could never be healthy, no matter how much one person loved the other.

"Maybe you're right," I admitted.

Holly lifted her head. "Seriously?"

"Well, yeah. Makes sense."

"I haven't said that before because I didn't want to seem like a flake."

"Yeah, but I already know you're a flake."

"Hey!" She crushed her cigarette out and shoved me onto the lush grass beneath the steps. "You'll pay for that, Wallace!"

"You wish!"

We rolled around on the lawn, tickling and tackling each other, ignoring the bemused looks of passersby. Eventually she pushed away from me and we lay on our backs, gazing up at the night sky.

"You know," she said, "Becca thinks we wrestle all the time because secretly we want to sleep together."

I was silent for a moment. Then I looked at Holly and she looked at me and we both busted out laughing.

"No offense," I said when I caught my breath. "But—yuck!"

"I agree," she said, still snickering. "You're totally not my type, dude."

"Yeah, well, you're too butch for me." I ducked the inevitable punch my crassness elicited.

We watched the moon rise, lying together on the lawn in companionable silence. Then we headed back to our dorms.

"Are you really going to tell her?" Holly asked just before we parted ways.

I nodded. "I think so. I can't hold out like this anymore. I'm too young not to have a girlfriend."

"And too cute," Holly added. "I'm telling you, you've got to take advantage of this little boy look while you can. Eventually you're going to get old and fat like everyone else." She ruffled my hair.

I swatted her hand. "Zip it."

"You doing the deed tonight?"

My smile faded. "Nah. Tennis isn't supposed to get home until late, and I want to tell her in person. Why don't you cancel Thursday so it's just her and me?"

Holly, Jess and I had gotten into the habit of eating dinner and watching the NBA on Thursday nights at Jess's. Sometimes Becca even came along, and on those nights it felt like such a comfortable, fun double date that I almost couldn't stand it.

"Will do." Holly held out her hand.

I slapped it. "Thanks, man."

"What have you got to lose, right?"

Everything, I thought. But I didn't say it. Holly would only accuse me—rightly—of melodrama.

At my dorm, I succumbed to a fit of laziness and rode the elevator to my floor. I was almost to my room when I saw Taylor Lewis from the tennis team leaning in the doorway of one of my neighbors, Grace Chang. Taylor noticed me and turned with a smile.

"Hey, Cam. What's up?"

"Not much." I stopped in the hallway, glancing into the room to wave at Grace lying on her bed in sweats, a thick book open before her. "Hi Grace."

"Cam." She returned the wave.

I liked Grace. She played volleyball and, like me, sometimes trained with the track team. She was a senior, though, so she was taking it easy her last semester. No sports commitments.

"How'd you guys do this weekend?" I asked Taylor, hoping I didn't sound too eager.

"Great." Her eyes lit up. She was dressed still in her SDU

Tennis sweats, sneakers and a baseball cap. They must have just gotten back from San Francisco. "I was telling Grace we won the tournament. We're number one in Big Eights and number five nationally."

"That's awesome. Did Jess win?" I asked, trying to keep my voice casual. Out of the corner of my eye I could see Grace watching the exchange.

"Actually, she had a rough day yesterday and dropped a couple of sets. But today she kicked major butt. She's still number one in Division II. Can you believe it?"

I shook my head. "Amazing."

A few minutes later Taylor left and I lingered, chatting with Grace. She was studying for her organic chemistry midterm later in the week. I told her I'd heard track had come in third at SDC the day before. She said she thought they would have been better this year. Then she sat up a little, pushing her shoulder-length black hair behind an ear.

"I don't mean to pry," she said, "but I was wondering. What's this I've been hearing about you and Jess Maxwell?"

I glanced down the hall. Empty. "It's nothing," I said. "You know how gossip is."

Grace was straight and had been with the same guy for two years. She and I usually stayed away from the subject of romantic relationships. Or at least the subject of who I was dating.

She nodded. "It's not really any of my business. I was just going to tell you to be careful with her. She's not as tough as everyone thinks."

Frowning, I moved a step further into the room. "What do you mean?"

"Well…" She hesitated. "Shut the door, will you?" When I'd complied, she added, "I don't want this getting around. You're obviously close with her so I trust you won't repeat this. Agreed?"

"Sure, agreed." Now I was curious. I sat down on the chair at her desk and waited.

"Do you remember that storm we had last year in January?"

I nodded. Thunderstorms were rare in the San Diego area,

and often led to flooding and mudslides. "I was at home but I saw it on the news."

"I was here and it was pretty bad. The power went out in the gym. I was in the locker room at the time, and so was Jess. She looked pretty nervous even though she said she wasn't. But when the lights went out, she went totally quiet. Then I could hear her breathing and it sounded almost like she was hyperventilating. In the flashes of lightning I could see her face. She was crying. She was just sitting there on a bench, shaking. So I went over and sat with her. She kept repeating something about the rain and the lightning and the ocean. It didn't make any sense to me.

"After the wind died down, the lights came back on. Jess seemed dazed at first, like she didn't know where she was. Then she apologized for scaring me. She asked me not to tell anyone. I said I wouldn't and asked if she wanted to talk about anything, but she just pulled away and shut off again. Ever since then she's always acted like it never happened. Sometimes I think she doesn't remember."

None of what Grace said really surprised me. I'd known there was more to Jess than what she showed. But it still shook me, knowing that there was this pain so deep inside her that no one could touch it. Not even me.

"Something must have happened to her," I said. "I always thought there had to be something."

Grace nodded. "The storm seemed to trigger her reaction. Maybe I should have told her coach but she seemed fine after that, like it was an anomaly. I told myself she was probably just afraid of the storm. But there's something more, isn't there?"

I nodded. "I think so. I'm just not sure what."

Back in my room a little while later, I checked voice mail. A couple of new messages, one from Alicia and one from Mel. Nothing from Jess. I glanced at the clock. Almost eleven. Maybe she was still getting settled in at home.

I called Mel and shot the shit with her, ever alert for the call waiting beep. Then I tried to study. I had a ten-page teaching methods paper due on Thursday in lieu of a midterm, among other things. Personally I preferred exams, with quantifiable data you could understand and memorize. Papers were too subjective.

Jess never did call. By eleven thirty I'd picked up the phone several times to dial her number, but each time I realized she might be wiped out from the trip and in bed already. It would have to wait until tomorrow, I finally decided. I wasn't tired though, so instead of calling Jess, I dialed a different number. Alicia picked up on the first ring.

"Told you I'd call," I said, reclining on my bed. I could hear music playing in the background at her end. "It's Cam, by the way."

"I know. What are you doing?"

"Trying to work on that collaboration paper. Unsuccessfully, I might add."

"Me too," she said. "It's putting me to sleep."

We talked for a while about our classes and midterms. Friday was the last day of classes before spring break. Then, a glorious week of freedom. Alicia was off to Mexico to visit her maternal grandmother; the tennis team was leaving for Tucson Friday afternoon for eight days; Becca was going to Aruba with her father and his third wife; and I was going home with Holly to L.A., from whence we planned to launch day and overnight trips to Las Vegas and San Francisco and anywhere else I could almost afford to go.

Finally Alicia ended our innocuous chatter with a not-so-subtle hint. "You know, Cam, the better I get to know you the less you seem like a chicken. Why don't you just tell the girl already?"

I opened my eyes and looked up at the familiar brush strokes in the ceiling paint. I had spent so many hours on the phone staring up at this ceiling and talking to Holly and Jess and Mel. And now Alicia.

"You're one to talk."

"Totally different situation. Anna doesn't even know I exist, but you and Jess, you're already friends."

She was right and we both knew it.

"Holly thinks I should tell her too," I admitted. "You know, either get together with her or get on with my life."

"Sounds like good advice, my friend."

We hung up a little while later. The universe was starting

to align, I thought. Clearly it was time for me to overcome my fears and leap.

Unfortunately, Jess seemed unaware of the motion of the universe. I got a message from her on Monday when she knew I'd be in class, telling me that they'd won and that she was really busy with midterms and Thursday night wasn't going to work for her. Holly told me later that she'd received basically the same message. So much for my Thursday night confession plan.

I called Jess back and left a message, but Tuesday came and went without a peep from her. I was starting to think something was wrong. Before the tournament in San Francisco, we'd talked on the phone every night even on days we found time to see each other. Now, suddenly, it had been five days since I'd seen or talked to her. Maybe she really was just busy with tennis and midterms, I told myself. I was somewhat occupied as well.

Midterms meant cramming and staying late in the computer lab and trying not to fall asleep in the library. Drinking coffee and smoking more than I should. Working with Holly on our paper. Studying. I didn't have enough time to do well in my classes and worry about Jess, so I pushed her odd silence out of my mind and concentrated on transition sentences and the laws of supply and demand and the presence of U.S. troops in Italy a full year before D-Day. I tried to call Jess a couple more times, but her machine always picked up. She never called me back, either.

On Friday morning I had my Macro exam, which I thought went okay, considering. Afterward, I looked for Jess at the cafeteria to no avail. It was increasingly clear that she intended to leave for spring break without talking to me. The question was, why? Had Alicia let my secret slip to someone else? Had Jess discovered my true feelings for her and was now avoiding me?

Tennis was leaving for Tucson at three, Taylor had informed me when I ran into her that morning. At two forty I stationed myself in the main lounge of the gym, stretching in my running gear. The team would have to pass through here before they boarded the bus.

At a quarter to three, Jess entered the lounge. She stopped when she saw me. "Cam," she said, scanning the area. But we were the only ones there.

I tried not to notice how good she looked in her navy SDU sweats. Her hair was pulled back in its usual ponytail, a few wisps curling about her face. I hadn't seen her in a week, and I'd sort of been hoping my crush would have waned with the lack of contact.

"What're you doing here?" I asked, pretending I hadn't in fact set a trap for her.

"We're leaving for Arizona in a few minutes." She was still standing where she'd stopped, about ten feet away. "What are you doing?"

"Just working out before Holly and I take off." A blatant lie, but she didn't have to know that.

"That's right, you guys are going to L.A." She paused. "Anyone else going with you?"

Frowning, I looked up at her. "No, it's just the two of us. You knew that."

She shrugged, glancing over her shoulder as a couple of tennis players walked through the lounge. They said hi, she said hi, and then she looked back at me, her eyes unreadable. "I gotta go. Have a good break, Cam." And she turned away.

I jumped up. "Jess, wait."

She stopped and watched me cross the distance separating us, the darkness of her eyes revealing her mood.

"What's going on?" I asked. "Last week everything seemed fine and then you go to San Francisco and now it's like we're not even speaking."

More tennis players passed by, watching us curiously.

"Nothing's going on," Jess said, fiddling with the shoulder strap on her duffel. "I just had midterms."

"Usually we study together," I pointed out. "Come on, you're clearly avoiding me. This is weird even for you," I added, trying to tease her a little, get her to loosen up.

She stared at me, her eyes even darker. "I have to go."

I caught her arm as she started to turn away again. "Wait. Please."

But she jerked her arm out of my grasp. "Don't touch me," she said, her voice low. "I don't have anything to say to you."

Her bitter tone caught me off-guard. "What are you talking about? What happened?"

"Nothing happened." She lifted her chin. "I just don't think we should hang out anymore, that's all."

She didn't think... I took a step back. "Oh." I blinked rapidly. My heart felt like it was being pulverized. My stomach too. Suddenly I wished I hadn't eaten that huge burrito at lunch.

"Cam." Her voice softened and she reached out for a moment as if she might touch me. But then more voices, more of her teammates. Her hand dropped. "Look, we'll talk when I get back, okay?"

"Whatever." I turned away. I could feel my throat closing, tears beginning to prick my eyes. I wasn't going to cry in front of her, damn it.

"Cam," she said again.

But I didn't answer. I hurried out of the lounge, leaving her standing there. I wasn't going to be her punching bag, I told myself, trying to swallow my tears. One of these days she was going to have to deal with her shit. She couldn't pull this on-again, off-again bullshit and expect people to stick around.

I headed outside for an impromptu run, passing the team bus idling in the gym parking lot. I didn't care, I told myself, feet pounding against pavement as I tried to outrun the memory of what Jess had said. Anger and hurt carried me up Prospect Street in the middle of the day, along the beach, back through town in a wide loop. When I got back to the gym the bus was gone. I wouldn't see Jess for at least a week.

I headed home on my bike, trying not to think about her. Holly and I were going to have a good time on break, and Jess could jump in a lake for all I cared.

In my dorm I showered and threw some clothes, toiletries and CDs into an overnight bag. The phone rang just as I finished packing my book bag.

"You ready to go sit on the freeway for the next few hours?" Holly asked.

"Totally. I'll meet you outside."

"This is going to be so much fun!"

"I know." I smiled, starting to feel a little better. I didn't need Jess. "Bring your camera, okay?"

"Already packed. See you in a few."

I zipped a pair of running shoes into a side pocket on my duffel, Doc Martens into the other. As I turned away from the dresser, I caught a glimpse of the picture I'd placed next to the Wallace family photo, and I paused. It was from the soccer-tennis party at Mel's, a shot of me, Holly, Jess, and Mel raising our beers to the camera. Jeni had given me a copy of the photo right before winter break.

"One of these girls is not like the others," I murmured.

I slung my bags over my shoulder and headed out, turning off the light and locking the door behind me.

CHAPTER SIXTEEN

Spring break, Huntington Beach. In Holly's Spanish villa home, I tried to forget about Jess and the more confusing aspects of my college life. On the drive up, I'd told Holly what had happened at the gym, insisting that I was never going to speak to Jess again. It was over, I said. Totally over. Holly had just nodded sympathetically and let me rant as I vowed to use spring break to get over Jess Maxwell. Holly's family home would provide a respite from real life and engender an extended decompression session, aided by sunshine and, of course, the backyard pool and hot tub.

Each night that week we stayed up late watching Letterman. Every morning we got up around ten and hit the beach, where we roller-bladed for miles along the paved beachfront, almost biting it in the sand a dozen times a day. We got sunburned but not unpleasantly so, hanging out in her backyard going from the hot tub to the swimming pool and back again. Despite my upbringing in rainy Oregon, fifteen years of soccer and two summers working outdoors had trained my Scotch-Irish skin not to burn badly, while Holly was one of those L.A. blondes who had been tan since toddlerhood. We ignored her mother's warnings of skin cancer and only applied sunscreen when absolutely necessary. At twenty, we figured we had a few years left of deep-frying our skin in the ocean sun without worrying about melanoma.

Midweek, we ventured to Vegas. Holly lost all of her money and then some on blackjack the first hour we were there. Meanwhile I won forty bucks on a slot machine and refused to spend another penny. Holly called me cheap but I didn't care. My portion of the road trip was covered. I even came out ahead. We wandered the glitzy city, hanging out in fancy hotels in our shorts and tank tops and, once the sun had set, our SDU Soccer sweatshirts. After a scrumptious seafood dinner and a final fruitless assault on the slots, we drove off across the desert back to L.A. as night fell. The Vegas lights lit up the sky behind us for the first hundred miles. Holly said she'd read that astronauts could see two human-made objects from space: the Great Wall of China and the Vegas Strip.

We'd planned another road trip to San Fran, but we never made it up to the city by the bay. Too much effort would be required to drive that far, we agreed Friday afternoon as we drank virgin daiquiris by the pool.

By the time Sunday rolled around, I was feeling nicely decompressed. In fact, I hadn't missed Jess at all, I announced as Holly and I drove back to school in my Tercel.

"Really?"

I could tell from her tone she didn't believe me. "Really."

"Huh. What's your plan, then?"

I had actually spent some time the previous day by the pool considering this very question: *What next?*

"I'm fine talking to her," I said, "but only if she makes the first move."

"Wow," Holly said, shades masking her blue eyes. "You were

so pissed last week I didn't know if you would ever talk to her again."

"Neither did I," I admitted, checking over my shoulder before switching lanes to pass a slow-moving Beamer. At mid-afternoon on a Sunday, all four lanes of the 405 were full. Typical. "I guess I just needed a little distance. Now I think maybe I got too close, from her perspective. She has such a hard time letting anyone in. I should at least give her a chance to explain."

"You don't seem pissed anymore," Holly said, looking over at me.

"I don't think I am."

Toward the end of the week, whenever I'd thought of Jess I'd pictured her in the locker room as Grace had described, shaking and crying as the storm raged outside. The image still made my heart hurt. Jess wasn't like other people. She hadn't meant to lash out at me, I was certain. In a way, I wished I hadn't sprinted out of the lounge like that. She'd seemed almost like she wanted to take back what she'd said, but I hadn't given her the chance. Instead I'd turned away, deserted her. Although admittedly, she'd deserved it.

"You never seem to stay mad for long," Holly said.

"Unlike some people." I smirked a little. "Remember freshman year when Coach made that comment about placing your shots? You didn't forgive him until like halfway through sophomore year."

She nodded. "I would hope I've matured somewhat since then. After all, in a matter of weeks we'll officially be seniors."

"Don't remind me."

Only a month and a half of school remained. Then finals and graduation and back to Portland for the summer. Back to Oregon for the last time, I promised myself.

We drove onto campus just before dinner.

"Can you feel it?" Holly asked as I parked the car in the half-full student lot near our dorms. "That back-to-school tension already seeping in?"

"Unfortunately, yes." We grabbed our bags from the backseat and headed toward the dorm. "When does Becca get back?"

"After dinner. What about tennis?"

"They were supposed to get back last night. You know what? I think I'll get cleaned up and go over there right now. To Jess's, I mean. That way she can't avoid me."

"I thought you were going to let her make the first move," she reminded me as we neared my dorm.

"Guess I've been around you too much this week," I said. "I'm feeling distinctly impatient all of a sudden."

"About freaking time." She enveloped me in a quick hug, her bags threatening to knock me over. "I'll be around later. Or at Becca's. Give me a call if you want to talk."

"Will do. Thanks for the awesome week, dude."

"Quality time well spent." She started to walk away, then added over her shoulder with a final grin, "I think my mom got quite an education too."

One afternoon in L.A. while watching a spring break show on MTV, we hadn't realized until way too late that Mrs. Bishop was standing in the doorway of the den. She'd overheard a conversation full of choice phrases like, "total hottie" and "nice ass" and "I'd do her." Holly and I had both looked up in time to see her mother disappearing down the hallway. When we joined her later for dinner, Mrs. Bishop acted like nothing had happened, though her initial smile looked a tad forced. Holly was sure her mother had heard those sorts of things before from her children. But in the past, it had probably been Holly's hyper-straight brother and his fraternity brothers doing the verbal babe ogling.

When I opened my dorm room door, the first thing I noticed was the message light blinking on my phone. I dropped my bag, shut the door, and launched myself across the bed. It was great to be back in my own room after a week in one of the Bishops' guest rooms with a Laura Ashley bedspread, matching wallpaper and lacy curtains. Flowers just weren't me. The room smelled a little stuffy, so I opened the window next to my bed as I dialed voice mail. Three new messages. The first one was from an on-campus extension I didn't recognize, dated the Friday before break at 2:58 p.m. I frowned. I should have gotten it before I left. Campus voice mail must have been overloaded.

Jess. I closed my eyes and listened, trying to feel nothing at all at the sound of her voice. "Hi, Cam. You just took off from the lounge. I don't know. I just wanted to say I'm sorry. I think we need to talk. I know I blew you off all week when I should have just asked you... Anyway, call me when you get back, okay? I didn't mean what I said about not wanting to hang out. Just—give me a call."

The message ended. "Shit," I said out loud. I knew I shouldn't have run off the way I had. Could have cleared the whole thing up before break. At least she wanted to see me. At least she hadn't meant what she'd said. Relief flooded me even as I realized that sometime soon, probably in the next few hours even, I was going to tell Jess Maxwell I loved her, for better or worse. God, I hoped it wouldn't be worse.

The second message was from Mel, dated yesterday afternoon. "Came back a day early. Just called to say hi. Give me a call when you and Holly get back."

The third message was from Jess again, dated earlier today. She sounded infinitely more upbeat. "Hey, Cam. Tennis was great. Arizona was beautiful. I even sent you a postcard, but you probably won't get it because we all mailed our postcards on Friday. Anyway, give me a call when you get in and we'll talk, okay? I should be around. I—um, see you."

Now that I had heard her voice and knew she wanted to talk too, I felt a little calmer. Our friendship apparently wasn't over, after all. Of course, she hadn't heard what I had to say yet.

I took a quick shower and changed into shorts and a clean T-shirt, all fresh smelling from the Bishops' fabric softener. Holly and I had done our laundry this morning before we left, taking advantage of the free washer and dryer. I pulled on my Sambas and headed out. I wasn't even going to call ahead.

On Jess's quiet tree-lined street, I parked my car behind her Cabriolet. As I locked the door and walked up the long driveway, I tried not to feel nervous. I was going to tell her how I felt, that was all. I was going to hear what she had to say and then I was going to tell her. Period.

I rang her doorbell but got no answer. After a few minutes of indecision, I went around to the front of the house and rang that bell.

Sidney appeared at the door, smiling when she saw me.

"Hello, Cam. Haven't seen you in a while. Come on in."

She held the door open and I stepped past her. Their living room, to the left of the entryway, was decorated in dark reds and blues with hardwood floors and warm cream walls. It reminded me of an upscale version of Jess's apartment.

"Thanks," I said. "I was just wondering if you knew where Jess was. Her car's here but she's not answering."

"She borrowed Duncan for a walk. Said she was stiff from the bus ride home. She should be back anytime."

This explained why Duncan wasn't snuffling eagerly around my legs and crotch. "Okay. Thanks."

"Who is it, Sid?" Claire called from the kitchen.

"It's Cam," Sidney bellowed back. "Why don't you come in?" she added to me. "I'm sure Claire has some fresh lemonade in the fridge. It's her favorite spring treat."

"Bring her on back," Claire called out just then. "We can have a glass of lemonade."

"Okay, darling," Sidney hollered back. She waved me through the living room. "Why didn't I think of that?"

In the kitchen at the back of the house, Claire was chopping piles of vegetables for dinner. She took a break and we sat at the finished oak table that occupied the back portion of the kitchen, sharing a pitcher of lemonade. Sidney and Claire seemed like opposites, Sidney so gruff on the outside and Claire so talented but slightly clueless when it came to people instead of pianos. We talked about spring break and SDU and their alma mater, Smith, a women's college in Massachusetts where they had met thirty years earlier. When I said I couldn't believe they'd been out of college that long, Claire called me a wonderful liar.

Ten minutes after I arrived, the front door slammed and we heard the sound of Duncan's toenails on the floor as he trotted through the living room. I felt my shoulders tense as Jess appeared in the doorway.

"Hey you guys," she started. Then she saw me and stopped, biting her lip. "Cam."

I stood up. Duncan was at my side in an instant, and I rubbed his back obligingly. "Thanks for the lemonade," I said, nodding at Sidney and Claire.

Sidney looked from me to Jess. "Just leave your glass," she said. "We'll see you kids later." Claire started to say something, but Sidney quieted her with a glance.

I brushed past Jess, heading for the front door. After a second, she followed.

"Do you want to come up?" she asked once we were outside.

The late afternoon sun angled through the trees, dappling the street and the front lawn, while the house cast its enormous shadow over us. This really was it. By the end of the day, Jess might well decide she didn't want to be my friend, after all.

"If you want me to."

She shot me a quick look but didn't say anything as we made our way up to her apartment. I watched her walk up the stairs ahead of me, leg muscles rippling beneath her shorts. Why did she have to be so damned hot, I thought, scowling. Her tan was darker after a week in the sun, while my face was now overrun with freckles. Holly had thought it hysterical that people in L.A. saw me in my baseball cap and baggy shorts and mistook me for the younger brother she didn't have.

Jess waved me into her apartment and locked the door behind us. We stood in the hallway between the closet and her Sabatini poster, watching each other. Sunlight from the kitchen window lit the apartment. Jess looked so good to me in her shorts and white T-shirt, her shoulders straight, eyes questioning, and I realized it had been more than two weeks since I'd last seen her.

In the kitchen, I pulled out a chair and dropped onto it as she kicked off her sandals and padded barefoot to the fridge.

"Want a soda? Or a beer?" she asked, hand on the door.

I shook my head, slouching down in the chair. "Nah, I'm okay."

I still loved her, more than ever somehow. The realization elated and depressed me at the same time. There were those extremes again, the same old roller coaster. But did I want to take the ride? Did I have a choice?

She leaned against the unopened refrigerator door, facing me. "So."

"So." Deliberately I tipped my chair back. It always bugged

her when I did that. Whether she was concerned for my safety or the longevity of the chair she never said.

Her eyes flickered, and she crossed her arms across her chest. "I think we should talk."

My pulse quickened, and I let the chair dip to the floor. "I think you're right."

Sunlight wavered in the apartment as trade winds brushed through the branches of the trees in the backyard. I knew this room so well, the color of the walls, the framed Picasso poster over the table, the shape of the light fixture overhead. I knew Jess too, the twist of her ponytail at the back of her head, the line of muscle in her arms and legs. But only these physical impressions, I reminded myself. Only outwardly.

"Did you get my message when I called from the gym?" she asked.

"Not until today. Phone mail must have been down again."

Nodding, she glanced out the partially open window into the backyard. Birds were singing as the sun slowly angled toward the horizon. It was only five thirty. We would have another couple hours of daylight yet.

"I guess I owe you an explanation," she said finally, expelling a short breath. "The thing is, you were right. Something was going on." She hesitated. "You know that tournament a couple of weeks ago? The one in San Francisco?"

I nodded.

"You called me the day I left but I didn't pick up," she said. "I was here, but I didn't want to talk to you because—well, I thought you were dating that girl, Alicia, and you hadn't told me." Her eyes were slightly defiant as she regarded me.

"Alicia? How did you know—" I stopped, realizing how that sounded. "Where did you hear that?"

She didn't answer for a moment. Then she said, "Julie saw you at the coffee shop on Main with her and I saw you outside the cafeteria together. Then when I got home from San Francisco, I ran into Cory Miller at the gym and he said you took her to the dance."

Everything clicked into place—Jess must have been the woman Alicia had seen at the cafeteria shooting daggers at us.

But why would she be upset at seeing us together? I didn't think she was the possessive friend type. I felt a glimmer of hope.

"You thought I was dating this woman and that's why you were avoiding me?" I clarified. She nodded. "Why didn't you just ask me?"

She shrugged and focused on the poster of the Picasso dove, red and orange flowers trailing through its feathers. "I'm asking now. Are you, Cam? Going out with her?"

"No, I'm not. She has a crush on someone else on the soccer team. I went to the dance with her, Holly and Becca. It wasn't a date."

Jess was watching me now, eyes shadowed. "Cory saw you, though. He said you were dancing together, like, together."

"We were. I had a good time. But why do you care?" I knew I was pushing, but I wanted to hear her say it. I was tired of feeling like the lecherous lesbian looking for a convert. "It's not like you and I are anything more than friends. Right?"

As my words hung in the air, she blinked and looked out across the backyard again. "Right," she said. "You don't owe me anything. You can date whoever you want."

Abruptly she pushed away from the fridge and headed down the hallway, stepping into her sandals on the way. She was reaching for her keys when I caught her.

I moved between her and the door. "Where are you going?"

She stared at the floor. "I don't know."

"Jess." My hands on her shoulders, I pressed down until she looked up at me. I could see tears in her eyes threatening to spill over, and felt my own throat tighten. "Don't run away," I said, my voice as gentle as I could make it. "You don't have to leave."

Shrugging my hands off, she took a step back. "Stop it, Cam."

"Stop what?" I took a step toward her, slid my arms around her waist, felt her shiver against me. God, I'd wanted to do this for so long. "Don't you know how I feel about you?"

"No." Suddenly she pushed me away, shoving me hard against the door. "I don't want this."

The doorknob had nearly impaled me, but I ignored the

pain. "You don't want me to love you? Well, too bad, because I already do."

I stared at her, hardly able to believe I'd finally told her. Now what?

The object of my affection seemed less than overjoyed by my pronouncement. A tear spilled over and trickled down her cheek. She swiped at it and gazed down at her feet again.

"No, you don't," she said bleakly. "You don't even know me."

I'd been prepared for her to cringe away in disgust, to pat my arm patronizingly, even to—yeah, right—leap toward me in joy. But I wasn't prepared for her to tell me that I didn't know her.

I touched her arm, more hesitant this time. "What do you mean?"

She walked away without answering. After a moment, I followed her back down the hall and into the living room, increasingly confused as she sat down on the couch and curled her feet under her body, wrapped her arms around herself, rested her chin on her arms. Unsure what else to do, I dropped down on the opposite end of the couch and waited.

She gazed at me, her eyes dark and sad. "You're not going to let this go, are you?"

"Of course not. You can't convince me I don't love you."

Despite my bravado, though, every time I said it out loud and she didn't respond, I felt a little less sure of myself. My family is hardly demonstrative. We rarely hug, let alone freely verbalize our deepest feelings.

Sighing, she plucked at a couch cushion. "Fine. Then I'm going to tell you something, and it might change your mind."

As if that would happen. Unless... she hadn't killed anyone, had she? Tortured any innocent animals? Of course she hadn't. I knew her well enough to be sure of that much.

"When I was a senior in high school," she said slowly, brow furrowed, "I was—well, I was raped. I told my mom but she accused me of lying. That's why I don't have a relationship with her." She stared down at the cushion, avoiding my eyes.

Raped? "Oh my God. I'm so sorry, Jess. I had no idea."

I reached for her hand, crushing her fingers between mine

as a rush of feelings swirled through my mind. Shock that someone could have hurt her, rage at the faceless man, anger with her mother. How could a parent do such a thing? It turned my stomach. And yet, suddenly everything clicked into place: why Jess flinched whenever anyone came too close; why she had constructed massive emotional walls to retreat behind at the first sign of trouble. The mystery that was Jess dissolved, leaving before me a scared, hurt girl in place of what I'd believed to be a strong, resolute woman.

But maybe she was both of those people simultaneously, I thought—strong and frightened, brave and uncertain, stoic and vulnerable. And all at once, I loved her even more for this complexity that had been there all along, hidden just beneath the surface.

Then something else occurred to me. "Wait, is this why you thought I couldn't love you? Because some asshole—are you serious?"

She pulled her hand away and nodded, hugging herself again.

My throat tightened and I moved toward her, shifting on the couch until our legs were touching.

"Jess," I said, brushing back a curl that had escaped from her ponytail, "what happened in the past could never change the way I feel about you. I love you." She looked at me, eyes nearly black, and I half-smiled. "You're stuck with me. I'm not going anywhere."

"Don't you see?" she asked, her voice raw. "I'm damaged, Cam. I won't ever be the same. I can never undo what he did. After it happened I drove all the way to the ocean and I walked down to the water and I thought about walking in, just being done with everything. That's what my dad did. But I didn't want to be like him, so I stayed on the beach all night and in the morning, I asked Barbara, my art teacher, for help. I stayed with her until I came here. She asked, but I never told her what happened. I never told anyone. I just wanted to forget it. Only I can't. I wish I could make it go away, but I can't."

I leaned back beside her, unsure what I should feel. Anger, horror, relief? Thank God she hadn't killed herself, I thought, rage at the unknown man and her pathetic mother bubbling up again inside me. I'm not particularly violent, but at that moment I found myself fantasizing about hurting another person. If I ever met the man who had preyed upon her, I vowed to myself, I would kill him.

"Was it someone you knew?" I asked, my face flushing with the heat of suppressed rage.

"Yeah, it was." She blinked. "You're disgusted, aren't you?"

"Disgusted? No way." I caught her hand in mine again and gave it a squeeze. "I was just thinking about what I'd do to the bastard if I ever got my hands on him."

She winced a little, and I took a deep breath. The last thing she needed right now was the threat of more violence.

"I'm sorry," I added. "I don't mean to upset you. It's just..." I trailed off. What could I say that wouldn't make matters worse?

Shifting again on the couch, I moved closer, tugging her toward me. She resisted at first, but when I didn't let go, she seemed almost to fall into me, hiding her face in my neck.

"It's okay," I said softly, my lips against her hair. "I've got you." And I held her gently, there on the couch in her third-story apartment while the seconds ticked past and the light faded beyond the windows.

After a little while, she murmured, "So you love me, huh?"

"I do." I was glad I couldn't see her face. What would she say now that her revelation had failed to send me packing?

"Good," she said, breath warm against my chin.

"Good?" I repeated.

"I think so. I mean, I knew I liked you and I thought you felt the same way, especially after the party at Mel's. I wanted to go home with you that night, I really did. I just wasn't ready."

That meant I hadn't imagined the Kiss Me look she'd given me at Mel's. Funny—the party seemed like a million years ago.

"Are you ready now?" I asked.

"I don't know. I was terrified of telling you. I thought it would change the way you felt about me, the way you look at me."

"You don't have to worry." I leaned away so I could see her face. "Something like that could never change the way I feel about you. I don't think you're damaged. I think you're beautiful and resilient and amazing, even more so now that I know how strong you really are. Okay?"

"Okay." She leaned her forehead against my chin. "Would it be all right if you just held me?"

"Of course. Come here."

We stretched out side by side on the couch and I wrapped my arms around her. Half on top of me, she slipped one arm around my waist and rested her face against my shoulder. Outside the streetlamps flicked on one by one, while in my arms Jess cried, softly at first, then harder until her entire body shook with gut-wrenching sobs. Her tears soaked my T-shirt and slid down my neck, and I held her tighter, stroking her hair and whispering soothing words, wishing I could take her pain and sorrow into me and dilute it somehow, relieve her of the burden of what had happened to her before we'd ever met. But I was as powerless as anyone else to change the past.

Powerless—that was exactly what the man who had raped her wanted. To rob her of choice, to inflict physical and emotional pain, to erode her confidence in herself and the people around her. How could you trust strangers when someone you knew could do such a thing?

As a lesbian, I'm used to being accused of hating men. I usually prefer to think of myself as a lover of women, not a hater of men. But as I held Jess in my arms, the sobs ripping through her, I felt the ember of rage that had ignited inside me at her admission growing stronger, feeding on the images that curled through my mind: Jess with a man's thick-fingered hand over her mouth, a heavy male body pressing her into a mattress or against a wall or onto a floor, blood between her legs, under her fingernails, on her lips where she'd bitten herself as he forced himself into her. I didn't hate men as a whole because of what had happened to her. My brother and dad were good men who would be outraged by the bastard who had assaulted Jess. But just then I hated a man I had never met more than I had ever hated anyone before.

I shut my eyes against the awful pictures, but it didn't help. Then I thought about Jess lugging around this horrible memory she thought she had to hide from everyone, this history she seemed to believe divided her from her peers, made her damaged goods, unlovable.

She wouldn't be alone with this anymore, I decided as her sobs eased and her body relaxed against mine and her breathing took on the regular rhythm of sleep. I would be whoever she needed me to be. No matter how she felt in return, it was enough that I loved her. For some reason, this realization was freeing. At that moment, I didn't need anything from her except to be allowed to try to help however I could. I had never felt anything quite so selfless before, I thought, slightly in awe of the strength of my own sentiment.

I closed my eyes and kissed Jess's hair as she slept in my arms. I only wished she could be this at peace always.

A little while later she started awake, and we sat up and turned on the lights. Her tears had dried. In the lamplight, she blinked and smiled at me shyly.

"I'm glad you came over tonight," she said.

"Me too."

Despite what she'd told me, I felt a growing sense of peace. She hadn't sent me away and I didn't have to hide anything anymore. Seemed like a win-win to me.

I stood up and stretched my hands above my head, my muscles tightening and then releasing. "Hey, are you hungry?"

She stood up next to me. "I could be. You want to make some dinner?"

"Definitely. You still have to tell me about Arizona."

"And you have to tell me about L.A."

Which reminded me... "Can I use your phone? I told Holly I'd call her."

"Sure. Is pasta okay?" she added, heading into the kitchen.

"Awesome."

While Jess poked through the cupboards, I dialed Holly's room.

"Hola," I said when she answered. "I was just over here at

Jess's and remembered I was supposed to call you." *Hint, hint.* In the background I heard a door slam. "Am I interrupting?"

"You could say that."

We were both speaking in code for our respective audiences.

"What, a fight?"

"Mm-hmm."

"Glad I called then."

She laughed shortly. "Me too. What's up with you? You're still there, so obviously she didn't kick you out. Or else—maybe you didn't tell her?"

"No, I did. We're making dinner right now."

"That means you've been there a couple of hours, you confessed, and you're only now eating dinner. Hmm," Holly said. "Does this mean what I think?"

In other words, had we slept together? That was the way her mind worked. Mine too, usually.

"Not quite," I said, looking over at Jess, who was setting a pot of water on the stove. "I have to help with dinner, since I'm the one who dropped in. Can't leave all the work to Jess."

The subject of our conversation looked over her shoulder and smiled. "Sure you can." She pulled a jar of tomato sauce from the fridge. "Tell Holly I said hi."

"I heard that. Give her a big kiss for me, Cam."

"She says hi, too," I told Jess.

She held up a bottle of red wine questioningly. I nodded.

"Wuss," Holly said.

"Anyway," I said into the phone, "want to meet for lunch tomorrow so you can tell me what's going on with you and Becca?"

"Sure," she said, "and vice versa. In the meantime, don't do anything I wouldn't do," she added. Jackass.

I hung up and walked over to the stove, resisting the urge to wrap my arms around Jess's waist from behind. After all, it wasn't like she'd said she loved me back. Then again, she hadn't said she didn't, either.

"What can I do?" I asked, peering into the water.

"It's pasta," she said, pouring tomato sauce into another pot. "Not much to do."

"Tell me about Arizona, then. How was the trip?"

I leaned against the counter and listened to her talk about the week in the desert—double sessions on the courts, days off when they hiked to the top of mesas, nights hanging out around a campfire. They had outlined their team plans and goals. This was the year they were going to win nationals, they'd decided.

That rung a bell. I remembered a soccer meeting early on in the fall before Jamie and I were at each other's throats. With a couple of wins behind us and the whole unknown season yet ahead, we'd talked about our goals for the season. A national championship was the ultimate objective for plenty of teams, realistic or not. Tennis, though, would have a significantly better shot at it than we'd had.

"What did you and Holly do all week?" Jess asked as we sat down at the table a little while later, plates heaped with steaming pasta and red sauce.

"We were a lot lazier than you. Mostly we laid out."

"I can tell. Nice freckles," she teased.

"Hey now, not all of us can have perfect tans."

"I don't know. Yours looks pretty good to me."

"Thanks. You look pretty good yourself."

She glanced away. "What else did you guys do? You couldn't have spent the entire week by the pool."

We sat in the kitchen talking over our meal as if nothing had happened, trading stories of our separate spring breaks. This was the way it was supposed to be, I thought as I took a sip of wine to wash down the pasta. Jess seemed lighter than usual, almost as if telling me about the rape had somehow lessened the power the memory held over her. I knew it couldn't be as easy as that, but I hoped that telling me would signal the beginning of something good for her.

After we'd cleaned up the kitchen, we returned to the living room and switched on the TV. Curled up together on the couch, shoulders and thighs touching, wineglasses on the coffee table, we watched the *Movie of the Week*, a made-for-television film about a couple's struggle to rescue their daughter from a religious cult. I wasn't really focused on the movie, though. I was just happy to be in Jess's apartment with her beside me and everything out in the open. Happy to look at her and smile and have her smile back even though the girl in the movie was being drugged by the cult leader at that exact moment. Happy that Jess had decided not to walk into the ocean three years before.

She fell asleep again, her head on my shoulder, before the movie ended. I stayed awake with my arm around her shoulders, hand stroking her hair, cheek resting against her forehead. So this was what it was like to really love someone, I thought, new feelings rising and falling inside me. There was tenderness, vulnerability, protectiveness. If anyone ever tried to hurt her again, I would kill them. It wasn't even a very fierce thought this time, more a matter-of-fact promise I was making to myself. I wouldn't let anyone hurt her again.

My eyes wandered from the television to the painting on the wall, the one I'd guessed on my first visit was supposed to depict a storm. And all at once, I understood—it was hers. Jess had painted the night she'd been raped, the night she drove to the ocean and sat on the damp sand thinking about ending her life. She displayed the image now in her living room, I supposed, to remind herself that she'd chosen to live. That she'd decided to be strong.

I wondered how long she could continue to be strong. I wondered what I would have done in her shoes. I wondered if the storm was still somewhere inside her just beneath her collarbone, maybe, waiting to deluge her again. Not if I had any say. But realistically, I knew I probably didn't.

When the movie ended, I hit the power button on the remote.

"Come on, Jessie," I said softly, squeezing her shoulder. "Time to make the doughnuts."

Her eyelids fluttered, and she looked up at me, blinking in the semi-dark room. Outside the window the sky was black, stars pricking the canopy of night. "Oh. Hi." She yawned.

"Hi," I said. "Time to get you to bed."

She sat up. "Are you staying?"

"Sure. This couch and I are buds." I patted the cushion.

"No, I mean, with me." She gestured toward her bedroom.

Gulping, I glanced toward the bedroom. "Are you sure?"

She nodded.

"Okay then." Didn't have to ask me twice. Actually, she already had, probably because even in my most optimistic moments, I hadn't pictured ending the night in her bed.

We got ready in shifts. I changed into the boxers she loaned me while she used the bathroom. Then, while I was brushing my teeth and taking my contacts out, she changed clothes and pulled the covers down.

I left the nightlight on in the bathroom and crossed to the bedroom, aware of the creak of the wood floor beneath my feet. Sidney and Claire had to have noticed that I hadn't left yet. Then again, they were probably happy that Jess was hanging out with a lesbian. One of the family, so to speak.

She was already curled up under the forest green comforter, bedside lamp glowing. I hesitated, looking at her questioningly. Her hair was down, flowing about her shoulders in a dark wave. She smiled, shy again, and patted the bed.

"It's okay, Cam," she said, her voice calm. "I promise."

Taking a deep breath, I closed the bedroom door partway behind me and crossed the room. I couldn't quite believe this was happening. Then I was climbing into bed beside her and sliding down beneath the cool sheets and warm comforter. My feet brushed against her leg and she pulled away with a laugh.

"Your feet are freezing!"

I had heard that complaint before. I shrugged, grinning nervously at her. "You know what they say. Cold feet, warm heart." I had used this same line before, too. I burrowed down in the bed until my head was on the pillow facing her. "So."

"So."

We were only a few inches apart now. This close, I could see tiny laugh lines fanning out from her eyes.

"You have beautiful eyes," I said. Another line. I had to stop.

"I was just thinking that about you. Yours change all the time. Right now they're green."

"Because of the comforter."

She smelled clean, a combination of shampoo, soap and toothpaste. And something else that was just her.

We were both quiet. I was afraid to move, afraid I might trigger some awful memory. But she was looking steadily at me with the open, vulnerable look I'd only glimpsed a couple of times. I moved closer and lifted my hand to her cheek. Her skin was so soft.

"Jess," I whispered.

She met me halfway. Our lips brushed, softly, lightly, just for a moment. I pulled away a little, but she was too close. I couldn't focus on anything except her eyes, half-closed and shining. I closed my own eyes and kissed her again.

We kissed for what felt like hours, bodies pressed together beneath the sheets, legs intertwined. I kept my hands shoulder-level, afraid of scaring her. The last thing I wanted was to remind her of the last time presumably she'd been this close to another human being. Eventually she pulled away, kissed me once more sweetly, and shifted onto her back, staring at the ceiling. Her breathing wasn't steady.

Neither was mine. I watched her, feeling my pulse pounding at my neck. She was so beautiful.

"You okay?" I asked.

She looked over at me and nodded. "Better than okay." She lifted her hand to brush my hair off my forehead. "I'm really glad you're here."

"So am I." I hugged her against me. This was what life was all about, I thought, closing my eyes and burying my face in her hair.

Jess turned out the light a few minutes later. We fell asleep holding each other. In the middle of the night I woke up, disoriented. Then my eyes focused in the dim light from the doorway and I saw Jess, asleep on her side, face turned toward me. I lifted my arm to her waist. In her sleep she moved closer to me. I smiled and sank back into darkness.

So this was love.

CHAPTER SEVENTEEN

Jess and I skipped our classes the next day and lay around her apartment eating bread and fruit and cheese, drinking Gatorade and watching old *Laverne and Shirley* reruns. Among other things. Half the day we spent in bed. Jess wasn't as nervous as she had thought she would be, she said. Still, we took it slowly. I didn't want to hurt her, not ever, so I let her set the pace, pleasantly surprised when she pushed me down on my back that first morning and had her way with me.

Every time I opened my eyes to see her leaning over me, I felt the same thrill that it was her lips on my collarbone, her fingers trailing over my taut belly, her hand tracing circles on my inner thigh. For so long, I had viewed Jess as cool, remote, asexual even. In reality, her interest in my body was unabashedly prurient. She seemed fascinated by the texture of my skin, the sounds that escaped the back of my throat as she caressed me, the slickness between my legs after she had kissed her way across my stomach.

Took a little longer for her to let me return the favor, but eventually she did, biting her lip as I slid my hand under the tank top she'd slept in. Despite the desire flooding through me, I went slowly and let her call the shots, and didn't take it personally when she stopped my hand at the waistband of her boxer shorts. I knew it would probably be a while before she could let go completely and trust me with her body. Good thing I had a healthy ego when it came to sex. Not to mention, ample experience "helping women reach their full orgasmic potential," as Mel had once jokingly put it.

On Tuesday, we reluctantly left the apartment and returned to real life. In the days that followed, school quickly reasserted itself in the form of classes, homework, practice, matches, all trying their best to keep us apart. We fought the pull of other commitments as well as we could. I started spending nearly every night at Jess's apartment, even the ones pre-competition, parking my car behind hers outside Sidney and Claire's house and letting myself into the upstairs apartment with the spare key Jess presented me with a week after I'd started staying over.

"Is it too soon?" she asked worriedly as I stared at the key in its tiny jewelry box sitting between us on the kitchen table.

We had just finished dinner, and I had been wondering how she would react if I suggested we make it an early night. I'd been thinking about her all day, my palms damp as I remembered the way she'd gazed at me the night before, all sexy and in charge, as she did wonderful things to me.

Now I looked from the tiny box up into her eyes and smiled. "What took you so long?"

In response, she pulled me up and led me toward the bedroom. Seemed I wasn't the only one who'd been having X-rated fantasies all day.

Friends become lovers, we were officially dating from the night I told her I loved her, unofficial honeymooners from the first morning we awoke wrapped around each other. We shared most meals, talked on the phone incessantly when we were apart, and even Holly claimed to find our cuteness nearly unbearable.

"Payback's a bitch," I told her unapologetically one Saturday afternoon as we lounged in the tennis stands watching my girlfriend pummel the top singles player from CU-Rancho Cucamonga. Becca had chosen not to attend the match, and I was just as happy—gave Holly and me some needed best friend time.

I hadn't told her about the rape, and I wasn't sure I ever would. Not without Jess's permission, and even though matters were progressing in the bedroom—Jess had taken my hand and moved it under her boxers for the first time the night before—I doubted she would be comfortable with anyone other than me knowing her history anytime soon.

"So how's the sex?" Holly asked, lowering her voice so that no one around us would hear.

"Dude!" I shoved her sideways. "None of your effing business, that's how."

Holly rolled her eyes. "You Oregonians are so uptight."

"Yeah? Well, you Californians are too loose."

"And that's supposed to be a bad thing?" she asked, arching a superior eyebrow in my direction.

She might have had a point, not that I would have admitted as much to her.

At the end of our second dreamy week together, Jess confessed that tennis somehow no longer seemed quite as important. Secretly I was pleased by this admission, but outwardly I scolded her. She was still number one in singles in the country, and SDU, the top-seeded Division II team, was due to host nationals in a matter of weeks. She couldn't afford to lose focus now.

As they always do after spring break, the weeks began to slip away in a blur of warm weather, spring fever and rising academic pressure. They went even faster this time because I desperately wanted to slow everything down. Despite the auspicious beginning, my growing relationship with Jess felt tenuous somehow, as if everything could suddenly end without warning. We were a couple now, double dating with Holly and Becca for real, holding hands on campus and around the city when it seemed safe to do so, attending LGBA functions together, even occasionally dirty dancing at eighteen-and-up nights at Zodiac.

But at times even now Jess retreated to that place no one else could reach, her eyes blank and body rigid. Sometimes after we made love, she closed her eyes and turned away from me, shutting me out entirely as she took deep, calming breaths. I understood where she went to at those moments—and why—but I was still powerless to bring her back. I could only quell the urge to touch her and wait for her to soften toward me and everything else around her. She was well worth the wait, but I wasn't always sure she'd come back to me.

The days and nights marched inexorably past, taking us closer to summer and our inevitable parting. With tennis season in full swing, my girl was busier than I was. Sometimes I only saw her late at night for a cuddle session and the perennially too-short sleep of the exhausted. She spent three weekends in April away, traveling throughout the region for various tournaments and away matches. I slept in the dorm then and got caught up with my other friends, who teased me about spring mating season and my recent vanishing act. Alicia was envious I'd gotten the girl when she hadn't, but she graciously congratulated me over lunch the week after spring break, agreeing that there were indeed other fish in the sea, even for her. Mel's roommate had asked her out, and she was thinking of saying yes. The hockey player was no Anna, but she had a nice smile. Had to start somewhere, I told her, trying not to glow too brightly.

April came and went while I was too love-struck to notice, and then suddenly, somehow, it was only a week until finals and I was finishing up end-of-term projects and studying for my Macro and Word War II exams. I went into the econ final with a solid B. Not bad considering I hadn't cracked my textbook even once during the semester. Even if I bombed the exam—which I didn't plan on doing—I couldn't get lower than a C+ overall, according to my calculations. No matter what, my eligibility was safe, and I had won the bet. Laura was not just a little pissed that I had managed to make a mockery out of her beloved Macro. She wasn't nearly as annoyed as Holly, though, who, in accordance with the terms of our wager, had to pack my room for me at the end of the term.

Tennis nationals were slated for the week between finals and graduation. I was supposed to go home as soon as I finished my tests, but I decided to stay an extra week to watch Jess play in the tournament. Holly stayed too. In fact, she had no plans to go home except for a brief visit. She and Becca were going to try living together in San Diego for the summer. Becca was planning to look for a job in her field, marine science. But there wasn't much you could do with a bachelor's degree anymore, she kept telling Holly. She was putting off grad school until Holly graduated so that they could plan a future together.

The week before commencement, I helped Holly and Becca move into their new apartment, a one-bedroom place a mile north of San Diego's business district. They had the top floor of a two-story house on a quietish street a few blocks from University Avenue, and Holly had a job at Starbuck's on Fifth. Afternoon and evening shifts only, she told me as we hung her posters throughout the apartment. No early mornings for her.

Jess was busier than ever that last week, getting ready for nationals. Every day she had double practice sessions, and nearly every night there seemed to be some sort of team event. I felt like I barely saw her, even though I was staying at her apartment the week between finals and commencement. I spent a lot of time working out, hanging out with Holly at the beach before her shift, riding my bike around town, and reading magazines and paperback novels—my respite after a semester of academic study—under an umbrella in the tennis stands while Jess and the rest of the team practiced.

She might have said tennis didn't seem as important anymore, but you couldn't tell to look at her. At least, I couldn't tell. I tried to tamp down rising jealousy as she worked on and off the court on a single goal—playing the best she possibly could at nationals. There would be time later for us, I told myself as Jess crawled into bed each night with a half-hearted kiss for me, falling asleep on my shoulder almost before I turned off the bedside lamp. But time was dwindling for us. When tennis season ended, so would my sojourn in Southern California.

National semis were Saturday, finals on Sunday. Sidney and Claire came to all of Jess's matches, waving occasionally from under their sun umbrella on the hillside overlooking the courts. Holly and I sat in the stands in baseball caps, tank tops and shorts, cheering on SDU and sunning ourselves at the same time. Becca didn't come either day, citing her job search. Holly thought she might be envious of the sports thing Holly, Jess and I all had going. Momentarily, I felt sorry for her. It passed quickly.

On Saturday, Jess rolled through her matches without dropping a set while SDU beat its opponents easily to advance to the team finals. After the match, as I waited for Jess to come out of the field house with the rest of the team, I thought I saw a tall, slim woman in a familiar tan and gold suit disappear into the crowd. Was she Jess's mother? I was tempted to run after her, but the tennis team exited the field house just then, laughing and chatting a million miles a minute. I didn't mention the woman to Jess. No need to risk knocking her off her game.

I thought about her later, though. Would she come back for the finals? Who did she think she was, anyway? I pictured telling her off. I saw myself decking her. I imagined asking her what she'd been thinking when she turned her back on her own child, if she knew the damage she'd wreaked. But in the end, I knew I probably wouldn't get a chance to enact any of my fantasies. It was Jess's life, her decision to talk to her mother or not, assuming my hunch was right and the mystery woman was Jess's mom.

That night we ate leftover pasta and salad at the apartment, careful not to load up on too many carbs. Then we went to bed early so that I could give her a full body massage to work out the kinks from the day's matches and get her relaxed and ready for the finals.

In the bedroom, she took her shirt off and lay on her stomach. I straddled her hips and went to work on her back, kneading lotion and a bit of tiger's balm into her muscles and trying to ignore my own tingling. I'd been flying solo in that regard all week. Jess had told me she'd make it up to me somehow, but I wasn't sure how she planned to accomplish that one.

"That feels so good," she murmured, turning her head on the pillow to sigh softly. "You're amazing."

Not the context I'd hoped for such accolades, but it would have to do. After all, a national championship hung in the balance.

"Face forward, Ms. Tennis Pro," I said, working on her lats. "Even out your shoulders."

"Mmm." She buried her face in the pillow.

After ten minutes, my hands were tired and Jess's breathing was deep and even. I lay down beside her, running my hand across her back and feeling the muscles beneath my touch. My hand drifted over her hair, silky strands soft against my fingertips. She turned her face toward me, blinking in the lamplight, and smiled sleepily.

"Thanks, Cam. That felt awesome."

"My pleasure," I said, sliding my fingers down the side of her face. "I'm going to miss you so much."

I didn't mean to say it out loud. We should be focusing on tennis, both of us, specifically on finals the following day. Not on our impending separation, slated for first thing Tuesday morning when I would climb into the Tercel and point my wheels north.

Her eyes narrowed. "I know. I've been thinking." She hesitated. "Do you really have to go home for the summer?"

A spark glimmered in my chest. She didn't want me to leave? But I couldn't enjoy the feeling long.

"I wish I didn't have to," I said, "but I told the Parks guys a while ago I would work this summer. I can't back out now."

"I knew you would say that," she said, closing her eyes again. "You're so good."

"We can't all be California flakes," I said, but the joke felt hollow even to me.

I had thought more than once how perfect it would be, the two of us in La Jolla hanging out with Holly and Becca on the beaches and at the parks and around town when we weren't working, taking weekend trips to the mountains and Baja and L.A. But La Jolla in the summer was Jess's turf. I hadn't wanted to invite myself into her life. Now it was too late to do anything other than reluctantly head home for the summer and wish I'd had the nerve to say something sooner.

"Does this mean you would want me to stay if I could?" I asked.

"Of course I want you to stay," she said, eyes closed, voice and body relaxed. "I love you. I'll always want you to stay."

She'd said it, finally. I leaned my chin on her shoulder and kissed her cloud of hair. "I love you too," I murmured.

In response, she snored, and I laughed quietly. Such was the life of an intercollegiate athlete.

While my girlfriend slept, I took the phone into the kitchen and called Holly to tell her about the latest happy milestone Jess and I had managed to achieve.

"Great, now you two will be even more obnoxiously cute," Holly said, but I could hear the smile in her voice. "Bet you're glad now you don't ever stay mad," she added.

"My friend," I replied, "I'm ecstatic."

Now if only life could continue this unfailingly happily. Somehow, I doubted it would. But I had hope. After all, I was from Oregon.

On Sunday, Jess woke up at six a.m. and never went back to sleep. She told me this later—I didn't wake up even when she left the apartment to take Duncan for an early walk. I know, some girlfriend, right? Jess had to meet the team for breakfast at a bagel shop near campus, so she left after her walk. But she came home between breakfast and the match for another massage.

Her muscles had tightened since the previous night's bodywork. I kneaded a knot below her shoulder blade until she grunted in pain.

"You're tense this morning," I said, relenting a little.

"No kidding," she muttered.

"You know you guys are going to kick ass. All you have to do is maintain your focus."

"Right."

She was unusually quiet. Understandable, since it was nationals.

"Are you okay?" I asked, working my way down her spine.

She hesitated. "I'm not sure I can do this."

"What do you mean, exactly?" I asked, pressing down against the small of her back. "What can't you do?"

"I'm not as good as everyone thinks," she explained, voice

muffled against her hands. "It's like, when I'm on the court, I have this anger inside me that makes me win. You know? But it's not really inside of me. That's the problem. It's outside of me. I have to keep it there or I wouldn't be able to handle it."

I tried to choose my words carefully. "Are you saying the emotion you use to win comes from the assault?"

Her muscles tensed even more beneath my hands. We hadn't talked about the rape other than that one time. I'd wanted to, but I hadn't wanted to push her. Besides, the timing never seemed quite right, with tennis and the end of the semester propelling us forward.

"Yes," she said, her voice quiet. "I was never this good before."

I sat back on my heels. She turned over and watched me, eyes shuttered in the old way.

"Jess," I said, taking her hand in mine, "you know that saying—what doesn't kill you makes you stronger?"

She nodded.

"I know it sounds cheesy and clichéd and all of that, but it's true. You survived something terrible and it didn't kill you. It made you stronger. That strength is deep inside you, where your athletic ability comes from. In here." I touched her forehead. "And in here." I placed my hand on her chest, above her heart. "And especially in here." I tickled her stomach.

She squirmed away, smiling reluctantly. "At least one of us thinks I can do it."

"I believe in you," I said, and lay down beside her. "Now come here."

My arms around her, we lay quietly, listening to each other breathe as the sun climbed higher beyond the window.

When it was time, we left the apartment and drove to campus, where I dropped her at the gym. She kissed me as she left the car, her lips pressing firmly against mine. Then she was sliding out the passenger door, bag in hand, and striding toward the gym entrance. She looked back at me once and I flashed her a thumbs-up. She nodded and disappeared inside. As I went to park the car, I tried to contain my pride. This was it.

The top nine singles players from each team met each

other in the finals. Jess was seeded number one. Her opponent, a woman named Michelle Argot from Hawaii-Pacific, was a former Division I top ten player who had blown her knee two years earlier and struggled back. A senior, she was ranked just behind Jess in our division. They had met once over spring break in Tucson. There, I knew, Jess had lost the first set and been taken to a tiebreaker in the second, but ultimately she'd won the match with two service breaks in the third set. That boded well, I thought, crossing my fingers.

The stands were packed. Holly and I scored seats in the second row only with difficulty. When Jess took the court to warm up, I felt pressure on my bladder—just like a soccer game. Meanwhile, out on court, Jess didn't appear nervous at all. Her movements were careful and controlled, graceful as ever. I couldn't believe she was my girlfriend. I wondered if my head was swelling visibly with the pride my chest couldn't quite seem to hold.

Jess had first serve. Tucking an extra ball into her tennis skirt, she took a deep breath and looked toward the stands. *Do it*, I thought as her eyes found mine. *Kick her ass.* She nodded slightly like she'd heard me, bounced the ball twice, and tossed it up. The match was underway.

Sometimes in sport you feel so strong and good and skilled that it's like you are the ball or the racquet or the bat. Everything clicks and the sun is perfect overhead, never in your eyes, and even the wind seems to gust in your favor. It's almost as if you are the game and the game is you. You're in the zone. Jess, it quickly became evident, was having one of those days, buoyed along by the gods of sport or whatever inner strength it was that made her swing powerful, her shots accurate, her serve deadly. At first, everything she did was just right.

But it rarely lasts long, that perfect synchronicity between body and mind. Something gives and you return to mortality, after the match or game if you're lucky. For Jess, the come-down occurred in the middle of the second set. She'd won the first 6-4 and was leading the second 3-1, thirty-love on her serve. Three more games, and she would be the undisputed national champion, no matter what the rest of her team did.

She served and moved in immediately to play the net, but Michelle anticipated her step and angled a clean shot crosscourt. Jess did something she had done a thousand times before—she scrambled and reached for the distant ball. A drop shot, all she could manage, and the ball skipped over the net, bouncing twice before Michelle could manage more than a few steps. Jess hit the ground and rolled. Forty-love. The fans went wild.

Then the clapping died away as Jess stayed down holding the back of her right leg, face twisted in pain.

I grabbed Holly. "Her hamstring!" She'd had problems with it during the winter season.

"But I thought it was okay now," Holly said, grimacing.

"So did she." Despite the heat of the day, I shivered a little. This was not supposed to happen.

We watched as Carrie, an SDU athletic trainer, sprinted out onto the court, bag of medical tricks in hand. Adrienne, Jess's coach, followed, her steps quick. I resisted the urge to jump the barrier and run out with them, holding tightly instead to Holly and waiting with everyone else.

After a few moments, Adrienne conferred with the chair umpire. He granted Jess a ten-minute injury time-out. After that, he said loudly enough for those of us in the first few rows to hear, Jess would have to play—or forfeit the match.

Adrienne and Carrie helped Jess off to the side of the court and began working on her there. Steve, the student trainer, squatted down next to Jess as she said something. Then he stood up and headed for the stands.

"Cam," he said, catching my eye. "Can you come down here?"

I scrambled down from my seat and followed him around the edge of the court, barely aware of the eyes of the crowd on my back. She had to be okay. She was only three games away.

When I reached her, Jess was holding a bag of ice to the back of her right thigh. Her eyes were red and full of tears, but she managed to fake a smile as I squatted down next to her.

"Hey, champ," I said, a hand on her shoulder. "How you doing?"

"Not so good," she said. "I was almost there, but now..." She shook her head, staring down at her leg.

I glanced over at Carrie, who was checking her watch, Ace bandage in hand. "Can she play?"

Carrie shrugged. "If this were any other match, I'd say no. But she'll have the summer to recover. It's up to her."

"What do you think?" I asked Jess.

"I don't know," she said, her voice low. "It's bad, Cam. Really bad."

"Okay, but this is it," I said, tightening my grip on her shoulder. "This is the championship match. And you know what? I don't think you'll let yourself just bow out. You've come too far to quit now. What do you say? Want to get back out there and give it a try?"

Jess looked at me staring hard at her at the edge of the dark green court, restless spectators murmuring in the background. She squinted into the sunlight, and then all at once, she nodded. "Okay. But if I never walk again, you'll be the one pushing the wheelchair."

"Deal." I held out my hand and she slapped it. "Now get out there and finish her off."

While Carrie wrapped Jess's leg, I went back to the stands. Everyone around me asked if she could play. I told them she was damn well going to try.

Moving gingerly, Jess headed onto the court. The trainer had sprayed her leg with a deep numbing spray, anesthesia in an aerosol can. Not a long-term fix, but at least it would temporarily dull the pain. Back in position again, she took a few practice swings, wincing each time her weight shifted onto her bad leg.

This was going to be ugly, I thought, slouching down in my seat.

Jess held on to win one last point on her serve to go up 4-1 in the second set. On Michelle's serve, though, she barely moved. She didn't score a single point. 4-2. Her serve again, only this time Michelle upped the pressure. Jess lost again. Now it was 4-3, back even on serve. I was starting to get nervous. So were the other SDU fans.

When Jess asked for a break, the chair umpire granted a short time-out. She went to her bench, waved Adrienne and Carrie away and hung her head, a damp towel draped over her face. She sat motionless, invisible to the crowd. I wondered where she was—in her sunlit apartment upstairs at Claire and Sidney's house? On a storm-swept beach west of Bakersfield? Snuggled under the covers with me on a laid-back Sunday morning? Wherever it was, I hoped it was galvanizing her. She would have to break Michelle again to win.

When the time-out ended, Jess rose, tossed the towel aside and walked toward court, barely limping. She was ready. Whether or not her leg would hold, that was the question.

Whereas earlier in the match Jess had been in the zone, now she had to work desperately hard for every point. Sweat poured down her face, dripped from her shirt, darkened the edges of her white tennis skirt. A scowl seemed etched permanently into her face as she switched to a long serve-and-volley game, wearing Michelle down slowly, relentlessly, moving her from one side of the court to the other. She let Michelle make all the attacks and most of the unforced errors. With this strategy, she managed to hold her next serve.

With Jess up 5-4 in the second set, Michelle broke herself with a double fault at thirty-thirty and another at thirty-forty. Then, on match point, she returned a crosscourt volley well over the end line. And just like that, the match was over.

The shocked silence in the stadium was broken by the chair umpire's calm, "Game, set, match to Jessica Maxwell, San Diego University."

Jess dropped to her knees while Holly and I screamed and threw our arms around each other. The stands erupted around us, the pent-up tension of the past half hour released in cheering and whistling. Jess had done it. Despite her injury, she was the new NCAA Division II national tennis champion.

She finally allowed herself a smile as she shook hands with her opponent and the chair umpire. Then she waved at the stands, briefly, and headed for the bench. She would prefer not to have the attention, I knew, now that the match was over and she wasn't out there playing her guts out anymore. Adrienne and Carrie met her at the edge of the court, and the stands began to empty as people wandered off to watch the remaining top matchups. So far, two other SDU players had won. Things were looking good for a possible team championship as well.

"Go get her," Holly said. "And come find me later, okay? We've got some celebrating to do tonight."

"Yeah we do!"

On the other side of the court, Jess was listening to the trainer and nodding, her forehead lined. She glanced up, straight across to where Holly and I stood beside the emptying stands. She nodded at me almost imperceptibly.

"See ya," I said, clapping Holly on the back as we headed in opposite directions.

Adrienne was still standing beside Jess when I reached them. The coach glanced at me, then returned her attention to the trainer. I stood behind the bench, eavesdropping.

"For the next hour," Carrie was saying, "I want you to ice fifteen minutes, then walk and stretch for twenty. Then ice fifteen, walk and stretch for twenty. Keep moving around or you're going to seize up, which you definitely don't want. No running, either. I'll take another look after the last match."

She handed over four Advils and a water bottle to wash the pills down, then patted Jess's shoulder and stood up. "Good work," she added. "You showed a lot of courage out there. You should be proud of yourself, kiddo."

Jess glanced back at me and smiled, then returned her attention to the trainer. "Thanks, Carrie. Thanks a lot."

"You're welcome."

Carrie nodded at me, eyes gleaming knowingly. I had it on good authority from one of the student assistants that our head trainer was a softball-playing, died-in-the-wool dyke herself.

Adrienne, however, was a straight mother of two young children. As Carrie walked away, Adrienne looked from me back to Jess again. "She's right. You did show a lot of courage out there, Maxwell. You earned this victory."

"Thanks, Coach," Jess said. Then she focused on the next court over where Julie Seaver was battling the second seed. "How's everyone else doing?"

Adrienne gave her an update on the team competition, congratulated her again on her win, and strode away with a final nod to me.

I sat down on the bench next to Jess and threw my arm across her shoulders.

"Awesome match, champ! I knew you could do it." Not the time to tell her I had doubted her inner strength. Probably there wouldn't ever be a right time for such an admission.

"Thanks, Cam." She leaned into me. "Couldn't have done it without you."

A mild glow centered in my belly, and I didn't even mind her sweatiness. Must be love.

"You're amazing," I said. "You don't even know how incredible you are, do you?"

She smiled some more, her eyes tired. The adrenaline appeared to be wearing off. "I can't believe I won. It doesn't feel real yet. I still feel numb."

"That's just the ice talking. Dude, you came back from an injury to win! You know, triumphing over personal tragedy and all of that."

"Ha, ha," she said, swatting me.

We were sitting on the aluminum bench at the edge of the empty court on an early summer's day, smiling into each other's eyes. And I suddenly thought, *This can't end, not ever*. But what if it did?

A shadow crept across us. My arm fell away from her shoulders as we looked back, squinting in the sunlight. I had an impression of a slightly familiar patrician woman in a tailored suit with a gold necklace and matching earrings. Then Jess jumped to her feet, the Ace bandage around her leg unraveling, the bag of ice tumbling to the ground.

"What are you doing here?" she demanded, eyes suddenly flat, voice harsher than I had ever heard.

I stood up too. The stranger was definitely Jess's mother—she had the same high cheekbones as her daughter, the same long waist. Only Jess's muscles were bulkier and more clearly defined, while the lines about the older woman's eyes were etched deeper.

"I didn't mean to upset you," the woman who had to be my girlfriend's asshole mother said. "I just wanted to congratulate you, Jessie. I wanted to tell you how proud I am. Your father would have been too."

Her eyes were a pale blue, her hair in its tight bun streaked with golden highlights. She was beautiful in a cool sort of way and very well put together. But she didn't sound nearly as confident as she appeared.

"Thank you," Jess said, her voice clipped. Her eyes were dark, narrowed against the sun and something else. "But you don't get to be proud. This has nothing to do with you."

I tried not to squirm as they stared at one another. "I can leave you two alone," I offered, "if you want."

Jess blinked at me. "You don't have to go, Cam." She glanced back at the woman. "My mother and I have nothing to say to each other. Do we, Mother?"

The older woman clutched a small white purse to her side. "I hope that's not true," she said, her voice uneven. "I'm sorry about everything, Jessie. I've tried to tell you, but you won't answer my letters, you won't return my phone calls. I divorced Harvey years ago. He moved back to Connecticut."

Harvey? Who was Harvey? And then an idea occurred to me, too horrible to entertain seriously. It couldn't be.

As if she could sense the wheels spinning in my head, Jess shot me a quick unreadable look before glancing back at her mother. "I know. Gram told me."

Her mother took another step forward, stopping as her nyloned knees brushed against the bench. "I wish I could take it all back. I would do it all over differently if I could." She hesitated, looking down at the ground for a moment. Then she took a deep breath and said, "I know I don't deserve it, but I am your mother. Can't you find it somewhere in your heart to even consider giving me another chance?"

For a moment, I thought Jess wavered. Her eyes glistened as she stared into her mother's face. Then a tear spilled over, slipping down her sweat-dampened cheek and breaking her reverie. Scowling, she swiped at it and stood straighter.

"No," she said firmly. "You're right. You don't deserve it."

"Jess," I protested inadvertently, feeling my throat tighten. How could she turn away her own mother? And yet, this was the same woman who had, apparently, brought Jess's attacker into their lives to begin with.

Jess cast a wounded look my way. "Don't, Cam," she said, her voice low. "You don't understand."

"It's okay," her mother said, looking at me. "She doesn't deserve a mother like me. She deserves so much better." She lifted her chin. "I understand, honey, and I don't blame you. When you're ready, if you're ever ready, Gram knows how to get in touch with me."

Jess looked down at the dark stain that had begun to seep onto the court from the melting bag of ice. She didn't say anything.

"Congratulations, Jessie," her mother added. "I do so love you." Then she nodded at me, turned and walked quickly away. In a few moments she had disappeared into the passageway between the courts.

"Fuck, fuck, fuck," Jess said. She blinked, and the tears spilled over again. She stooped to pick up the ice, wincing as she bent her leg. "Shit." She dropped onto the bench.

I knelt beside the bench, trying to take the bag from her. "I've got it."

But she shoved my hands away and arranged the ice again, securing it to her leg haphazardly with the Ace bandage.

"Don't touch me," she said, her voice hoarse. "How could you do that? How could you take her side?"

I inhaled deeply. She was upset from seeing her mother, I told myself, not to mention emotionally drained from the roller-coaster match she'd only just finished. I was feeling fairly overwhelmed by the day's drama myself, and I hadn't won a national championship or faced down an estranged parent.

"I'm sorry it seemed like that," I said. "But I'm on your side."

"You have no idea," she said, shaking her head. "I went to her for help, and she told me I was ungrateful, that I couldn't be happy for her. She said I was just jealous of their relationship." Her voice broke again, and she pressed her hands over her face.

She was right. I couldn't possibly know what it would be like to be raped by my stepfather and then abandoned by the one person I should have been able to trust. Her mother should have taken Jess to a hospital, should have called the police, should have kicked the son-of-a-bitch to the curb faster than you could say

"Prison." But she hadn't done any of those things. Instead, she had turned her back on her child. Now Jess was reciprocating.

I took a risk and sat down on the bench, wrapped my arms around her and pulled her against me. She resisted at first, actively trying to push me away. But I stayed where I was and refused to let go, and eventually she gave in, leaning into me and pressing her face into my shoulder.

She cried like she had our first night together, the salt of her tears mingling with her sweat against my bare neck as she sobbed. The sounds were so gut-wrenching that I felt tears stinging my own eyes, a lump in my own throat. So much pain, terror, hurt, rage. It didn't seem possible she could survive as wounded as she was.

But more than anything, Jess was a survivor. She'd proven that fact over and over again. My pep talk earlier in the day had contained elements of truth—the pain she'd suffered had made her stronger, even as she maintained it had left her permanently damaged. But maybe strength and injury weren't contradictory states of being. Maybe, instead, they were intimately connected.

"I love you so much," I murmured, stroking her hair and kissing her forehead, "and I'm so freaking proud of you."

"Good," she mumbled through her tears, tightening her grip on me.

We stayed at the edge of the court like that, me propping Jess up while tennis matches played on around us, the crack of racquets, grunts of battle, cries of myriad fans echoing throughout the complex as, slowly, her tears abated and her breathing settled back to normal.

Finally she checked her watch, unwrapped the Ace bandage, and looked at me, eyes bloodshot and swollen but clearer somehow too.

"Time to move around," she said, and cleared her throat, laughing a little at her own hoarseness. "You ready, Wallace?"

"Ready, Maxwell."

Standing up, I held out a hand. She took it and let me pull her up.

As we headed for the passageway where her mother had disappeared, Jess added, "Thanks for sticking around."

"You got it," I said, looping my arm through hers. "I told you—you're stuck with me."

"Yay." She tugged me closer and we crossed the court arm in arm while the midday sun beat down and tennis fans cheered all around us just out of sight.

CHAPTER EIGHTEEN

You know how people are always saying that anticipation is worse than what you actually fear? Yeah, well, that wasn't the case for me. Leaving La Jolla—and Jess—for the summer sucked even more than I'd anticipated.

We spent Sunday night celebrating NCAAs with the tennis team and Holly and even Becca, Jess limping on crutches around the off-campus apartment of one of her teammates, laughing and drinking more than I'd ever seen her do before. The pressure was finally off. In addition to facing down her mother, she had finally lived up to the hype of her preseason All-American selection and number one ranking throughout the year. Talk about a momentous weekend.

The next morning, though, I woke up to find her sitting in the chair beside the bed watching me sleep.

"Good morning, Miss National Champ," I said, yawning and stretching.

She shook her head and frowned.

I mock-frowned back. "Is it not a good morning?"

"In case you've forgotten, this is our last day together for three entire months."

"Well, when you put it that way." I pulled a pillow over my head. "I'm going back to sleep."

She limped to the bed—I could hear her uneven gait through the pillow—and threw herself on top of me. "The better to tickle you, my dear," she said, reaching under the covers to find my sensitive armpits.

Naturally, this led to a different form of physical interaction much more satisfying than tickling, and we occupied ourselves for some time that morning—finally!—before the growling in both of our stomachs could no longer be ignored. Then we got up and fixed a big breakfast. We'd worked out that I was good at eggs and she highly skilled at French toast, so that's what we made that morning, drinking coffee (me) and tea (her) and both of us talking almost without taking a breath. There seemed to be so much to say and not nearly enough time.

The whole day was like that. We had lunch with Sidney and Claire in the backyard, a combination celebratory/send-off meal. They carefully guided the conversation away from the immediate future and on to topics like favorite foods, the tennis tournament, SDU classes and professors we'd especially liked. The last thing Jess and I wanted to talk about was how we'd be spending the next three months until we saw each other again, and Jess's landlords seemed to understand instinctively.

After lunch, they suggested we borrow Duncan for a neighborhood stroll. Twenty-four hours of Carrie's ice on, ice off routine, minus a few hours of naked fun this morning, had left Jess's hamstring in considerably better shape. She no longer needed crutches.

As we walked slowly away from Sidney and Claire's house, I said, "I'm glad you have them. They take such good care of you."

"I know. They've been amazing."

I hesitated. "Have you ever thought of telling them what happened? Or your teacher back in Bakersfield?"

This time, Jess didn't flinch away at the mention of the rape. She tilted her head slightly, pursed her lips and said, "I've thought about it. But I don't want to always wonder if they're thinking about it whenever they look at me."

"What about someone else, maybe a professional?" I hazarded.

"I've thought about that too," she admitted, "but I haven't gotten much past the thinking stage. Can't tell you're a psych minor or anything."

"Gotta proselytize. It's in the contract."

We walked in silence for a few minutes while I pondered what she'd said. Then I asked, "So do you ever wonder that with me? You know, if I'm thinking about it?"

"No," she said, nudging me with her shoulder. "I know your mind is on other things. For example, what we did this morning."

"True," I agreed. "I fantasize about your French toast all the time."

"Who wouldn't, really?"

When we reached the park at the end of the street, Duncan tugged on the leash. I unhooked it from his collar so that he could snuffle about the bushes. Then I leaned against a tree and tried to memorize the way Jess looked, midday sun glinting in her hair and reflecting from her sunglasses.

"Stop looking at me like you're taking a picture," she said.

"Yes, ma'am."

But I couldn't keep from looking at her like that throughout the day, our last together for what seemed like forever.

That evening, we had a marathon dinner at a fondue restaurant in town with Holly and Becca, where we relived the tennis tournament and heard about Holly's new barista job and Becca's job search, again carefully avoiding the topic of my impending absence from the city where the three of them would all be going about their lives while I lived at home with my parents and mowed lawns, trimmed hedges and painted fences, no doubt wishing I could be here with them. I even suspected I would miss Becca. Once you got past the poor little rich girl act she wasn't so bad. Really.

After dinner, the four of us walked to Seal Beach and watched the seals settle in for the night as the sky darkened and the tide receded and the day grew closer and closer to an end. Finally Jess hinted that it was time to go. We walked back to the cars, where I hugged Holly and Becca goodbye, forcing a grin as they drove off toward their apartment in the city. *Not jealous*, I told myself as I waved until Becca's car was out of sight. But I was a lousy liar.

Back at the apartment, Jess watched me pack my bags and putz around checking for forgotten objects. I'd managed to make myself quite comfortable in her space in the ten days since Holly had helped me move out of my dorm room. I couldn't believe now how quickly the time had gone. If I could have any superpower, I've often thought, I would pick mastery of time. Then nothing terrible would ever have to happen because I'd be able to go back and prevent any tragedy from ever happening. Of course, then I'd get stuck living in reverse, and that would no doubt be unsettling. But think of all the lives saved. Certainly it would be worth losing the rhythm of my own life if I could have a positive impact on hundreds or even thousands of others, wouldn't it? Not that they'd ever know I'd saved them, of course, and there was part of the rub.

"Hey." Jess's voice interrupted my metaphysical reverie.

I turned from my search of the couch cushions for my missing Walkman. "Yeah?"

"Come here for a sec."

I followed her into the bedroom, where she opened the drawer in her bedside table and pulled out a small object wrapped in the funny papers. "This is for you."

"I have something for you too," I said, and retrieved a bag from my backpack.

I sat beside her on the bed and made her open the bag first. It contained a small jewelry box and a mix tape stocked with tunes from the Indigo Girls, Melissa Etheridge, Fleetwood Mac, the *Some Kind of Wonderful* soundtrack, and "I Can't Tell You Why" by the Eagles. As she read the names of the songs from the cassette case, she started laughing, and I wasn't sure if I should be hurt or not.

"Sorry—I love it. Just, open yours," she said, smiling sideways at me.

Turns out she'd made me a mix tape too, with nearly the same exact songs on it. Apparently we'd both paid attention to our relationship's soundtrack.

"Open the box," I said once we had recovered from our mutual mirth.

She lifted the lid carefully and pulled out the silver locket I'd picked out for her weeks before, etched with stars on the outside and containing tiny pictures of each of us—our official athlete photos from the SDU Sports Information office—on the inside.

"Now we both have necklaces," I said, nervously fingering the sun pendant she'd given me at Christmas, which I rarely took off.

"I love it," Jess said, tracing the engraved stars lightly. She hesitated and added, "I love you."

It was the first time she'd looked me in the eyes as she told me she loved me, and I couldn't help grinning. "Good thing."

"It is a good thing." She reached under the bed then, pulling out a small flat, rectangular package wrapped in brown paper. "I have one more thing for you. I thought it might give you something to think about for next fall."

It had to be a painting, I thought as I tugged at the string and slid the paper away from the canvas. I held my breath, not sure what I'd find as I turned it over. And then I had to laugh—Jess had painted a close-up of a white soccer ball resting on a gorgeous lawn of springy, bright green grass, the stalks of which were enormous, as if the viewer were an ant or other invisible creature looking up at the giant leather ball, the words "SDU Soccer" and the stitches holding the individual panels together clearly visible.

"Dude, this is awesome," I said.

"You thought it would be something serious, didn't you," Jess said, biting her lip.

"Yeah, but I love it. It's perfect. You're perfect."

"Hardly," she said, but she returned the hug I gave her. Then she kissed me, lightly at first and then more seriously, devouring my lips with hers until I felt a little dizzy.

"Get rid of this, please," she said, tugging at my T-shirt. "And these." With a pull on my shorts.

"Gladly." I paused briefly to place our gifts to each other someplace safer than the comforter cover. Then I stripped down and slipped under the covers with her, my hands and mouth running over her body, which opened so easily to mine now. She loved me, but what was more, she trusted me. That was the better gift, really.

Later, when we lay sated and quiet next to each other, as much of our naked skin touching still as was humanly possible, Jess murmured, "Now that we've given each other the sun and the moon and the stars, guess there's not much else, hmm."

I loved that she was as appallingly cheesy as me.

"I don't know," I said, and kissed her shoulder. "I'm sure we'll think of something."

We lay in her bed under the slanted ceiling together as the last of the summer light leaked from the sky and darkness seemed to settle on the house more heavily than it usually did. The bedside lamp was on, and we moved without talking so that we could look into each other's eyes, both of us clearly trying to memorize what we saw. As her eyes seemed to grow lighter, more transparent, I wondered if this was the last time we would ever be together. Three months apart was a long time—longer than we'd been dating, even. What if Jess changed her mind? What if she got used to being alone again and decided she didn't want me anymore at the end of the summer? What if by leaving now I was ruining any chance we had at a future together?

Jess lifted her hand and smoothed it over my brow. Her eyes intent on mine, she said, "I've been meaning to ask you this all day—is now when we talk about monogamy?"

This was so far from what I was expecting that I burst out laughing for the second time that night.

"What?" Jess asked, looking worried. "Is this not the right time? Sorry, I'm new at this relationship thing."

I laughed again. But a little while later, after we'd agreed on a monogamous summer, nothing seemed funny anymore as we lay in her bed wishing we could hold off morning.

CHAPTER NINETEEN

As I drove away the next day, suffice it to say that we both bawled and it was awful and I almost turned around half a dozen times, possibly more. Only the Wallace family sense of honor—*I Have Given My Word to the Portland Parks Department*—compelled me to continue forward when I glanced in my rearview mirror and saw Jess standing alone on the street beside her car, watching me leave her. I wiped away tears as I headed toward the freeway and turned north toward Oregon. Why was I doing this? Just then, money for school seemed seriously unimportant.

The day after I got home, I was up early and off to work downtown, and my summer of sullenness officially commenced.

"What's your problem?" my friend Joe asked me that first day. We were out for the afternoon together on an irrigation job.

"I had to leave my girlfriend in San Diego," I groused.

"Oh, poor you," Joe said.

His girlfriend, Jennie, lived in a tiny forest town out on the eastern side of the state, not far from the Idaho border. He left her for eight months every year to come work in the city, where the wages and benefits were too good to pass up. During those months, he was lucky to see her every other weekend.

"Shut it," I said. "At least you live within driving distance."

"Yeah, if you don't mind an eight-hour trip every couple of weeks."

Okay, so he had a point.

My parents were more receptive to my whining, and happily reminisced about the summer after their junior year of college when my mom went to work in a resort town a hundred miles north of San Francisco and my dad would hitchhike up on the weekends to visit her. Then they'd take a bus into the redwood forests and wander the trails there, feeling as if they had traveled back in time to an era with no cars, no telephones, no universities. A time that contained only them and the primordial forest.

I, of course, was less than sympathetic to this turn of conversation. For one thing, I'd heard these stories innumerable times. For another, my parents currently got to see each other whenever they wanted and had done so for the last twenty-nine years. Kind of unfair to compare their long-ago separation, which, incidentally, hadn't been nearly as extended or remote as Jess's and mine, to the visceral heartbreak I was currently experiencing. I mean, couldn't they see my heart literally breaking inside my chest as I pined away for the love of my life? They thought I didn't see the condescending smiles they exchanged when I described my emotional state. Just made me grouchier.

The only way around the distance, Jess and I decided my first week at home, was to talk every night and write copious letters. Nearly every evening I took the cordless phone out into the backyard and sat in one of the deck chairs watching birds and red squirrels flit about my parents' garden while Jess and I talked for an hour about our days, our jobs—she was working as a camp counselor at the Y for the third summer in a row—or nothing at all.

Hummingbirds who guzzled sugar water from the various feeders hanging around the yard were my favorite. I came to know them by the sounds they made as they fed—the high-pitched chirps accompanied by the buzzing of their wings, like a hundred bumblebees circling overhead. On the weekends I helped my mom clean and refill the feeders, and sometimes the birds were so anxious for food that they would hover outside the kitchen window watching us and dive bomb us as soon as we emerged with the refilled feeders. Napoleon's complex, my mom called it.

Sometimes I took the phone into my bedroom and Jess and I ventured down the road of phone sex, me always praying my mom and dad wouldn't happen to pick up the phone themselves and accidentally receive an ear full. Occasionally I wondered if Jess preferred sex via telephone to the real thing—this way she didn't have to cede any control over her body to anyone else. Personally, I found the long distance line to be a poor substitute, but hey, it was better than nothing.

After a couple of weeks, the phone bill arrived and my mother sat me down to have a talk about the cost of long distance phone calls to Southern California. I glowered through the whole lecture, though I knew she was right. What was the point of me coming home to work and save money for school if I was going to blow hundreds of dollars a month talking to Jess? For that, I might as well have stayed in La Jolla for the summer.

"I know," I finally said when she paused. "I just miss her so much."

"You really love this girl, don't you?" my mom asked.

"I really do. You would too if you met her."

From then on I timed our calls, and we took turns so that we were both spending money, since my parents had made it clear that any communication expenses I incurred were my sole responsibility. Harsh but fair, I had to admit.

We went on like this for weeks, both of us working long hours outdoors at physically strenuous jobs during the week, good-naturedly arguing about which was more taxing—diesel-operated weed whackers or large groups of seven-year-olds. On the weekends, I would traipse around the city taking photos and writing accompanying letters to send to Jess. She returned the favor, sending photos and pictures she painted of Sidney and Claire's backyard and the ocean at sunset and my favorite, a collage from Seal Beach.

But the letters and pictures and phone calls weren't enough. I missed her deeply, in an almost sweet way. It was like when you get a bruise from soccer and you test it all the time, pressing on it to see if it still hurts just as much. Only in this case, the pain didn't ever really fade. In this case, I wouldn't be able to heal until the summer was over and we were back together again.

I turned twenty-one the Friday before the Fourth of July, which fell on a Tuesday this year. The guys on the crew were psyched about the holiday—we'd get Monday and Tuesday off paid, which meant a four-day weekend. I should have been stoked to be turning twenty-one, but summer birthdays were often less than memorable. You were lucky if school friends even remembered, let alone sent anything on time. Jess told me the night before that she'd sent me a package. It should be waiting for me when I finished work today.

"Happy birthday, Cam," Jim, my boss, said as I was leaving the Park Bureau building just across the street from Chapman Square.

"It's your birthday?" Joe echoed, pausing as he changed out of steel-toed boots into beat-up sneakers.

"Yeah. I'm legal today," I said, and waved as I ducked out into the summer evening.

I had to hurry if I was going to catch my bus. But as I rounded the corner, I stopped dead. There directly in front of me, leaning against my Tercel at the edge of the curb, was Jess. She smiled as she saw me, straightening up and pushing away from the car. It was the best smile I'd ever seen. Best birthday present ever.

"Tell me again how this happened," I said that night as we lay in my childhood bed in the dark, naked flesh to naked flesh. We'd had dinner with my parents, and then we'd gone out for a drink—my first legal alcoholic experience—with Todd, Ben and Josh, guy friends from high school, and their respective girlfriends. We'd had a good time, and I'd been happy to show off Jess, who was of course the most impressive of the assembled g-friends, in my entirely unbiased opinion. But the entire time I had buzzed with sexual energy. We'd been apart for nearly six weeks now, and I couldn't wait to get her into bed. It was all I could do not to nibble on her ear or feel her up in the Irish pub my buddies took us to, especially after I got a couple of shots of tequila into my belly. But I refrained, and so did she—barely, she admitted later—and we waited until we got back to the house to slide our hands down each other's pants.

We didn't, however, make it all the way upstairs. Our first encounter took place on the staircase, and we both had the rug burns to show for it afterward. I was aware the entire time that either or both of my parents could at any moment stumble out of their bedroom in their matching bathrobes from Christmas 1983, but I couldn't seem to help myself. Jess couldn't either.

Eventually we made it up to my bedroom, where we shushed each other as we made love again just down the hall from where my parents were sleeping. My mother used a machine that simulated ocean waves to drown out city noises. I hoped it also drowned out the sounds of lesbian lovemaking two doors away.

We were finally winding down when I asked Jess to tell me again the story of her sudden appearance in my Portland life.

"It was your mom's idea," she said, her arm under my neck and her fingers toying with my hair, standing up now all over my head from our exertions. "The night she talked with you about the phone bill, she started thinking about how and when to get me here for a visit. Your birthday seemed like the perfect opportunity, so your parents pooled their frequent flyer miles and sent me the ticket. I asked for time off work, and because I'm the best counselor they have—okay, I actually didn't give them a choice—my boss at the Y agreed I could take next week off."

"I can't believe my mom lied to Jim."

My mother had reportedly told Jim that I would need to miss the following week at work for an important family event. In reality, Jess and I were going to spend a few days at my uncle's condo at Mt. Hood. By ourselves.

"She loves you that much," Jess said, her hand stilling.

I knew she was thinking about the differences between our

mothers. I snuggled closer in the narrow bed, my arm across her chest, my chin on her collarbone.

"She already loves you too," I said. "So does my dad."

"You don't know that."

"I do know that. For my parents to talk that long about tennis voluntarily? It was you they were interested in, not the sport, I can guarantee it."

Over veggie burgers, spinach and kale from the garden, and homemade sweet potato fries, my parents had been warm and caring and accepting. Which hadn't been a surprise to me, but I'd noticed Jess's shy smiles of gratitude as they invited her into our home and tried to make her feel like part of the family. They were good eggs, and so was she. I'd felt damned lucky as we sat outside on the deck that evening drinking beer and lemonade and trading stories.

At one point my dad had said, "Cam tells us you're quite the painter."

Jess had stared at me. "She does, does she?"

Now, as we lay murmuring together in the dark, Jess said, "So when did you figure out the storm painting was mine?"

I froze, my eyelids the only part of me moving as I blinked, trying to decide how to answer. We'd never discussed the fact that I knew the painting's creator nor that I'd deduced its meaning.

"It's okay," she added, her hand gentle in my hair. "I know you know, Cam. I'm glad, in a way. You know me better than anyone and you still love me."

"Of course I do," I said, kissing her chin because it was the nearest thing to my lips. "I figured it out the night I told you that, in fact."

"You did? I didn't realize."

"Well, I do tend to hide my superior intelligence beneath this jockish exterior," I said, trying to lighten the moment.

"You don't always have to do that, you know," she said. "Make a joke out of everything, I mean. I promise I won't cry."

"It's okay if you do," I said quickly.

"Kidding, Cam."

A little while later, I could feel sleep tugging at me, trying its hardest to extinguish my consciousness for the night. But I didn't want to give in yet. We only had a week together and then she'd be back in San Diego again and I'd be here refusing to wash my sheets so that I could hold onto the scent of her as long as possible.

I blinked myself awake and said, "I wish you didn't have to go back to La Jolla next weekend."

"I know, but it'll be good for me to go back."

I couldn't keep the whine out of my tone—it had been a long day, and happiness had lowered my defenses. Or maybe it was the tequila. "What, you'd rather hang out with a bunch of second graders than me?"

"No," she said, running her hand lightly up and down my arm. "But I do have some things to work out."

"Like what?"

"Like maybe I thought over what you said, you know, like talking to someone about what happened. Someone professional, I mean."

I was glad it was dark so she didn't see my chin drop, though she may have felt it hit her shoulder. "Seriously?"

"Seriously. I actually went to see a woman last week, a therapist who specializes in cases like mine. It's still early, and it's obviously not going to be easy, but I think I might be ready to deal with what happened. I need to if I'm going to get beyond it."

From the outside, she already seemed to have gotten beyond the rape—successful student three-quarters of the way through college, All-American singles Division II National Champion, girlfriend to another Division II success story, if I did say so myself. But it didn't matter what I thought, only what her life felt like to her.

"I'm so proud of you," I said, and leaned up to kiss her.

She pulled me on top of her and deepened the kiss, sliding her hands down to my hips. Quickly any notion of sleep fled, and I only had time to think, *Again?* Then I stopped thinking, lost in the feel and taste and touch of her skin against mine. It was just too good. She was too good. I had never loved anyone else like this, and somewhere in the back of my brain, I knew I never would again.

We did wonderful things to each other, and when we'd finally gotten our fill, we lay pressed together in my twin bed, light from the streetlamps leaking in the window, the faint sound of the ocean reaching us from down the hall.

On the edge of sleep, I knew all at once we'd be okay. Jess wasn't going to suddenly change her mind or freak out about what had happened to her, and I wasn't going to get distracted by soccer this fall and drift away from her. Like Holly and Becca, we were beyond the beginning of our relationship now. We had made it through an uncertain takeoff, and now we were safe together in midflight, the sky wide open before us. I wasn't afraid anymore, and I thought Jess probably wasn't, either. At least, I hoped not.

"Hey," she murmured beside me.

"Yeah?"

"Can you move over a little? My arm's asleep."

"Of course," I said, and shifted to make room for her.

**Publications from
Bella Books, Inc.**
Women. Books. Even Better Together.
**P.O. Box 10543
Tallahassee, FL 32302
Phone: 800-729-4992
www.bellabooks.com**

CALM BEFORE THE STORM by Peggy J. Herring. Colonel Marcel Robideaux doesn't tell and so far no one official has asked, but the amorous pursuit by Jordan McGowan has her worried for both her career and her honor.
978-0-9677753-1-9

THE WILD ONE by Lyn Denison. Rachel Weston is busy keeping home and head together after the death of her husband. Her kids need her and what she doesn't need is the confusion that Quinn Farrelly creates in her body and heart.
978-0-9677753-4-0

LESSONS IN MURDER by Claire McNab. There's a corpse in the school with a neat hole in the head and a Black & Decker drill alongside. Which teacher should Inspector Carol Ashton suspect? Unfortunately, the alluring Sybil Quade is at the top of the list. First in this highly lauded series.
978-1-931513-65-4

WHEN AN ECHO RETURNS by Linda Kay Silva. The bayou where Echo Branson found her sanity has been swept clean by a hurricane — or at least they thought. Then an evil washed up by the storm comes looking for them all, one-by-one. Second in series.
978-1-59493-225-0

DEADLY INTERSECTIONS by Ann Roberts. Everyone is lying, including her own father and her girlfriend. Leaving matters to the professionals is supposed to be easier! Third in series with *PAID IN FULL* and *WHITE OFFERINGS*.
978-1-59493-224-3

SUBSTITUTE FOR LOVE by Karin Kallmaker. No substitutes, ever again! But then Holly's heart, body and soul are captured by Reyna... Reyna with no last name and a secret life that hides a terrible bargain, one written in family blood.
978-1-931513-62-3

MAKING UP FOR LOST TIME by Karin Kallmaker. Take one Next Home Network Star and add one Little White Lie to equal mayhem in little Mendocino and a recipe for sizzling romance. This lighthearted, steamy story is a feast for the senses in a kitchen that is way too hot.
978-1-931513-61-6

2ND FIDDLE by Kate Calloway. Cassidy James's first case left her with a broken heart. At least this new case is fighting the good fight, and she can throw all her passion and energy into it.
978-1-59493-200-7

HUNTING THE WITCH by Ellen Hart. The woman she loves — used to love — offers her help, and Jane Lawless finds it hard to say no. She needs TLC for recent injuries and who better than a doctor? But Julia's jittery demeanor awakens Jane's curiosity. And Jane has never been able to resist a mystery. #9 in series and Lammy-winner.
978-1-59493-206-9

FAÇADES by Alex Marcoux. Everything Anastasia ever wanted — she has it. Sidney is the woman who helped her get it. But keeping it will require a price — the unnamed passion that simmers between them.
978-1-59493-239-7

ELENA UNDONE by Nicole Conn. The risks. The passion. The devastating choices. The ultimate rewards. Nicole Conn rocked the lesbian cinema world with Claire of the Moon and has rocked it again with Elena Undone. This is the book that tells it all...
978-1-59493-254-0

WHISPERS IN THE WIND by Frankie J. Jones. It began as a camping trip, then a simple hike. Dixon Hayes and Elizabeth Colter uncover an intriguing cave on their hike, changing their world, perhaps irrevocably.
978-1-59493-037-9

WEDDING BELL BLUES by Julia Watts. She'll do anything to save what's left of her family. Anything. It didn't seem like a bad plan...at first. Hailed by readers as Lammy-winner Julia Watts' funniest novel.
978-1-59493-199-4

WILDFIRE by Lynn James. From the moment botanist Devon McKinney meets ranger Elaine Thomas the chemistry is undeniable. Sharing — and protecting — a mountain for the length of their short assignments leads to unexpected passion in this sizzling romance by newcomer Lynn James.
978-1-59493-191-8

LEAVING L.A. by Kate Christie. Eleanor Chapin is on the way to the rest of her life when Tessa Flanaghan offers her a lucrative summer job caring for Tessa's daughter Laya. It's only temporary and everyone expects Eleanor to be leaving L.A...
978-1-59493-221-2

SOMETHING TO BELIEVE by Robbi McCoy. When Lauren and Cassie meet on a once-in-a-lifetime river journey through China their feelings are innocent...at first. Ten years later, nothing — and everything — has changed. From Golden Crown winner Robbi McCoy.
978-1-59493-214-4

DEVIL'S ROCK: THE SEARCH FOR PATRICK DOE by Gerri Hill. Deputy Andrea Sullivan and Agent Cameron Ross vow to bring a killer to justice. The killer has other plans. Gerri Hill pens another intriguing blend of mystery and romance in this page-turning thriller.
978-1-59493-218-2

SHADOW POINT by Amy Briant. Madison Maguire has just been not-quite fired, told her brother is dead and discovered she has to pick up a five-year old niece she's never met. After she makes it to Shadow Point it seems like someone—or something—doesn't want her to leave. Romance sizzles in this ghost story from Amy Briant.
978-1-59493-216-8

JUKEBOX by Gina Daggett. Debutantes in love. With each other. Two young women chafe at the constraints of parents and society with a friendship that could be more, if they can break free. Gina Daggett is best known as "Lipstick" of the columnist duo Lipstick & Dipstick.
978-1-59493-212-0

BLIND BET by Tracey Richardson. The stakes are high when Ellen Turcotte and Courtney Langford meet at the blackjack tables. Lady Luck has been smiling on Courtney but Ellen is a wild card she may not be able to handle.
978-1-59493-211-3